RITA THE RESCUER

Rita
Superhero

D1375018

Please return/renew this item by the last date shown on this label, or on your self-service receipt.

To renew this item, visit **www.librarieswest.org.uk** or contact your library

Your borrower number and PIN are required.

LibrariesWest

Also by Hilda Offen:

Rita on the River

Rita Rides Again

Rita and the Romans

Rita at Rushybrook Farm

Rita and the Flying Saucer

Arise, Our Rita

Rita and the Haunted House

RITA THE RESCUER

Rita Superhero

Hilda Offen

troika

For Katie and Helen

Published by TROIKA

First published 2019

1 3 5 7 9 10 8 6 4 2

Text and illustrations copyright © Hilda Offen 2019

Originally published under the title *Rita the Rescuer*

The moral rights of the author/illustrator have been asserted

All rights reserved

A CIP catalogue record for this book
is available from the British Library

ISBN 978-1-909991-87-3

Printed in India

Troika Books Ltd
Well House, Green Lane, Ardleigh CO7 7PD, UK

www.troikabooks.com

There are four children in the Potter family –
Eddie, Julie, Jim and Rita.

   Because Rita is the youngest, the others
sometimes leave her out of their games. They
say they have to spend all their time rescuing
Rita – she falls in the mud, she gets stuck up
trees and loses her wellingtons. Poor Rita!

"Take me with you!" begged Rita one day.

"You're too young!" said Eddie. "You can't push or pull."

"You're too young!" said Julie. "You can't skip or jump."

"You're too young!" said Jim. "You can't run or kick."

Eddie, Julie and Jim went off to play
with their friends. Rita was left alone with
the cat.

"You'd like some milk, wouldn't you?"
said Rita and she went to get it in from
the doorstep.

"What's this?" she cried. "A parcel –
for me?"

Rescuer's Outfit said the label inside.

First Rita unpacked some boots, then gloves and tights, a tunic, a belt and a cloak.

"Oh!" she said. "That's just what I need."

And she put them all on as fast as she could.

In the street some children were jumping over a rope.

"Let me try!" said Rita.

"You're too young!" they said and they held the rope even higher.

But Rita wasn't put off.
She drew a deep breath, gave
a hop, step and jump and –
up she soared!

Rita could hardly believe
what was happening.
"Look at me! Look at me!"
she shouted.

Rita's leap carried her high above the roof-tops. She could see for miles. Down in the next street she spotted Basher Briggs who was snatching her brother Jim's football.

GIVE THAT
FOOTBALL
BACK!

Rita's roar was so loud
that all the windows
round about rattled.

Basher turned pale.

"I'm off!" he said and he dropped the
football and ran away as fast as he could.

"Thanks a lot," said Jim.

"You're welcome!" said Rita. "Now for my
next rescue!"

She could hear someone close by yelling
"Help! Help!"

A pram had rolled into the river.
Worse still, there was a baby inside!
The current was sweeping it away and
no one could reach it.

Quick as a flash, Rita dived into the water. She grasped the pram firmly and swam to the river bank.

The ducks quacked and the people cheered.

The mother hugged her baby and shook Rita's hand.

"You deserve a medal!" she said.

Rita was about to reply when she heard a scream. There, on the other side of the river, was her sister Julie. She was being chased by a bull!

In a split second, Rita was there.

She flung herself in front of the bull, who
stopped dead in his tracks.

"Bull – you're a bully!" said Rita.

She stared straight into his little red eyes,
while Julie escaped over a gate.

The bull looked ashamed and shuffled his
hooves; but Rita was already on her way.

It was Lavinia Smith's wedding day.
There she was, with her flowers and her
bridesmaids – but the car had a flat tyre.
Mrs Smith looked furious and Mr Smith
was in a panic.

"Oh no, the foot pump doesn't work!"
he cried.

Rita came bounding over a hedge.

"Leave this to me, Mr Smith," she said. "It won't take a minute."

She gave a mighty puff.

"There you are. That's fixed it!" she said.

"Thank goodness for the Rescuer!" cried Lavinia as the car roared away down the street.

Nearby in Jubilee
Gardens a large crowd
had gathered beneath
a tree.

"That cat's going to
fall!" someone yelled.

"Our poor little
Rufus!" cried Mr and
Mrs Rumbold.

20

"Hang on, Rufus!"
called Rita. "Here I
come!"
She whooshed through
the air like a whirlwind.
"Ooh!" gasped the
crowd.

"Got you!" said Rita
and she snatched Rufus
to safety just as his claws
slipped from the branch.

"Thank you! Thank you!" cried Mr and
Mrs Rumbold, but Rita was off again –
she had heard another call for help.
Eddie's go-cart was out of control and
hurtling down the steepest hill
in town.

Rita ran
like a greyhound.

22

She grabbed the go-cart and braked so hard with her heels that sparks flew in the air.

"Phew!" said Eddie, as they screeched to a halt. "That was a very close thing!"

At the foot of the hill a crowd stood and stared.

Mr Carter's mare, Rosie, had fallen down a hole in the road. No one knew how to get her out.

But help was at hand.

Speeding down the street came

– a jet plane?

– a javelin?

– a flash of greased lightning?

No! It was Rita the Rescuer.

Rita dived down into the hole.

"One – two – three –heave!" she cried.

She raised Rosie above her head.

"Up you go!" she said and she lifted
Rosie out of the hole and placed her
back safely on the road.

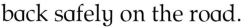

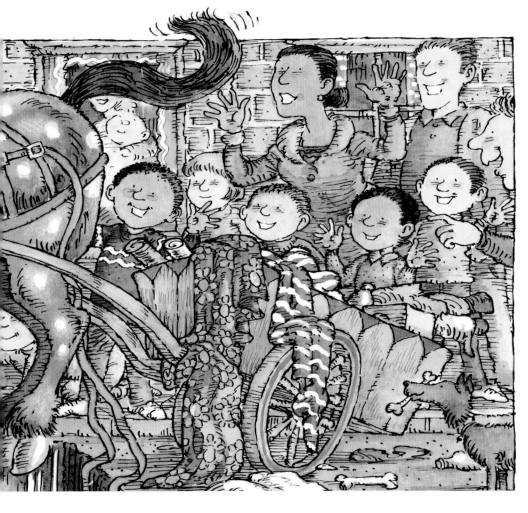

"What strength!" cried the crowd.
"What muscles! Did you ever see anything
like it?"

They cheered and they clapped and Rosie
swished her tail.

"Goodbye, everybody!" said Rita.
"I'm off home for my tea!"

But she stopped on the way to hit two thousand runs –

to kick four hundred goals –

and to skip up to three thousand and eighty.

"What a busy day!" said Rita, back home in her room. She took off the Rescuer's outfit and hid it under the bed.

"Everyone's talking about the Rescuer!" said Eddie at tea-time. "She's terrific! Who can she be?"

"Where can she come from?" asked Julie.

"However does she do those rescues?" cried Jim.

Rita could have told them, but her secret was special. So she smiled to herself, picked up her spoon, and started eating her beans.

Look out for other Rita titles from Troika Books

RITA THE RESCUER
Rita and the Haunted House
HILDA OFFEN

RITA THE RESCUER
Rita and the Romans
HILDA OFFEN

RITA THE RESCUER
Arise, Our Rita!
HILDA OFFEN

RITA THE RESCUER
Rita at Rushybrook Farm
HILDA OFFEN

RITA THE RESCUER
Rita and the Flying Saucer
HILDA OFFEN

RITA THE RESCUER
Rita Rides Again
HILDA OFFEN

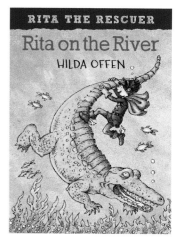
RITA THE RESCUER
Rita on the River
HILDA OFFEN

numerous short stories. ...

translated into fifteen lan...

teaches creative writing at ...

larly visits schools to give ta...

lives in West Yorkshire witl...

   Visit Martyn online at ...

D1375015

Other books by Martyn Bedford

Flip
Never Ending

Twenty

Questions

for

Gloria

MARTYN BEDFORD

WALKER
BOOKS

First published 2016 by Walker Books Ltd
87 Vauxhall Walk, London SE11 5HJ

2 4 6 8 10 9 7 5 3 1

Text © 2016 Martyn Bedford
Cover photograph © 2016 Sylwia Gruszka

The right of Martyn Bedford to be identified as author of this work has
been asserted by him in accordance with the Copyright,
Designs and Patents Act 1988

This book has been typeset in Joanna

Printed and bound in Great Britain by Clays Ltd, St Ives plc

British Library Cataloguing in Publication Data:
a catalogue record for this book is available from the British Library

ISBN 978-1-4063-6353-1

www.walker.co.uk

In memory of Uncle Jim.

And "Uncle" John Barker, who was like a second dad.

Q1: Let's start at the beginning, shall we?

Detective Inspector Katharine Ryan:

This interview is being audio- and video-recorded with parental consent and the agreement of the interviewee. We are in Interview Suite 1 at Litchbury Police Station on the 14th of June. Time, 10.12 a.m. The interview is being conducted by myself, Detective Inspector Katharine Ryan, of the West Yorkshire Police Service. Also present, for the purposes of Interview Support of a juvenile, is the interviewee's mother. Can you state your name, please?

Mrs Elizabeth Ellis:

Oh, yes. Liz – I mean (Clears throat) Mrs Elizabeth Mary Ellis.

D.I. Ryan:

Thank you. I am interviewing... Could you please say your full name?

Gloria Ellis:

Gloria Jade Ellis.

D.I. Ryan:

That's great. How old are you, Gloria?

Gloria:

Fifteen. Sixteen in October.

D.I. Ryan:

Are you happy for me to call you Gloria? Only, your mum calls you Lor, so—

Gloria:

Gloria is fine.

D.I. Ryan:

Right. OK, as I've explained, Gloria, this is an interview, not an interrogation. You're here of your own volition, your own free will to—

Gloria:

I know what "volition" means.

D.I. Ryan:

I didn't mean to sound patronizing, I just want to make sure there are no misunderstandings about the nature of what we're doing today. So, as I say, you're here of your own volition to help us figure out what's been happening. That's all. Are we OK with that?

Gloria:

(Nods)

D.I. Ryan:

For the recording, please.

Gloria:

Yes, I'm OK with that.

D.I. Ryan:

Excuse me. (Presses intercom button) Are the levels OK, Mike?

Recording Technician:

(Voice only) Yep.

Gloria:

The recording guy is called Mike?

D.I. Ryan:

How many times you been ribbed about that, Mike?

Recording Technician:

Eight hundred and sixty-three. That's just this month. (Laughter)

D.I. Ryan:

Believe it or not, we have a Sergeant Pete Sargent and a dog-handler called David Barker.

Gloria:

You're making that up.

D.I. Ryan:

10.15 a.m., interviewee accuses interviewing officer of lying. (Laughter)

OK, this is all good. So, Gloria, thank you for coming in this morning. You've been home less than twenty-four hours and I imagine the last thing you want to do is sit here going over everything and answering a pile of questions. You too, Mrs Ellis — I appreciate your co-operation.

Mrs Ellis:

We just want to know what he—

D.I. Ryan:

It must be so good to have her back.

Mrs Ellis:

It is. It is. (Snuffles) Sorry, I promised myself I wouldn't do this.

D.I. Ryan:

Take your time.

(To Gloria) How about you – glad to be back with your mum and dad?

Gloria:

(No response)

D.I. Ryan:

You certainly look a lot better for a decent night's sleep, a shower and a change of clothes.

Gloria:

Look, I know you have to be friendly, win my trust and all that, but d'you think we could—

D.I. Ryan:

Rapport, they call it. With someone your age, I'm supposed to ask what music you're into, your favourite movie, your best subject at school. Your hobbies.

Gloria:

I make my own earrings. You want to talk about that?

Mrs Ellis:

Lor, why are you being like this? She's on our side.

D.I. Ryan:

No, Gloria's right – we should cut the crap and get on

with it. Get you out of here and back with your family as soon as possible.

OK, let me just explain the process. In a moment I'm going to ask you to tell me all about the events of the past fifteen days. Take as long as you like. While you're speaking, I won't interrupt or ask questions unless I have to, just to make sure I've got things straight in my head. OK? We'll have regular breaks, of course. And you can call a time-out at any point if you're tired or it all gets a bit too much.

Good. So, one last thing. I have to be clear that you appreciate how important it is for you to be totally honest with me today. Try to recall as much as you can, as accurately as you can, yeah?

Gloria:

The whole truth and nothing but the truth. (Crosses her heart) So help me, God.

D.I. Ryan:

I'm being serious.

Gloria:

Me too.

D.I. Ryan:

The thing is, people have been very worried about you. Your mum, your dad. All of us. A girl your age goes missing for as long as you did… Well, you can imagine what we thought. And we're so pleased and relieved that you're back with us. But if we're to make sense of it all,

I need you to take me through everything that happened to you while you were gone. Step by step.

Gloria:

He said you'd do this. Get me to play the victim.

D.I. Ryan:

No one's getting you to… That's not what we're doing here, Gloria. We have fifteen days unaccounted for. Fifteen blanks. I can't fill in those blanks without your help. That's all.

Gloria:

(No response)

D.I. Ryan:

Do you think you can do that for me?

Gloria:

(No response)

D.I. Ryan:

Just … say it like it was. In your own time, in your own words. Yeah?

Gloria:

(Shrugs)

D.I. Ryan:

Gloria?

Gloria:

(Nods) Yeah.

D.I. Ryan:

Excellent. So. Let's start at the beginning, shall we?

Q2: How can you disappear from yourself?

D.I. Ryan doesn't look like a detective, in her ripped jeans and trainers and black short-sleeved Dorothy Perkins top. The outfit must be for my benefit, to put me at my ease. I read somewhere that when children give evidence in court, the barristers and judge take off their wigs and gowns to appear less intimidating. The room's playing its part, too. On TV, it's always bare walls, hard seats and a lightbulb behind wire mesh. This "interview suite" reminds me of a hotel reception: a triangular coffee table, comfy purple chairs, a leafy plant in a tub, art prints on the wall and a blue-tinted water dispenser that stands in a corner like an ice sculpture.

I'm so tired I could curl up and go to sleep. It's going to take more than one night in my own bed to wipe out the last couple of weeks.

Imagine their expressions if I called a time-out now, before we've even begun.

For all her smiles, D.I. Ryan looks frazzled, edgy. She wants to find him, bring him in. But first she's got me to deal with. She tells me to take as long as I need, but I can taste her impatience. Mum and Dad are the same. Not that they've been interrogating me since I got back – the police probably told them to lay off the questions. The questions are there, though, hanging unspoken in the air. Meantime, they make do with holding my hand, squeezing my shoulder, rubbing my back, kissing the top of my head, asking if I'm OK, if I want anything to eat or drink, if I'm warm enough or too warm, or telling me how good it is to have me home. That's when they're not staring at my fake-blonde hair like they're trying to figure out if I'm an impostor pretending to be their daughter. Or simply gazing at me the way I imagine they did when I was a baby.

During one of my naps, I half-woke to see them in the bedroom doorway, Dad's arm round Mum's shoulders, watching me.

I just want to be left alone. I can't say that to them.

They were afraid I was gone for ever. Then I turned up. It's a miracle. I'm a miracle. And they can't quite believe I won't vanish again.

It's funny, I never thought of myself as missing. How can you disappear from yourself?

I did make a start at explaining things yesterday, at home, once the police doctor had given D.I. Ryan the go-ahead to speak to me.

It wasn't what they thought, I tried to tell her.

That didn't get me very far. It hardly helped that I slurred

14

like a drunk and couldn't string two sentences together. I was exhausted, she decided. The interview could wait.

"We'll try again tomorrow, when you're fresher. Less confused." D.I. Ryan sounded like a teacher who suspects a student is lying but is giving them another chance to tell the truth.

I was in bed by the time Dad showed her out. I overheard him ask if she thought I was in post-traumatic shock.

"It's possible," came her muffled answer. Then something I didn't catch.

"Did the doctor ... examine her?" Dad said. "You know, properly."

I thought I'd missed D.I. Ryan's reply, but she must've just taken her time answering. "No," she said. "I can't authorize that until we know whether the boy did anything."

"You're not seriously telling me you think he *didn't*?"

"Mr Ellis, I'm saying we need to hear it from Gloria."

Then the front door opened and the hallway echoed with the clamour of the reporters, photographers and camera crews behind the barrier across the street from our house.

I nuzzled down under the duvet, shut my eyes, and imagined myself somewhere else.

Apparently, while I was away, I'd gone viral at *#wheresgloria?*.

Yesterday evening I was watching the TV news and a reporter was doing a live report from outside our house. If I'd gone over to the window and pulled back the curtain, I could have waved to myself. It's weird and a bit scary to think of so many people missing me, worrying about me, looking for me. When my parents showed me some of the stuff online and in the newspapers, it was as if I was reading about someone else. Some other Gloria.

But that's me, now. That's become my story.

Only, "Where's Gloria?" has become "Where *was* Gloria?" And "What did he do to Gloria?" And "Where's the boy who took Gloria?"

Where *is* he? It's all I can think about. Every minute since it ended.

D.I. Ryan wants to hear it from the beginning. The first of the fifteen days, I presume she means; the day I went missing. It started a couple of weeks before then, though.

It started with an appearance, not a disappearance.

It was a regular Monday morning at school and the tutor room was lively, with start-of-the-week blues drowned out by the chatter of what-did-you-do-at-the-weekend? Mr Brunt had just taken the register. The windows were open, letting in the drone of a lawnmower from the school field and the scent of cut grass. It had set off Tierney's hay fever. Even with red eyes and a snotty nose, she's still pretty. Like a grief-stricken princess. She sneezed three times, all over our desk.

"Thank you for sharing those with us, Tierney," Mr Brunt said. "If you have any more lined up, please turn

16

around – the chaps in the back row missed out that time."

I'd like to say there was a sign, an omen – sunlight bathing the room in a strange aura, a blue butterfly fluttering in through the window and settling on my sleeve – but there was nothing like that. I don't recall what I was thinking about (forgotten homework, probably, or whether Mum had signed my planner), or my mood (switched off, I expect; wishing away the day, the week), but it seems bizarre that those moments weren't electrified with anticipation.

Mr Brunt clapped his hands, as he always does ahead of class announcements. As usual, he followed the clap with, "Right then, 10GB, listen up."

The whole time he's been our form tutor, Mr Brunt has worn nothing but variations of brown (suits, ties, shoes, socks, the occasional sweater). Even his white shirts have turned beige. He must have been teaching since the days when desks had inkwells.

He barely got started on his announcements that morning before the door opened and a boy let himself into the room. Tall and gangly, with very black, very fine, very straight hair down to his shoulders. Dusky, in a Mediterranean-meets-the-Indian-subcontinent kind of way. But for his height, his boy-sized nose and the scruffy stubble on his chin and upper lip, he might have passed for a girl. It wasn't just the long hair; there was something feminine in his manner and the way he moved. A kind of grace. His school uniform was way too small for him, exposing two stripes of hairy shin and a pair of knobbly wrists encircled in numerous multicoloured bangles.

He hadn't knocked before coming in. Mr Brunt wouldn't like that.

"Who'd he?" Tierney whispered through hay-feverish nostrils; not a, *Wow, he's cute*, more of a *Who's this freak?*

One or two people sniggered.

He was tall enough to be Year 12 or 13, but he wouldn't have been in uniform if that was the case. I didn't recognize him, anyway, and I'm sure I'd have remembered him if I'd seen him around school. The guy showed no trace of self-consciousness. Head held high, he surveyed the room with an easy confidence.

"Shall we try that again, young man?" Mr Brunt said.

I thought he was going to ignore the question. At last, with a half-smile, he turned to the tutor. "Try what again, sir?"

Posh-spoken, polite. If he had any idea what he'd done wrong, he didn't show it.

Mr Brunt was a few centimetres shorter and seemed displeased by having to look up at him, as if the boy was to blame for it. The teacher pointed. "The door."

The new arrival looked genuinely perplexed. "What about it?"

"I'd like you to knock on it before entering my tutor room."

"But I'm already in your tutor room."

"Then could you please go back out, knock on the door, and come in when I say so."

"I could very easily do all of those things, but – if you don't mind me saying so, sir – it would be a poor use of my time. And yours, for that matter."

An odd sound escaped Mr Brunt's mouth. The rest of us were utterly silent and still.

The boy continued. "You've already established that you prefer people to knock before entering – fine, point made, I'll know for next time – so what you're doing now is attempting to assert your authority over me through a process of ridicule." He shrugged. "So, no."

Just like that: No.

I didn't dare breathe or so much as glance at Tierney, sure if I caught her eye I'd burst out laughing. In any case, I couldn't tear my gaze from the two figures at the front, face-to-face like boxers at the start of a fight. Or lovers in a TV drama. That was it: there was no aggression in the boy's tone or body language; he was relaxed, almost seductive. As I sat there, enthralled, I pictured him leaning forward to kiss Mr Brunt on the lips.

As if he'd had the exact same thought, the form tutor took a half-step backwards.

Unlike some teachers, Mr Brunt doesn't tend to lose his temper with us, individually or as a group; I don't think I've heard him shout. Not properly. But we know where he draws the line and there's no doubt when we've crossed it. That

19

morning, though, he seemed bewildered. A confused old man who'd gone walkabout from a care home and somehow found himself in a room full of teenagers.

"You're, you ... what did you ... this is totally ... young man, I want you to..."

He must have started the sentence ten times. Then he gave up trying to get the words out and simply stood there – shoulders sagging, head tilted to look up into the boy's face – as if awaiting further instructions. It was shocking to see him like that.

The boy rescued him.

"We haven't got off on the right foot, have we, sir?" he said, still wearing that half-smile. He offered his hand. "Hello. I'm Uman." He pronounced it *Oo-maan*. "You must be Mr Brunt."

The form tutor stared at the hand like he'd never seen one before. Maybe he'd noticed all those bangles – a flagrant breach of school dress code – and was debating whether to confront the boy about that, too. "Uman?" he repeated.

"Padeem. Uman Padeem."

Mr Brunt frowned, then took the hand and shook it, or at least allowed his own to be shaken.

Still holding the teacher's hand, Uman Padeem said, "I'm the new boy."

I've seen the effect Uman has on people many times since then, but that morning it was almost literally unbelievable –

20

as if the episode had been staged, with the form tutor and the new boy in cahoots to play a practical joke on the class.

"What's wrong with Brunt?" I whispered to Tierney.

She just shook her head.

"Tier, he looks like he's been drugged."

"Or hybdodized."

"Or *what?*"

"*Hyb-do-dized.*"

"That's what I thought you said."

In the hours and days that followed, this was one of the theories about Uman Padeem's "effect" – that he cast a hypnotic spell over people. In that tutor room, though, all we could do was watch – bemused, awestruck – as Mr Brunt capitulated.

"New boy?" he said. "I wasn't inform— Let me check if I have…" He went over to his desk and fumbled at his computer. "You sure you're meant to be … ah, yes, here we are."

When he'd finished reading, he stood up. Straightened his tie. Studied Uman with the strangest expression. I know what it conveyed, now, but back then I couldn't read it at all.

"Well," he said, raising a hand towards the rows of desks, "you'd better join us. Uman." He spoke the name as if testing it. "And, um … welcome to 10GB."

"Thank you, sir."

Whatever he'd read on that PC, the confrontation over Uman's failure to knock before entering the room was no longer an issue. The new boy had defied the teacher,

21

spectacularly, and got clean away with it. I'd have expected him to look smug; most of the other boys in the class would have taken their seat with a smirk and a swagger if they'd pulled a stunt like that. Uman, though, had erased all trace of a smile from his lips. If anything, he looked sorry for Mr Brunt.

"There's a spare seat by the window," the form tutor said, pointing. "Next to Luke."

Uman Padeem glanced in that direction. Then he cast his gaze about the room, as he'd done when he first came in. This time he seemed to look more closely, as if assessing us one by one. His attention settled on our desk. First, on Tierney. Then me. Then Tierney again. I am *so* used to that. He can only have looked at me for a couple of seconds, but it felt longer. His face gave nothing away. I willed myself not to break eye contact.

Who the hell do you think you are? I distinctly recall having that thought as he stared at me; he might have messed with Mr Brunt's head but he wasn't going to mess with mine.

The odd thing was that, during his visual trawl of the room, none of us said a word; Mr Brunt, too, simply stood patiently beside him, waiting for him to finish whatever he was doing. What *was* he doing? I'm not sure any of us knew, but, despite its bizarreness, there seemed to be a general acceptance that he was perfectly entitled to do it.

Eventually, Uman moved. With a long-legged stride that somehow managed to be both ungainly and graceful at the same time, he picked a route between the desks.

Until he came to ours. Specifically, to Tierney's half of it. Of course.

"Hello," he said to Tierney. "What's your name?"

"Tierdey."

"Well, Tierdey, would you mind—"

"Her name's Tier-*ney*," I cut in. "With an 'n'."

Uman looked at me, with that half-smile in place again, then back at Tier. "Tier-*ney*, can I ask you to sit over there with Luke, please?"

Her expression was priceless. "Are you habbing a larp?"

"Is she speaking Danish?" Uman asked me.

"Hay fever," I said.

"That's a *language*? Wow, we never got past Latin and Mandarin at my last school."

That was actually quite funny, but no way was I going to show it. Anyway, who learns *Latin* these days? And what kind of school offers Mandarin?

I looked at Mr Brunt, wondering if he would intervene. Clearly not. Like the rest of the class, he just watched the scene unfold as if fascinated to see how it would end.

"So, Tierney with an 'n'." Uman nodded at the empty seat next to Luke. "How about it?"

"Doh way! Why should I hab to moob?"

"Because your friend looks by far the most interesting person in the room and – with all due respect to Luke – I'd prefer to sit with her."

23

* * *

Uman Padeem brought many surprises to 10GB that morning, but none greater than this: Tierney collected up her stuff and went over to sit with Luke.

I summarize this episode without interruption from D.I. Ryan. But she cuts in with a question now. Can't say I blame her. It's exactly the question I would ask at this point. It's the one I asked myself at the time — and Uman afterwards — without ever really producing a satisfactory answer.

"Gloria," she asks, "why did he choose you, do you think?"

"I don't know."

"You have no idea? You never spoke to him about it?"

"What, you don't think I'm 'interesting' enough for that to be the reason?"

Mum tsks. D.I. Ryan says, "You must have thought about it a lot since then."

"Does it matter why?"

"It might be a factor, yes."

"A factor."

"For his motivation."

Before I reply, I take a slug of water. I study her tanned kneecap through the rip in her jeans, the dusting of tiny blonde hairs. "He chose me because he chose me. That's all."

I just stop myself from adding, *Who knows what draws one person to another?* I don't think she'd appreciate a philosophical soundbite from a schoolgirl some thirty years younger than her.

Love at first sight, Tierney reckoned. But it wasn't that. With a choice between me and Tier – between me and most other girls in that room – what guy would pick me? I was never under any illusion that he even fancied me at first sight, let alone loved me. To be honest, it took me a while to figure out if he actually *liked* me. Or whether I liked him.

After Uman's explosive arrival in the tutor room, the remaining time before Mr Brunt dismissed us was an anticlimax.

Uman sat next to me. But he said nothing. And he did nothing, apart from have a coughing fit. Sometimes boys – less often, girls – will cough to disrupt a lesson; working as a team, taking turns, driving the teacher to distraction, but making it hard to prove they're doing it deliberately. Uman's coughs seemed genuine. (*Were* genuine, I know now.) They had the effect, though, of jolting poor old Brunt even further out of synch. As we filed out for first period, he asked Uman if he'd mind staying behind for a quick word. If that was OK. When Uman agreed, Mr Brunt's face was a mime of surprised relief that the boy would do as he'd been asked. The form tutor almost looked grateful.

As I reached the door, Uman called after me. "Wait for me in the corridor, yeah?"

"Wait for you in the corridor, *no*," I answered.

Really, he was something else. I left the room without a

backward glance and headed off to class (English, I think), hurrying to catch up with Tierney.

"What was that all about?" I asked.

"I doh – wadda dodal weirdo."

"No, *you*. Giving up your seat for him."

Tierney pulled her *so what?* face. "Doh big deal, really."

I let out a laugh. "Tier, that was so not like you."

"He'd dew."

"I know he's new but that doesn't—"

And so on. It was obvious, despite her trying to shrug it off, that Tierney was thrown by what had happened – what she'd done but, also, why she'd done it. She looked just as confused as Mr Brunt.

"Who is he?" I heard someone ask behind us. "Where's he come from?"

Uman Padeem was all anyone could talk about, the babble of our voices echoing along the corridor as class 10GB dispersed.

Q3: Why me?

I didn't see him again until morning break. Actually, I heard him before I saw him.

"Where did you get to?"

I turned to find Uman behind me in line for the snack kiosk. "What?" I knew what, of course, but I was irritated by his suggestion that I'd broken some kind of arrangement.

"You didn't wait for me," he said.

"That's right, I didn't." I turned away.

"Anyway, never mind – you're here now."

"No, *you're* here now. I was already here."

"Technically, we're both here, but I take your point." Then, before I could think of a comeback, "Where's your Danish friend?"

"She's gone to see the nurse to get some Piriton. And she's not Danish."

"Tierney," he said, as if suddenly remembering her name. "She's very pretty, isn't she?"

I exhaled. I still had my back to him. "Yes, she is."

"But you're much more complicated."

"Complicated. Thank you." I kept my voice flat and emotionless. "I can't tell you how happy you've just made me."

"Do I mean complicated or complex?"

"You don't even know me."

"I read people."

"You read people. Right."

We were at the head of the queue. I'd intended to buy a bag of dried apricots, but the annoying conversation with Uman had put me in the mood for chocolate. "You not having anything?" I asked, unwrapping an Aero as Uman followed me away from the counter.

"I don't know your name," he said.

His height was disconcerting. He was taller than my dad, but with an adolescent body and limbs, like he'd been stretched to adult-size. As for his face, I'd have killed for his eyes (almond-shaped, chocolate brown), his cheekbones (high, sharp), his hair (shiny as a model's in a shampoo ad), but the nose was a bit too big and the patchy stubble looked like a child had scribbled on him while he was asleep. He had the top half of a girl's face and the bottom half of a boy's.

"Why did you bother to sit next to me?" I asked. "You totally ignored me after that."

"Let me see if I can guess it." My name, he meant. He walked beside me, studying my face in profile as I headed out of the dining hall and into the yard. "Hmm, you look like a—"

28

"Gloria," I said. I couldn't be doing with this let-me-guess-your-name routine.

"Oh. As in the hymn 'Gloria in Excelsis'?"

That made a change. Most people ask if I'm named after the hippo in *Madagascar*. Some of the boys still greet my entrance into a classroom with *I like 'em big, I like 'em chunky*, even though the film's years old and I'm not exactly big or chunky.

"No, as in the Van Morrison song."

"I thought that was Patti Smith."

"She covered it."

"Are we going retro, here?" Uman asked.

I tried not to smile. "Apparently, Gloria is the two hundreth most popular girl's name in the UK."

"Would it embarrass you if I sang the chorus, right here, right now?" Uman asked.

Right here, right now was a yard swarming with students drawn outside by the spring sunshine. I didn't rise to the bait. Instead, I said, "No one calls me Gloria, anyway. My friends call me Lory, or Glo-Jay, the teachers all call me Lory – apart from Mrs Carmody, who thinks I'm Kate from 10SP – and, at home, I'm Lor."

I caught myself wondering why I was telling him all this.

"Glo-Jay?"

"My middle name's Jade." I offered him a piece of Aero. He shook his head. "Well, I'm going to call you Gloria."

"Because you like to be different."

"No, because it's a lovely name."

"OK, so – I'm going to have to find somewhere to puke, now."

Uman laughed. Then he coughed several times and couldn't speak for a moment.

I waited for him to recover. "You OK?"

"Consumption," he wheezed, dabbing at his lips with his cuff. The bangles on his wrist – about six of them, a mix of wood, plastic and metal – clicked against one another. "You should see the bloodstains on my handkerchief."

"Seriously, though, that's a nasty cough."

"I should be a character in a Victorian novel."

I spotted Emma, Molly and Bekah across the yard, looking our way, no doubt talking about us. Usually, Tierney and I spent break with them. It was my chance to detach myself from Uman, make my excuses and join the others. A few minutes earlier I'd have done just that. But he wasn't quite so irritating, now. Actually, it was surprising just how easy he was to be with, considering we'd barely met. Also, he was new. Unusual. OK, he was too self-assured for his own good, and he'd bossed Tier around and made a fool of Mr Brunt, but … well, he was the most interesting thing to happen at Litchbury High in a long time. And he was talking to me.

I produced a bottle of water from my bag and offered it to him.

He drank. "Thanks." His voice was less croaky and his

breathing had steadied. He took another sip and handed the bottle back.

"You won't be allowed to wear those," I said, indicating the bangles.

"I know. I was in Geography just now and Ms Vaux told me to take them off. I declined, naturally."

"You declined."

"We were discussing economic disparity between developing and developed nations," he said, matter-of-factly. "My bangles were an irrelevance."

"So you told her that?" Actually, having seen him at work on Mr Brunt, I could easily imagine it. *Ms Vaux, with all due respect...*

"For an intelligent woman, she took longer than I expected to grasp the point." Uman shook his head, as if disappointed in the Geography teacher. "We wasted several minutes on the bangles issue and, after that, I'm afraid Ms Vaux never quite recaptured her pedagogical mojo."

The laughter got stuck between my throat and the back of my nose. "Pedagogical mojo," I said. "I *loved* their first album but I felt they lost their way with the second."

Uman nodded. "You see, that's what I mean about you."

"What?"

"Complexity. You know what 'pedagogical mojo' means, yet you choose to misrepresent the meaning in order to disguise your intellect behind a veil of humour." He smiled. "That beats 'pretty', wouldn't you say?"

I fixed him a look. He was annoying again, with his assumptions about me. "You're quite posh, aren't you?" I said.

"And you're quite Yorkshire."

"Where are you from, then?"

"The accent says Berkshire," he said. "Ethnically, in case it matters to you, I'm something of a mish-mash. There's some Turkish in here and bits of one or two other places as well."

"So, why are you here?"

"I was born in Britain. Why wouldn't I be here?"

"No, I mean, why are you at Litchbury High?"

"Oh, OK." Uman hesitated. First time I'd seen him do that. "I've moved up here with my parents. On account of my father's work."

His dad – his father – had been head-hunted, he explained. Some big corporate law firm in Leeds wanted him to front up their something-or-other section. Uman had spent his whole life down south until now; he'd been at prep school, then boarding school since he was eight years old. May wasn't a good time of year to switch schools, he added with a grin, gesturing at himself – not if you were his height and hoped to find clothes your size in the school uniform shop.

"Anyway, I'll only be at Litchbury High till the summer vacation." Naming a ludicrously expensive boarding school in the area, he said, "I've got a place there in September."

If I'd thought about it, I would have realized his story didn't add up. For the sake of a couple of months – and given that his fees must already have been paid – why didn't he stay on at the boarding school down south, then join his family up here at the end of term? But before I had a chance to process what Uman had said, he threw me with a change of subject.

"I like your earrings." He reached out and held my left earlobe gently, examining the small, simple disc in the design of a primrose against a white background. His touch startled me, but I didn't pull away. "Delicate," he said. "Unusual."

"I made them myself."

"Did you?" He looked and sounded impressed.

A bell signalled the end of break. Uman dropped his hand back to his side.

Pulling a planner from his holdall, he flipped it open to the timetable. "Maths," he said. "In P-07, wherever that is."

"Same here."

"Good. We can sit together."

"No, we can't. I sit with Tierney in Maths."

"In which case, let's cut class."

"What are you talking about?"

"What's to stop us walking right out of here and doing something more entertaining?"

"Like what?"

"There must be an infinite number of alternatives – we are making a comparison with Maths, after all. But, frankly, I don't mind. I'd just prefer to spend this hour with you."

I stared at him. He seemed perfectly serious. "I'm not cutting class," I said.

33

"Why not?"

"Because it's crazy. Because you're crazy."

"You may have a point there, Gloria."

I liked hearing him say my name, which is odd, because I've never been keen on "Gloria" and have always insisted on being called by a shortened version of it.

"No, you're right," Uman said. "We'll go to Maths."

Perversely, I felt a twinge of disappointment. The idea of sneaking out of school might have been crazy, but it was also thrilling. The yard had almost emptied by then. As he made to head back inside I put a hand on his arm to stop him. "Uman, can I ask you – why?"

"Why what?"

"Why me? And don't give me that 'interesting-and-complicated' crap."

"OK, the truth: when I saw you this morning in the tutor room I realized right away how unhappy you are. How much your life" – he searched for the word – "*disappoints* you."

I Googled him. At lunchtime, I found a quiet spot by the tennis courts in WiFi range, switched on my iPad, and trawled the internet for Uman Padeem. He wasn't in any of the usual places – Twitter, Facebook and the like – and, as far as I could tell, he'd posted nothing on the photo-sharing sites. A more general search produced 225 results in 0.19 seconds, none related to "Uman Padeem", but only to one or other of his names, or to names that were similar: *Did you mean: uzma nadeem, umer nadeem, ayman nadeem, amman padam?*

It's possible to have lived for fifteen years without leaving a virtual trace. Possible, but not easy. Most people I know at school are out there somewhere on the web. Uman, it seemed, had never done anything sporty or musical, taken part in a charity fundraiser, acted in a play, won a painting or poetry competition, had his picture taken at a fête, fair, carnival parade or nativity, or done anything else that would have caused his name to appear on a school website or in a local newspaper.

Eventually, I gave up, opened the dictionary app instead and looked up "pedagogical".

How could he tell? Why was a total stranger able to see it when no one else, not even Tierney or my other friends or Mum and Dad, had noticed anything wrong?

I read people. That's what he'd said.

My first response was to deny it. "I'm not unhappy. Why would you even say that?"

"Because it's true. You want more out of life than it's giving you. You want change."

"Don't tell me what I want. You don't even know me."

So it continued as we headed to class. If Uman hadn't depended on me to show him the way to Maths, I'd have abandoned him right there in the corridor.

One time my brother's girlfriend did a tarot reading for me and I got pissed off with her when she started telling me about myself. A lot of her "analysis" was rubbish, but it was the things she got right that annoyed me the most – as if she'd intruded into a private area of my head. It was creepy. With Uman, it felt uncanny more than creepy. Like that guy on TV who performs tricks on members of the audience – hypnosis, mind-reading and that; it sends a shiver down your spine but you can't help smiling, shaking your head with wonder at how the hell he does it.

Uman insisted he wasn't telling me what I was – he was simply seeing it.

I didn't know what to make of it. Or of him.

I didn't sit with him in Maths. I said no when he asked if I'd meet up with him after school to show him the sights of Litchbury.

Yet there I was, at lunchtime, Googling him.

D.I. Ryan asks me straight out, "*Were* you unhappy with your life, Gloria?"

"Actually, yes. I had been for quite a while."

"All teenagers think they're unhappy, Lor," Mum says. "That their life is just so tedious."

"Mrs Ellis, please. Let Gloria speak for herself."

I give D.I. Ryan an example.

A regular here-we-go-again Saturday, the weekend before Uman turned up at Litchbury High. I was heading into town to meet up with the usual crowd in Caffè Nero for the usual hot chocolate with marshmallows, then back to Tierney's place for a DVD, popcorn and nachos. As usual. Sometimes we'd go to Molly's, or Bekah's, or Emma's, or mine – but, always, the romcom (horror, musical) and crunchy-munchies. If it was one of our birthdays we'd go right through to the evening at Pizza Express. It wasn't anyone's birthday that week. Even my outfit would've been predictable: purple Docs, odd socks, jeans and something baggy under the brownish fake-leather, fake-pilot's jacket. Burgundy beanie, worn on the slant, and home-made earrings – at the dangly end of the spectrum, what with it being a non-school day.

So far, so normal.

Or not.

Because, even as I walked into town, listening to familiar tunes on shuffle, passing the too-familiar sights of a route I'd taken so often it no longer looked real – the play area by the beck, the fire station, the pebble-dashed semis, the stone terrace behind the train station – I was aware of feeling flat. Not about anything specific, just in general.

"I'd been like it for weeks. Months, really."

D.I. Ryan waits for me to continue.

I backtrack to New Year's Day. I'm not sure that's when it started, but that was the first time I recall being properly aware of it. January 1st, a day of resolutions and renewal. I raised the blind at my bedroom window and gazed out over the same higgledy-piggledy rooftops and trim little gardens

37

and shiny cars and leafless treetops of the only place I've ever lived ... and I conjured up a tsunami. (No idea where from – the nearest coast is 100km away.) I saw it all as clearly as if it was happening right there: the whole town smashed to matchsticks and swept away by a huge surge of water. I couldn't have explained why. This is a "nice" town. Safe, quiet, pretty. Tourists come here. People who don't live here wish they could. I had no reason to dislike it.

Until I looked out on New Year's Day, I hadn't realized I did.

Tier reckoned I was just tired from the party. It was more than a morning-after downer, though. You don't hallucinate catastrophic tidal waves from your bedroom window because you've had several hours less sleep than usual and too much Smirnoff Ice. Or go on feeling like that through January and February, March and April. Not that it happened every day, or so full-on. It wasn't as if tsunamis played on a continual loop in my head. But there was a nagging sense of restlessness. Of dissatisfaction. With myself as much as anything. I'm sure a psychiatrist could've given me any number of good reasons why I shouldn't feel that way. But your mood doesn't listen to reason, does it?

Mine didn't as I hiked into town to meet my friends on a regular Saturday in the middle of May, two days before I even knew Uman Padeem existed.

"Uman said he entered my life because I was ready for him to enter it."

38

D.I. Ryan fixes my mum a look, as if daring her to interrupt.

I shrug. These things are unknowable. You can decide to believe them or not.

Whatever, I was running late. As usual. So by the time I got to Caffè Nero, my friends were already inside. I hesitated, peering through the window as though the customers were mannequins wearing clothes I might want to buy. Even though I stood to one side, the automatic doors kept opening and closing, as if in sympathy with my indecision about entering.

I spotted the others at our usual table near the back. Tierney and Bekah were facing in my direction, Emma and Molly had their backs to me. One empty chair: mine.

All I had to do was go through the doors, buy a drink and zigzag between the tables to join them, like I'd done a hundred thousand times. There would be loads of smiles and hey-ing and hi-ing and Yo, Glo-Jay-ing. They were my friends. They liked me. I liked them.

The two girls facing the front of the café hadn't noticed me yet. Tierney raised a mini-marshmallow to her mouth on a long-handled spoon and slipped it between her lips. She knows how attractive she is but acts like she has no idea. Alongside her, Bekah was messaging. Bekah is always messaging. Molly was in full swing on some anecdote or other, judging by the hand-flapping, the hair-flicking, the head-bobbing. Like a bee performing its waggle dance to tell the

39

rest of the hive where to find the food. It would be about Josh. It would be hilarious. Or tragic.

I pictured myself sitting in that vacant chair. Listening. Laughing. Or sympathizing.

At some point, one of them – almost certainly Tierney – would notice the latest earrings and I'd be confetti-ed with compliments, as if making my own jewellery from charity-shop bric-a-brac and bits of tat was just the coolest thing.

A hologram of my face stared back at me from the window, pale skin pixellated by the bustle beyond the glass. At their table, my friends enacted a scene so familiar it was suddenly the oddest sight – like they'd been reduced to the size of the dolls I used to play with and arranged for a make-believe tea party. Another tsunami moment. Only, instead of a torrent of water sweeping them away, I imagined going in there, gathering up my friends in my arms and taking them home to be stowed in the trunk under my bed.

I'm aware of the expression on D.I. Ryan's face as I say this. Mum's, too.

"I wanted to just turn round and walk away," I tell them. "They're my friends, we meet there all the time, but suddenly – that morning – I couldn't face it. Couldn't face *them*."

"Did you?" D.I. Ryan asks. "Walk away, I mean."

"No. Tierney spotted me just then. She waved and I waved back and went inside – I had to, once she'd seen me. But, also, it was like she'd snapped me out of a trance." I sit back in my chair. Rub my face hard, like I'm trying to scour

40

the skin off. When I lower my hands again, flecks of light fizz before my eyes. "The whole time I was with them that afternoon," I say, "I acted like everything was totally fine. Same old them, same old me. Same old, same old."

"Then, two days later, Uman appeared," D.I. Ryan says.

"Yep."

"And he was *different*."

"Yeah, he was. I'd never met anyone like him."

D.I. Ryan has called a break. Biscuits appear. Coffee, apple juice. Maybe I'll get used to it, but on my second day back, it still surprises me how easy it is to eat and drink whenever I like.

She's stepped outside to take a call just now. Like it's important.

As she returns to the interview suite I ask, "Have you found him?"

"No," she says. "No, Gloria, we haven't."

Q4: So, do you like him?

When we resume, she asks about Uman's attitude that first day at Litchbury High. Towards the teachers, me, everyone. The way he said what he liked, regardless of who he was speaking to and without thought for the consequences or people's opinion of him.

"He didn't care," I say. "He really didn't."

"You liked that – his recklessness?"

Did I? I suppose I must have done. It was exciting, in a way, witnessing his disregard for the rules of conventional behaviour. A *vicarious* thrill, to use an Uman-word. "It was like watching someone doing a bungee jump," I tell her.

As if the question follows on naturally, D.I. Ryan asks if I found Uman a bit scary.

"The bungee-jump thing was an analogy."

"I know, I meant more generally."

I see where she's going with this. When I was missing, the police must have questioned my school friends about the period leading up to my disappearance. And about Uman, of course. The things he did. The things we did. The things he "made" me do. She has all the dots in place and just needs me to join them up for her. But I'm not playing that game. I've tried to tell her – *have* told her – that she's got Uman all wrong. Got us all wrong. *He didn't do anything bad.* But D.I. Ryan, my parents – they go on twisting it.

Then they expect me to help them.

"No," I say. "I never found him scary."

As Tierney and I headed out of school that afternoon, I spotted Uman up ahead in the stream of students along Coronation Road. He was taller than just about everyone around him and, with his long dark hair, he was unmistakable. I remember thinking he must live on the same side of town as us, or he'd have left by the main exit. Tier's hay fever had eased, but she was complaining of feeling woozy from the antihistamine. It made me smile because it reminded me of Uman calling her my Danish friend.

"Where d'you think he lives?" I asked.

"Who?"

I gesture up ahead. "That new guy. Uman."

"Somewhere posh, if you reckon his old man's a big-shot lawyer. Don't let that put you off, though – some parents are happy for their sons to date a girl from the lower orders."

She'd been teasing me ever since Uman sat with me at tutor time.

We were crossing the bottom of Heatley Road, past the

usual huddle of after-school smokers in the bus shelter. The flow of students had thinned a little. I could see Uman fifty metres or so in front, a logo-less black holdall dangling from one of his long arms like a puppy he'd picked up by the scruff of the neck. That graceful but awkward stride – a cat-walk model with the slightest of limps, his hair fanned out behind him in the breeze.

"Let's follow him," I said.

"We *are* following him."

"No, I mean actually follow him. Find out where he lives."

Tier laughed. "What are we, private detectives or something?"

"Come on. Aren't you curious?"

"No."

"You are, I can tell."

"No, *you* are."

"Fine, I'll follow him on my own."

"Like hell you will."

We stayed close enough to keep him in sight but not so near that, if he happened to glance over his shoulder, he'd realize we were tailing him. We reckoned Uman was heading for The Ridings, where some seriously expensive houses sprawl in huge gardens as Litchbury gives way to country-side. But he surprised us by crossing the main road and taking the path that runs alongside a primary school field.

This was our route home.

44

My first thought was that Uman was going to my house – that I was following him but, in fact, he was trying to find me. It made no sense, because he could have had no idea where I lived. But, then, not much made sense where Uman Padeem was concerned.

"This is bizarre," I told Tier. "We've walked home this way a million times and suddenly I feel like I'm trespassing."

As we joined the path we glimpsed Uman at the far end. I was sure he would turn right, parallel to the railway line, and – although it was a roundabout route – head that way towards The Ridings. But, no. He turned left onto the footbridge that would take him over the tracks to the path on the other side. The one that led to the corner where my street meets Tierney's.

"How does he even know this route?" Tier asked.

It was a good point. The path was well used by people in the neighbourhood, but those from other parts of Litchbury – or who were new to town – wouldn't be aware of it.

Uman didn't live near us, that was for sure. If a new family had moved in, especially one that wasn't white, we'd have heard about it. Besides, a corporate lawyer who sent his son to boarding school could afford to buy several houses like ours and still have change for a yacht.

"Where's he going?" I asked.

The only way to find out was to keep following him.

But when Tier and I had crossed the footbridge over the railway line, the path on the other side was deserted. Unless he'd run, there was no way he could have reached the end so soon; and, with tall fences and hedges either side, climbing into someone's back garden wasn't an easy escape route. We quickened our pace. We'd still be able to spot him from the end of the path – my street was a dead end and Tierney's was long and straight, so no matter how fast he ran, he couldn't have disappeared on us altogether.

At the end of the path, though, there was no sign of Uman whatsoever.

"It's not possible," Tier said. "People don't just vanish."

"You may have a point there," a voice said behind us.

We turned to see Uman approaching along the path we'd just walked down, looking very pleased with himself.

"How d'you explain that?" Tierney asked.

I couldn't. We were at her place – officially working on a science project, but actually listening to music, browsing the internet, taking selfies and photoshopping them to make us look like freaks. I nearly always went round to hers after school. I preferred it there to being at home. I don't mention this to D.I. Ryan. Not with Mum sitting right here.

"I think he's got *supernatural powers*." Tierney made her voice go all spooky.

We laughed.

"Seriously, though," she said.

"Tier, we're not characters in a fantasy novel."

"Novels." She acted puzzled. "Are they the things that films are made from?"

46

Right above her were three shelves crammed with books. We lay head-to-toe on Tierney's narrow single bed, each of us on our iPad. Her bedroom smelled of peaches and cinnamon from the scented candles that burned on her windowsill.

"So, what're you saying?" I asked. "He dematerialized?"

"It's an option."

"And don't tell me he hypnotized us – we never got near enough."

Tierney had a theory that Uman used eye-to-eye or physical contact to assert his will over people: Mr Brunt, for example, at tutor time. Tierney herself. With Ms Vaux, in Geography, over his bangles. Individually, these "'episodes" – and the stunt he'd just pulled on us on the way home – might be explained away, somehow. Added together, though, they formed a pattern of weirdness. *Weirdery*, as we decided to call it.

"How did you *do* that?" I'd asked him, at the end of the footpath.

"Do what?" Uman said.

"You were in front of us and now you're behind us."

"Ah, but it's also the case that you were behind me and now you're in front."

"Come on, Uman, you must've done something."

"It certainly seems as if one of us did."

Tierney flashed him her prettiest smile. "Whatever you did, it was pretty cool."

"Hey, your English has really improved," he replied.

"My English?"

47

I tried not to let her see my amusement.

"But please don't flirt with me, Tierney," Uman said. "I'm only interested in Gloria."

Tier's eyes widened. "I *wasn't* flir—"

"Why were you following me?" Uman interrupted, addressing me.

"What?" I was still getting my head round what he'd said to Tier. "We weren't following you. We live here." I pointed along the street towards my house. "This is our route home."

"You need to be more subtle. Frankly, as surveillance goes, that was amateurish."

"You need to get over yourself."

"You're still upset with me about my remark at break time, aren't you?" Uman said. "I only hope it's delayed our impending relationship, not wrecked it altogether."

"Our what?"

"Anyway, I'm afraid I have to go now," he said.

His parents were expecting guests for supper and he had to finish his prep before they arrived. With that, he left, turning back up the path towards the footbridge. This hadn't been his route home at all, I realized.

"Just so you know, I really wasn't flirting with him," Tier said, in her bedroom.

"It wouldn't bother me if you were."

"You're my best friend, Glo-Jay. You're in an *impending relationship* with him."

I let out a snort. "Yeah, right. What is one of those?"

My bare feet were beside her head on the pillow. She squinted at them. "Your toenails need repainting, missy. Want me to do them?"

"Go on, then."

Tierney swung off the bed and went over to her dressing table. "What was all that about him upsetting you at break time?"

I hadn't told her what he'd said about me being unhappy. "Nothing. Just … he was, you know, being the way he is. I knocked him back."

"So, do you like him?"

"Uman?"

"*Yes*, Uman." She selected a bottle of nail polish. Put it back, chose another. "He told Ryan Jacques he has a tennis court in his garden."

"I hate tennis."

"What's tennis got to do with it? We're talking about the possession of a tennis court."

"Tier—"

"And what the hell's 'prep'?" she asked, still foraging among her make-up stuff.

"It's posh-speak for homework."

"It's his first day at a new school. How can he *have* any homework?" Tier held up two small bottles. "Aquamarine Glitter or Speckled Plum?"

"Both," I said. "Alternating toes."

As she painted me, I figured it out. Uman must have

ducked under the steps leading down from the footbridge, waited for us to overtake, then snuck up behind us. The discovery of a non-supernatural explanation was a bit of a let-down, to be honest.

But Tier was right – it was still a pretty cool trick.

Uman was so sure about "us". He had decided we were meant for each other and so it would come to pass. In a way, I found it quite funny, and I suppose I should have been flattered, but there was also something wrong about it. I don't just mean his arrogant assumption that I was his for the choosing. It wasn't right – wasn't normal – to breeze into someone's life and latch on to them in the way he had done with me.

Who was he? Why was he being like that? Why me?

The rest of that evening, that night, the next morning, I barely thought about anything else. Even when I was asleep, I dreamt of Uman. A nightmare, really: a rerun of the scene on the way home; only, this time, as I'm following him – alone, no Tierney – other people keep trying to obstruct me. Friends, my parents, my brother, teachers, strangers. They block the path, grab my arms – and all the time Uman is disappearing along a path that seems to go on for ever.

Please, I have to catch him!

I woke up, sure I'd shouted it out. But no one came to my room to see if I was OK.

Walking to school the following day, I made Tierney promise to sit next to me at tutor time no matter what. I'd decided to put the brakes on Uman – let him know that he couldn't take me or my friendship for granted, never mind a relationship. It was too much, too soon. That's what I would say to him: *Uman, it's too much, too soon.* We'd known each other twenty-four hours. He had to give me space, had to be less full-on, less … weird. I had it all rehearsed in my head.

But Uman wasn't in school that day.

Or the next. Or the next.

If the teachers knew why, they weren't letting on.

In those three days, his absence made his presence on the Monday seem all the more fantastical. It was almost as if we'd imagined him. Then, on the Friday morning – just when we were wondering if we'd ever see him again – he sauntered into tutor group, easy as you like. He'd shaved off his scruffy stubble and wore his hair in a ponytail, fastened with a purple scrunchie. The last to arrive, Uman apologized to Mr Brunt for being late and made straight for the vacant seat next to Luke. He didn't look in my direction.

Stunned silence. This entrance was somehow even more dramatic, more captivating, than the one he'd made on Monday.

Mr Brunt didn't ask where he'd been for the last three days, or demand a note, or ask if he'd been unwell and say that he hoped Uman was feeling better. None of that. He simply said good morning and carried on. If anything, this heightened the tension. Like a leopard had loped into the room and climbed onto one of the chairs and the tutor was pretending not to notice.

A boy at the back punctured the silence. "Nice ponytail, gayboy."

Mr Brunt looked up sharply. "Callum Rudd, I will not toler—"

Uman raised a hand to silence the teacher. It's OK, his manner suggested, I can handle this. Then, turning to address Callum directly, Uman said, "Your assessment of my sexual orientation is statistically inaccurate, I'm afraid. As a rough estimate, I'd say that eighty per cent of the people I find sexually alluring are female." Eyeing Callum up and down, he added, "But don't worry, you definitely aren't in the other twenty per cent."

The room exploded with laughter. Some students even applauded.

That day, Uman paid me no more or less attention than he did anyone else. He treated me the same as them, spoke to me no differently, behaved perfectly normally around me. Neither friendly nor unfriendly. We were two students who happened to be in the same tutor group and the same class for a handful of subjects. It was as if we'd actually had the conversation I'd rehearsed and he was respecting my wishes. Backing off, giving me space. Being less weird.

With me, anyway. With teachers, Uman scaled new heights of weirdery.

For example, in R.E. he informed Mr McQueen that he would prefer to spend the lesson reading poetry, as he'd already familiarized himself with the major religions and they had nothing more to offer him.

The teacher blinked several times. "I'm highly impressed, Uman," he said, heavy on the sarcasm. "Fifteen years old and you know all there is to know about religion."

"All I *need* to know, sir. And my name's pronounced *Oomaan*, not *You-man*."

"Well, Ooo-maaan, let me make it clear that, no, you cannot read poetry in my class."

"Would you rather I went to the library?" Uman pushed his chair back and stood up, gathering his belongings.

"Sit *down*, Mr Padeem. You're going nowhere."

Uman remained standing. "I'm afraid I don't take orders, sir. There should be a note about it on my file if you care to look it up."

A few people had laughed when Uman said he wished to read poetry. No one laughed now. On the interactive whiteboard behind Mr McQueen, the Microsoft logo flitted about the screen like a mutant moth butting repeatedly against a window. The teacher stood for a moment, gazing up at the ceiling panels, as if intent on counting them. He cleared his throat. Looked at Uman. This time, he asked him to sit down, with a "please", and without the sharpness of tone.

Uman sat down. He read poetry for a few minutes, then set the book aside and paid attention to the lesson. He joined in the discussion (about the Four Noble Truths of Buddhism, I think) and completed the written exercise we were set.

At the end, he approached Mr McQueen. "Thank you, sir. That was very stimulating."

Outside in the corridor, I fell in step with Uman. "Why are you like that with teachers?"

"I don't know." He sounded genuinely troubled by the question. "I can't stop myself."

I asked what he meant, but he said it was difficult to explain.

"You disapprove?"

"Not really. I'm not sure what I think." After a moment, I said, "The teachers cut you a hell of a lot of slack, don't they?"

"It certainly seems that way."

"It's like you have some kind of hold over them."

He coughed. Two sharp, harsh hacks. "It certainly seems that way," he managed to say.

"Or like they know something about you that makes them back off."

"It cert—"

"OK, I get the idea." I smiled, shook my head. "Jesus, you are off-the-scale irritating."

It was good to be talking to him again, though, even if he was giving me the man-of-mystery routine. At the lockers, I asked something else. "How come you've not been in school?"

"There were other things I preferred to do."

He made it sound so reasonable I couldn't help laughing.

"Why d'you ask?" he said, giving me a sidelong look.

"Oh, no reason. Just … nothing." It was a near thing, but I stopped myself from saying I was pleased to see him again. From letting him know I'd missed him.

"Three days earlier, you wanted him to stop bothering you," D.I. Ryan says. "What changed?"

"I don't know."

That's not true, though. What I mean is, I don't know how to explain it.

I must try, much as I'd rather be anywhere else right now than sitting here answering these questions. For her sake and for mine, I must try to answer because – in different ways, for different reasons – D.I. Ryan and I both need to make sense of what happened between me and Uman. Also, I have to be clear about it for Uman's sake. The police persist in regarding him as a perpetrator and me as a victim; the manipulator and the manipulated.

I can't let them think that's how it was.

With a shrug, I say, "I guess I didn't realize I liked him until I thought he was gone." I study D.I. Ryan's face. She has pouches of pale flesh beneath her eyes. I hadn't noticed them before. "Does that make sense?" I ask her.

She nods. "Yes," she says, quietly. "Yes, it does."

During his absence that week, I told her, the normality of my life – at school, at home, with my friends – was duller than ever. I missed the very thing I thought I'd wanted him to tone down: his oddness. I *like* oddness. Used to, anyway.

But as I've grown up I've become more and more conventional – worried about fitting in, increasingly self-conscious about drawing attention to myself by the way I behave, how I speak, the things I do, the clothes I wear, the—

Mum interrupts at this point to ask in what way my wardrobe – that's what she calls it, my "wardrobe" – can be considered conventional.

"And what about your earrings?" Mum asks.

She doesn't like my home-made jewellery. My "junk", she calls it. She's never forgiven me for sneaking off to get a third piercing in each ear when she'd drawn the line at two.

"Is that it?" I say, rounding on her. "I accessorize the tabs from drinks cans, wear purple Docs and a fake pilot's jacket that's too big for me, and suddenly I'm Lady Gaga?"

"Lor, I'm just—"

D.I. Ryan cuts in. "Gloria, Mrs Ellis. Please."

I slouch back in my seat. Fold my arms.

"You were saying," D.I. Ryan continues, after giving me a moment to calm down.

I consider not bothering to respond. In the end, I do. It can't sound all that coherent, but I try to explain that I envied Uman for breaking out of the constraints that life places on us. For being how he chose to be and not giving a damn what anyone thought of him.

That meeting Uman had made me see just how predictable I'd become.

Q5: What d'you mean, "how things were at home"?

I planned to follow Uman after school again on the Friday, this time without Tierney. The curiosity to see where he lived – to fill in some of the blanks about him – was eating me up. I'd be way more subtle about tailing him, for sure. *Clandestine*, that's the word. Last period on a Blue-Week Friday is Science; Uman was in top set, same as me, so it would be easy enough to keep tabs on him as we filed out at the end.

Only, Uman didn't turn up for the lesson. Back in school after missing three days and he was already cutting another class.

I felt like he'd cut me. As if he'd somehow known what I was planning to do and had left early to make sure I didn't. And now I wouldn't see him again till Monday. If he bothered to come to school, that is. I sat through Science with a scowl on my face, barely taking in a thing.

"Uman Padeem was an itch you had to scratch?" D.I. Ryan suggests.

I wouldn't have chosen those words, but it pretty much sums up how I felt back then.

Anyway, she doesn't want to talk about that any more. She'd like to move things forward. *Cut to the chase.* The day I went missing, she means. But I'm not there yet. I tell D.I. Ryan she needs to know how things were at home if she wants the full picture of my disappearance.

She glances at Mum, then back at me. "What d'you mean, 'how things were at home'?"

I begin with the story of how my parents met. D.I. Ryan interrupts, says this doesn't have any bearing on ... but I tell her it does. Reluctantly, she lets me continue.

California, 1993. Dad was twenty-seven, Mum was twenty-three.

Having been in a not very successful band in the UK, Dad had set off to America to try to *make it* in the *music business*. He ended up in San Francisco as a session musician. Meanwhile, Mum had realized she wasn't suited to a career in medicine and quit her training to go travelling. She'd been on the road nearly a year when she found herself living in a San Francisco youth hostel and waitressing at a diner. The diner where my dad and other musicians liked to hang out.

So Kev met Liz over a burger-and-fries and a bottle of Bud.

Mum watches me with a curious expression, like she's never heard this tale before. Or not told it herself a hundred times.

58

When Kev just happened to have a spare ticket for a Van Morrison gig, Liz just happened to be off-shift that night. If only we could time-travel back to The Mystic Theater, Petaluma, California, on the 12th December 1993, we'd witness their first date, first dance, first kiss. They've always disagreed over whether Van Morrison sang "Gloria" at that gig. Dad swears he did, Mum insists he didn't. But they do agree that they both loved – love – the song. Enough to name their only daughter after it.

They returned to England together, six months later, in the summer of '94.

One year after that, they were married. One year after that, they had my brother, Ivan.

"Van Morrison's middle name," I tell D.I. Ryan. "It's where the 'Van' comes from."

By then Mum had retrained as a secretary and Dad – his thirtieth birthday looming, weighed down by fatherhood and his continued failure to break through as a singer-songwriter – had finally drawn a thick line under his life as a musician and was completing an accountancy course.

"God, you make it sound so black-and-white," Mum says.

I look at her. Then, to D.I. Ryan, "Three years and four months after Ivan was born, they had me. Gloria. G-L-O-R-I-A. They had their 2.0 children. Their mortgage. Their safe, steady jobs." I realize, as I'm saying it, how horrible I must sound.

"Gloria, sorry, but what does all this have to do with 'how things were at home'?"

59

She doesn't get it. She doesn't get it at all.

"Excuse me." This is Mum. She says she needs the bathroom. As Mum bustles out of the interview suite, D.I. Ryan pauses the recording.

"You could go a bit easier on her, you know," she says after a moment.

I don't say anything.

She studies my face. "Your mum's a cyclist, isn't she? A good one, from what I hear."

"Uh-huh."

"She's certainly in fantastic shape for, what – forty-four, forty-five?"

I let D.I. Ryan know how much time, on average, my mum spends each day on her bike – training, or away at races all over the country.

"That's some dedication," the detective says, entirely missing the point.

She seems fine with us talking while the machine isn't running. While Mum isn't here. Like this conversation is so unimportant it's no longer part of the interview. I'm gripping the sides of the chair so tightly my knuckles hurt.

"Then there's Dad and his acting," I say.

D.I. Ryan frowns. "What?"

"He's in the Litchbury Players."

"Really? He doesn't strike me as the type for amateur dram—"

"Oh, he takes it very seriously. It must've been a real

60

wrench for him to skip rehearsals while I was missing. And Mum, her cycling. God, it must've been terrible for them."

She gives me a hard stare. It's the first time I've got the sense that she doesn't like me. "You have *no idea* what your parents went through during those fifteen days."

I don't respond.

Her stare hardens. "Gloria – It. Ripped. Them. To. Pieces."

She looks like she'd enjoy nothing more right now than to slap to my face.

I almost wish she would. I even flinch when she reaches out to hand me a tissue. Which surprises me because, until that moment, I didn't realize I was crying.

I thank her. We lapse into silence.

Mum was wheeling her bike out of the garage when I pitched up at home on that Friday afternoon, after Uman cut Science. She was all Lycra-ed up in yellow. We did the "Hey-how-was-your-day?" routine, but I could see she was irritated at being delayed by my arrival.

"You're home early."

"What time is it?"

"I don't know." (For cycling, she wears a stopwatch, not a regular watch.)

"Then how d'you know I'm home early?"

"I thought you'd be round at Tierney's."

I gave her the raised eyebrow. "Yeah, well, I would be, but

61

Tier's mum suddenly realized I wasn't her daughter and threw me out. I'm amazed I've got away with it as long as I have."

"Lor, much as I'd like to hear some more of your sarcasm—"

Mum bit back whatever she was about to say.

I watched her unhook the crash helmet from a handlebar and fit it on her head, the bike leaning against her hip. "There's food in the fridge, if you want to sort yourself out," she said, fastening the chin-strap.

I don't think I've ever spoken to Mum without her: (a) asking if I've eaten; (b) asking what I'd like to eat; or (c) telling me to get something to eat.

"I'll probably just have a couple of Pringles," I said.

She let that one go. "I'll be back before dark. Your dad's going straight to rehearsals after work, so I doubt he'll be home before me."

And off she went. Another typical evening in the Ellis household beckoned.

I don't tell D.I. Ryan any of this.

We just go on sitting quietly, avoiding eye contact, waiting for Mum to return. When she does, she looks like she's been crying as well.

The detective tells her, "We were talking about your cycling, Mrs Ellis."

"My *cycling*?"

"D'you mind me saying this, Gloria?" I shrug and D.I. Ryan addresses Mum again. "It bothered her, the amount of time you were spending away from home on your bike. And Kevin, with his drama."

Mum's face flushes. "What are you, a social worker, now, as well as a cop?"

D.I. Ryan exhales. "I just thought you should know how Gloria felt."

"We're hardly ever at home together, the three of us," I say. "And when we are, all we do is bicker and snipe at each other."

"That's not true, Lor."

It's been like that for ages, I tell D.I. Ryan. But it got a lot worse after Ivan left to go to uni last September. With my brother in London and me all grown up at fifteen, it was as if Mum and Dad no longer had any responsibilities towards either of us. Like our family had split into four separate individuals, each living his or her own life. As if I'd left home too.

"Oh, honey, how could you think we—"

"I actually overheard you on the phone to one of your friends saying, 'Now that Ivan's moved out it's like I've got my life back'."

I see the impact this has on Mum's expression. On D.I. Ryan's too.

In the hush that follows, Mum looks ready to start crying all over again. Eventually, her voice a little husky, she says, "I had no idea you felt like that."

It's hard to tell if she thinks I'm a selfish bitch or that she's a lousy parent. Or both.

I should feel relieved to have said all of this after shutting it away inside me for so long. But I feel crap.

"Let's get back to you and Uman, shall we?" D.I. Ryan says.

The following Monday, Uman was back in school. He sat with Luke again at tutor time and disappeared at morning break, so the first chance I had to speak to him was lunchtime. Even then he took some tracking down. I eventually found him sitting by himself on a strip of grass near the perimeter fence beyond the sports hall.

For some reason, he had taken off his shoes and socks, making his too-short trousers seem even shorter. His toes were long and thin, more like fingers, and surprisingly pale.

"Hey," I said, stopping on the path as if I just happened to be passing. In fact, the path continued only for another ten metres before hitting a dead end.

"My ankles swell up," Uman said, indicating his bare feet. The skin was patterned with indentations from his socks. Both ankles looked puffy, the insteps too.

"Your feet are *huge*."

"Size twelve, in their unswollen state. I can't take any credit for it."

"Even my dad's only a ten."

"Your father sounds like a good and wise man."

"For having size ten feet?"

"Absolutely. It shows an admirable sense of proportion. I lack that," he added, with a note of regret. "My feet, much

64

like my behaviour, have no capacity for self-restraint."

With Uman, you never quite knew when he was joking; just as you couldn't be sure if all those long words were part of the joke or just the way he spoke.

"D'you think they're connected?" I asked.

"My feet?"

"No, your foot size and your behaviour."

"Ah. You might be on to something there, Ms Inexcelsis."

I gestured at the grass beside him. "Mind if I join you?"

"Technically, you already have. What you mean, I think, is can you sit with me."

"You're only ever a nanosecond away from being a total smart-arse, aren't you?"

"You see," he said. "I knew you'd be like this from the moment I saw you."

"Like what?"

"Like you wouldn't take any crap from me."

"This was when you 'read' me, yeah?"

"Was that scepticism or sarcasm?" Uman asked.

"Both. But, then, you'd know that, if you could read me." I dropped my bag on the ground and sat down next to him; pulled out my lunchbox, which is bright yellow and shaped like a wedge of cheese. It had seemed amusingly naff when I bought it; just then, it looked childish. "So, your ankles," I said, fishing out a tuna mayo wrap. "How come they swell up?"

"I broke them."

65

"Both of them? How?"

Uman coughed, twice. I thought it signalled the start of one of his coughing fits, but it didn't. "I jumped from a height that was incompatible with ankle bones remaining intact." He frowned. "Are they bones or joints? Whatever, they broke. To be accurate, one broke, one dislocated. As a result, they sometimes swell up and, as you'll have noticed, I walk with a limp."

"Why did you—?"

"It's a boy thing," he said dismissively. "We climb tall trees, we ride bikes at breakneck speed, we dare one another to perform death-defying stunts. Inevitably, we hurt ourselves."

He didn't seem the type for all of that – he was the least boyish boy I'd met – and I got the impression his explanation was actually an evasion. The true story wasn't something he wished to reveal.

"Have you eaten?" I asked after swallowing a mouthful of wrap. Jesus, it was the sort of question my mum would've asked.

"I'm going to have mine in a minute."

He had no bag with him. "Do you actually *have* any lunch?"

"Not as such."

"So ... d'you want to share mine? It's tuna mayo." I indicated the wedge-of-cheese lunchbox. "Mum always makes way more than I could possibly eat."

66

"That's very kind, but no. Thank you."

I gave a suit-yourself shrug and took another bite of wrap. The ground was damp, I realized; moisture was seeping through my skirt. I wondered why Uman had chosen to sit on the grass when there was a bench just a short way back along the path. Why he'd sat so far away from everyone else, for that matter. Outside class Uman played the loner, but in lessons he didn't mind drawing attention to himself. Made a point of it, in fact. It was another of the things about him which didn't add up. Before I could suggest we move to the bench, he said, "You *were* following me last week, weren't you?"

I laughed. "Was it really that obvious?"

"What were you hoping to ascertain?"

"*Ascertain*. Nice one. You know Tierney calls you Thesaurus Boy?"

It was his turn to laugh. "I've been called worse."

"I quite like it. I feel more intelligent when I'm talking to you. I have to think."

"Thinking is good," Uman said. "We like thinking."

It was true what I'd said. Whenever I was with him I felt smarter, sharper, wittier. I felt stretched. Our conversations were casual, but there was always something bubbling underneath. "Subtext", Uman would probably have called it.

"You never say anything boring or predictable," I said.

"'The only people for me are the mad ones, the ones who are mad to live, mad to talk, mad to be saved, desirous

67

of everything at the same time, the ones who never yawn or say a commonplace thing, but burn, burn, burn.'"

I stared at him.

"Jack Kerouac," he said. "American writer. Very retro."

"Say all that again."

After he'd repeated the quotation, I turned it over in my mind. *Mad to live ... desirous of everything.* I liked that word: *desirous.*

"If you want the truth," I said, licking mayo off my thumb, "we followed you because we were hoping to *ascertain* where you lived."

Uman massaged his ankles, the bangles on his wrists jangling and clicking.

When he didn't respond, I said, "Is it just the three of you? Where you live, I mean. Or do you have any brothers or sis—?"

"If you'll excuse me, Gloria – my lunch has arrived."

A guy on a moped had pulled up at the kerb just the other side of the gates. He killed the engine and dismounted. "Mr Padeem?" he called to us, already opening the rear pannier. "One Triple Cheese Feast, one garlic bread, one coleslaw, one Diet Coke?"

"I still can't believe you did that," I said, when we'd finished sharing the food.

"I imagine it's against the school regulations," Uman replied.

"Ordering takeaway? Er … *yeah*."

"And you can't believe I would do something that contravened school regulations?"

"No, of course I believe you'd do it. I'm just saying it's *unbelievable*."

Uman frowned. Started to speak, then stopped himself.

"You were going to say something smart-arse again, weren't you?"

"Might've been," he said, mimicking a sulky child.

I laughed. So did he. "God, I'm full," I said. We had moved to the bench and were sitting at either end of it. I lay back, resting one hand on my bloated belly and using the other to stop my skirt riding up. "I don't even *like* Triple Cheese."

"You can rest your feet on my lap if it's easier," Uman said.

I raised my head far enough to look at him. "Easier for what?"

"Nothing, really. I just thought it would be nice to have your feet on my lap."

"Oh, in that case…" I kicked the empty pizza box against him. Lowered my head again. Gave a mock groan. "I swear I'm going to *buuuurst*."

"Or your head. If you turned the other way, you—"

"*Uman*, there is no part of me that's going to rest on your lap."

"You say that, Gloria, but if you did in fact 'burst', then

69

it's altogether probable that some fragments of your body would land there. Pot luck as to which parts they might be, of course."

I groaned again. "Please, don't make me laugh. It hurts my tummy."

We talked about rules; how you decide which ones to obey and which to break. It was like a class discussion in Citizenship ... only, it was nothing like a class discussion in Citizenship.

"Are you a rule breaker?" Uman asked.

"In my head I am, yeah."

"But not in practice."

"No. Not often, anyway. And nothing on your scale."

"Why is that, d'you think?"

"Don't know. Fear, probably. Fear of getting in trouble."

"And fear of standing out?" Uman suggested. "Fear of not fitting in?"

"Yeah, that too. As I've got older, I've become less daring, I guess."

He coughed. Just the once. "My father used to have a poster on the wall of his study – a cartoon showing rows and rows of identical grey houses with identical grey roofs, with just one house in the middle with a roof painted in pink-and-purple stripes. Outside, the owner – he's holding a paint pot and brush – is being frogmarched down the street by the police." Another cough. It took Uman a moment to catch his breath. "As soon as I was old enough to understand

70

that cartoon," he said, "I swore I would grow up to be a guy with a pink-and-purple roof."

I checked the time on my phone to see how long we had left before the end of lunch. Even as we discussed transgression, I was anxious about being late for class.

"Have you always been the way you are?" I asked. "Only, I can't believe you haven't been kicked out of about ten schools by now." Then, laughing, nudging his arm, "Maybe you *have*. Maybe that's your big secret."

"I haven't always been this extreme, no."

"So, how come? I mean, why have you become more transgressive?"

He nudged me back. "We were talking about you," he said. "How come we're talking about me again?"

"Because you're a stripy roof and I'm just plain old grey."

"Not on the inside. On the *inside*, Gloria, you're a kaleidoscope of pink and purple."

On the way to class at the end of the lunch break, I told Uman that if he still wanted someone to show him the sights of Litchbury, we could meet up after school.

"Does this mean we're friends?" he asked.

I threw one of his own lines back at him. "It certainly seems that way."

Q6: Did you start to have your suspicions about him?

D.I. Ryan:

Lunch OK?

Gloria:

Yeah, it was all right. Actually, no. It was terrible.

D.I. Ryan:

(Laughs) It's a real perk of the job, the police canteen.

Gloria:

Is this rapport?

D.I. Ryan:

Not really, but it'll have to do until the rapport turns up.

Gloria:

(No response)

D.I. Ryan:

OK, so. Good to go again, Gloria?

Gloria:

Uh-huh.

D.I. Ryan:

Interview resumes, 1.33 pm. Same persons present.

Now, this is still your story, your words – and it's all good. Really helpful. But I'd just like to clarify a couple of things before you pick up where you left off when we broke for lunch.

Gloria:

Clarify what?

D.I. Ryan:

So, it's clear Uman made a strong first impression on you. And, of course, there's everything that's happened between you since then, which we haven't come to yet. Already, though, I'm getting the idea that – how can I put it? That Uman became – has become – a very ... *dominant* figure for you. Not just back then, at the start, but still. Is that fair to say?

Gloria:

(No response)

D.I. Ryan:

What I want, Gloria, what I need to be sure of, is that you understand that you're safe. He can't get near you now you're home. Now you're here. He can't hurt you.

Gloria:

Why would Uman hurt me?

D.I. Ryan:

Gloria, listen to me, you do understand that, don't you? Uman has no hold over you any more.

Gloria:

I've always understood that.

D.I. Ryan:

OK, let me put it this way: did he make any threats towards you?

Gloria:

Threats?

D.I. Ryan:

About what would happen if you talked to the police?

Gloria:

No. Why would he?

D.I. Ryan:

Because… Look, in these situations, a bond can form between the two people involved – an affinity, but also a kind of emotional dependency, or what we call "empathetic identification". But the thing is, Gloria, I don't know whether you're trying to protect him out of some false sense of attachment or loyalty, or because you're still afraid of him.

Gloria:

Jesus, how many times do I have to tell you? He didn't *abduct* me. I wasn't his *hostage*.

D.I. Ryan:

Strictly speaking, no, you weren't. But—

Gloria:

Can I ask *you* something, Detective Inspector?

D.I. Ryan:

Yes. Yes, of course.

Gloria:

If you've already decided how things were between us, why d'you want to hear it from me?

D.I. Ryan:

I haven't already— All right, let me ask you this and then I'll shut up and you can carry on telling it in your own way. In that first week or so after you met Uman, did you start to have your suspicions about him? Your doubts. About his story.

Gloria:

What do you mean?

D.I. Ryan:

His background, his family. The posh kid moving to Litchbury because of his dad's high-powered job. Killing time at the local comp while he waits to start at a new boarding school.

Mrs Ellis:

Litchbury High is an *academy*. Not a comprehensive.

D.I. Ryan:

Thanks for that, Mrs Ellis.

So, Gloria? Did you realize that something about him didn't quite add up? And all of that business with the teachers, letting him behave how he liked. You were curious about that, weren't you? I know you were. You asked him about it after R.E. that time.

Gloria:

He was somewhere new, where no one knew him.

75

It was a chance to reinvent himself.

D.I. Ryan:

It was more than that, though. You know that, now.

Gloria:

I didn't know it then. Not to begin with.

D.I. Ryan:

What about the way he was with you? Do boys normally come on to you like that?

Gloria:

No. But boys don't normally look like Uman Padeem, or talk like him, or think like him, or do anything that even remotely interests me. Anyway, he didn't "come on" to me.

D.I. Ryan:

"Latched on" is the phrase you used, I think.

Gloria:

We latched on to each other. And anyway, Uman didn't make me feel the way I did about him. Didn't make me do the things we did. He had no hold over me.

D.I. Ryan:

You honestly believe that?

Gloria:

Christ.

D.I. Ryan:

Did it ever occur to you that Uman might be manipulating you?

Gloria:

No. Because he wasn't.

D.I. Ryan:

Sometimes it can be so subtle you don't even—

Gloria:

Uman wasn't exactly subtle about the fact he wanted to hang out with me.

D.I. Ryan:

Wasn't he?

Gloria:

That very first day, he was like: "Hey, Gloria, we're meant for each other."

D.I. Ryan:

Then he disappears for three days. And when he returns, he backs off, gives you *space*. Lets you make all the running. Then he's flirting with you again. Being interested in you, hanging out with you – reeling you back in. Only, he's so good at it you don't even realize.

Gloria:

I don't care what you think, he didn't trick me or manipulate me. It just wasn't like that.

D.I. Ryan:

OK, Gloria, tell me. What was it like?

Q7: The Hangingstones – what happened up there?

We headed down to the river, through the park, across the footbridge into the bluebell woods and back over the old stone bridge by the Waterman's Arms. It was a warm afternoon; people sat outside, drinking, eating ice creams or trays of chips from the kiosk next to the pub. Two toddlers fed bread to the ducks on the strip of mud we called "the beach" when I was little.

"Me and my brother used to build mud castles here," I said.

We stood and watched them, as if those kids were playing the parts of Ivan and me in a scene from my childhood being re-enacted for Uman's benefit.

"I didn't know you had a brother," he said.

"Ivan. He's nineteen." I explained the name. "His hair's longer than yours, actually. And he's grown this beard." I mimed a full-on beard. "He's down in London, at uni."

I started to say some more about my brother, how Ivan was my best friend when we were little (when we weren't fighting) and how much I missed him being at home since he'd moved out last September. But I got the sense that Uman wasn't really listening; or, rather, that he didn't want to hear it. He went quiet on me for a bit after that.

We made for the town centre. I showed Uman the remains of the Roman fort (a grassy mound, a tumbledown wall, an information board), the old church, the bandstand, Litchbury's famous café, where you queue for an hour to pay way too much for a crust-free sandwich the size of a drinks coaster. Uman didn't perk up until we hiked to the moor that overlooks the town. As I pointed out ancient rock carvings, told tales of UFO sightings and abductions and encounters with mythical beasts, he returned to his usual self. Engaged, talkative. Funny. *Where did you go just now?* I wanted to ask. But I didn't want to risk souring the mood, losing him again.

"There's a stone circle up here," I said.

"Seriously? Right, I *have* to see this."

"It's a bit of a trek, though. And it'll be muddy, in our school shoes."

He raised an eyebrow at me.

I smiled a little sheepishly. "I'm not being very pink and purple, am I?"

At the Twelve Disciples, we sat against adjacent stones and drank the drinks and ate the chocolate we'd bought in town. I apologized for the stones – a ring of stumpy, lichen-stained rocks, none more than a metre high, set in scruffy

79

grass and surrounded by heather that had been charred to fuzz in places by controlled burning.

"It's not exactly Stonehenge," I said.

"It's *better*." He took in the circle, the adjoining moorland, with a sweep of the hand. "No busloads of tourists taking photos, for one thing. Just you and me and the stones." He nodded to himself. "I can imagine a horde of Neolithic men in animal skins, conducting a ritual sacrifice here. A goat. Or a virgin. Or a virgin goat. Or is it Bronze Age? This is *real*. It has atmosphere. *Magnetism*. Don't you feel it? I bet our watches have stopped."

"I don't have a watch. I use my phone to tell the time."

"Same here, actually. But I bet *they've* stopped working."

We checked them. They were working just fine.

"Only one bar on mine, though." Uman held his phone up for me to see. "I told you: magnetism. We're sitting in a force field here, enclosed by an invisible mesh of ley lines and auras – aurae? – and ancient something or other. I doubt whether either of us will ever be able to pass through airport security without triggering the alarm. Or have babies."

I was taking a swig of water as he said this and most of it spurted out of my nose.

From the Disciples, we set off for Hangingstone Rocks. Last stop on the guided tour.

Following a stony track across bog and cotton grass and bilberry, I told Uman something I'd been meaning to say since that first day we met.

"I owe you an apology," I said, the words buffeted by the breeze.

"For what?"

We walked in single file, the trail was so narrow. I led, which meant I could hear Uman – his footsteps, his ragged breathing, his voice – but not see him. That suited me. Made me less self-conscious. I could almost pretend I was talking to myself.

"What you said last Monday, at break – you were right. About me being unhappy."

"Why's that worth an apology?"

"I lied. I told you I wasn't. I got cross with you – blanked you."

"If anyone should say sorry, it's me," Uman said.

"You? Why?"

"For presuming to tell you about yourself. It's arrogant. Intrusive."

Did he figure that out for himself or had I confronted him with it at the time? I couldn't remember whether I had. But I liked him for acknowledging it.

"I guess we're both sorry, then," I said.

"Sounds like a deal to me."

The noise of our progress along the track startled a bird out of the scrub up ahead. It flew fast and low above the ground, a blur of brown and red, wings clattering, before settling again farther off with a throaty cry that sounded like it was warning us: *go-back, go-back, go-back.*

"What's that?" Uman asked. "A *phoenix*?"

"Grouse. Male."

"I don't think we have those in Berkshire. Except as food, of course."

"I imagine your cook keeps some in the pantry in case you run out of venison."

"I wouldn't know," he said. "I don't associate with the servants. Not since the under-gardener ran over a croquet hoop with the lawnmower just before an important game."

We'd reached a steep descent and neither of us spoke as we concentrated on keeping our footing. When the ground levelled again, I picked up the thread of our earlier conversation.

"I don't know what you saw in my face that morning," I said. "Don't laugh, but I went into the loos later on and looked in the mirror to see if I could figure out what it was."

"What did you see?"

"Acne, mostly. If I'd joined up the spots, would it have spelled 'I AM UNHAPPY'?"

Uman laughed. "It isn't anything visible."

"What is it, then? An *aura*?"

"I can't explain it. There was just something in you that I recognized."

"I'm not depressed or anything. It's nothing as bad as that." I told Uman about my "tsunami" moments. "Everything's just the same old, same old," I said. "Friends. Home. School. I used to *like* school. But, lately – most of Year 10 – I just can't be bothered. With anything."

82

Uman listened to all of this in silence.

"God, I sound like such a spoilt, sulky brat," I said.

"No, you don't."

"You know what it is, Uman? What I'm really fed up with?"

"Yourself," he replied, simply.

"Yes. *Yes!* How do you even *know* that? And if you tell me you 'read' people..."

"I read people. Did I mention that already?"

I laughed. "Seriously, though, what do I have to be fed up about?"

"Unhappiness isn't a rational choice," Uman said. "Or happiness. You can't *decide* not to be unhappy any more than you can decide not to be tired if you've had a bad night's sleep."

Was that true? It sounded like it ought to be.

The track was wider now, and we walked side by side. His limp had worsened, I noticed. His breathing, too.

"You OK?" I asked.

"Not really. But, being male, I can't admit to it, so please don't ask again."

"It's only a couple of minutes to the Hangingstones."

"Then despite the pain, I shall endure without complaint, self-pity or melodrama." He coughed horribly. "But if I don't make it, just bury me where I fall."

I've summarized all of this. D.I. Ryan doesn't want every detail — *the day is slipping away, Gloria* — and I still haven't reached what she regards as "the beginning". But it began there, really. The events she most wants to hear about can be traced back to that day: eating pizza by the school fence; the guided tour of Litchbury; the hike across the moor. The Hangingstones.

The seeds were sown. The die was cast. Or whatever cliché she cares for.

"So, your feelings for Uman deepened that day?" D.I. Ryan asks.

"Yeah. I liked him. He was good to be with."

"Did he feel the same way towards you?"

"I don't know. You'd have to ask him that question."

But, of course, she can't ask Uman anything. My reply silences us. The desire to know where he is, to find out what has happened to him – to *see* him again – surfaces so strongly, it's all I can do not to shout out his name. I can't quite believe that if I cross the room and open the door he won't be standing right there, with that lopsided grin. I reach for the water, but my fingers are trembling so badly I don't trust myself to pick up the plastic cup.

"D'you need a time-out?" D.I. Ryan asks. When I shake my head, she studies me for a moment. Then, "The Hangingstones – what happened up there?"

"Did they hang people here, in *ye olden days*?" Uman asked.

"No, it's from the way the rocks look like they're hanging on to the side of the moor."

The rocks – huge boulders, really – were dumped on the hillside by a glacier during the last ice age, I explained. From just about anywhere in the town, you could see them silhouetted against the southern skyline – great grey blocks, perched (seemingly precariously) on a green swathe of heather and bracken and sheep-shorn grass. I'd loved the place ever since I was old enough to scramble with my brother on the rubble around the base of the rocks on family picnics. There's a picture at home of Ivan and me trying to push one of the boulders down the slope. We look like mice about to be sat on by an elephant. Behind the rocks is a disused quarry where the Victorians dug out the stone to build most of Litchbury. We studied it in Geography, I told him. Or History.

"Sometimes me and Tier come up here to watch the climbers."

There were several when we arrived that day, working in pairs on different pitches in the big U-shaped bowl, their Lycra suits, safety hats and synthetic ropes daubing bright colours on to the grey of the rock face. They climbed in silence, apart from the clink of a piton being hammered into a crevice, or the swish of rope being paid out, or an occasional echoey instruction. They'd drawn a small audience of hikers and dog walkers. For once, though, the climbers weren't the only attraction. A young guy had fixed a wire across the mouth of the old quarry and was setting himself to walk it. Twenty-five metres above the ground. Maybe thirty.

High enough to kill him if he fell.

"Oh wow, look at him," I said.

Beside me, Uman – still regaining his breath after the walk from the Disciples – said nothing. But I felt him tense up. I couldn't tell if it was fear or excitement, or both.

The shape of the quarry made it a perfect theatre, with us high in the upper circle. Scraps of cloud clustered overhead as if they, too, had gathered to witness the unfolding spectacle. As we edged closer to the rim to get a better view, the guy extended a leg and dabbed at the wire with his foot, like he was stepping into a bath and wanted to make sure the water wasn't too hot. His short dark-blond hair and pale forearms glinted in the late afternoon light and the breeze rippled his red T-shirt. He looked about twenty years old, slender as a ballet dancer.

No safety net. No pole. No helmet. Not even a belt-clip attaching him to the wire.

I started to point this out to Uman but he nodded, like he'd already noticed it. If the guy lost his balance, he really would fall to his death.

"I can't watch," I whispered.

But I couldn't not watch.

Against the slope of the moor in the background, the wire was almost invisible and, for one startling moment as he set off, he appeared to be walking on air. His progress was slow but sure. He took one pointy-toed step after another, arms outstretched at his sides, fingers spread and fluttering like the feathers at the tips of a kestrel's wings. Beneath him, the wire quivered and swayed from time to time and he would halt, perfectly still and poised, waiting for it to steady. A cluster of spectators had gathered at the top of the path that leads into the quarry and more were dotted around the outcrops above. The climbers had paused to watch him, too.

No one moved or spoke. It was as if we all held our breath. Mesmerized. Terrified.

I remember thinking, *Please, someone stop him.* But also not wanting him to be stopped.

It was too late for that, anyway. He would make it across. Or not.

I have a good head for heights. On the climbing wall at school, I'll be at the top and back down again before most of the others are halfway up. But watching this... My guts clenched, my skin went clammy, my mouth filled with the metallic taste of adrenaline.

I pictured him losing his balance, plummeting. Heard the impact. Saw him lying there on the dusty, rock-studded ground, a broken mannequin in a spreading pool of blood.

He made it, though.

He *made* it.

Ninety-six steps. I counted every one. With barely a wobble, he reached the other side, to a clatter of applause and whistles and whoops from his audience and a surge of collective relief so huge I'm amazed we didn't all hug one another. At the top of the crag, the guy gave an exaggerated bow. Waved. Smiled. Blew kisses.

Then, casual as you like, he packed up and left.

My hands were still shaking. Uman couldn't stop smiling, his eyes so glittery you'd have thought he'd been crying. He kept thanking me, as if I'd arranged the whole thing for his benefit. Even after the guy had gone, Uman stood at the rim of the old quarry for ages, staring at the space where the tightrope had been, as if watching the performance all over again.

Over the next few days, a change came over Uman.

He still turned up for school, or not – cut classes, or not; paid attention, or not – on a whim. The barriers of attitude he erected between himself and the teachers were still in place; he continued to challenge and disobey. To break rules. Just as before, he got away with it all. But it no longer seemed to interest him. It was as if he carried on behaving like that only out of habit.

He didn't go on about it, but I could tell this shift was rooted in the scene we had witnessed at the Hangingstones. If he'd had any idea how to walk a tightrope, I swear he would have gone back up there to fix one across the mouth of that quarry and given it a go.

I changed, too. I spent less time with my friends, more with him – in school (when he was there) and out. I stopped going round to Tierney's at the end of the day; instead, I'd head into town with Uman. He liked to tour the charity shops with me, browsing for bric-a-brac to turn into jewellery, or down to the riverside park. One afternoon, we bought a disposable barbecue and cooked sausages on the bank and splashed about, fully clothed, in the river. Just the two of us. Another time, we went into Leeds and blagged our way into an 18-certificate film. In a contest between the ticket-seller's refusal to admit us and Uman's refusal to be refused admission, there was only going to be one winner. Especially after she asked him for proof of identity and he launched into a monologue on Cartesian concepts of "the self" that must have left the poor woman wishing she'd been assigned to the pick-and-mix counter.

That was the first time I skipped a class to be with him. Design Tech, last period on a Wednesday. Sneaking out of the building was exhilarating. Also, surprisingly easy. It dawned on me that some rules – thou shalt not walk out of school in the middle of the afternoon, for example – remain unbroken not because they are actively enforced, but because the rule-makers assume no one would dare to break them.

D.I. Ryan nods to herself, like she's had the same thought.

On the train into Leeds, Uman and I pretended to speak German so the conductor wouldn't realize we were English PoWs on the run. I don't think I've ever laughed so much.

Another afternoon, we just sat in Caffè Nero and talked. About what, I've no idea. I just remember talking and talking and talking.

Tierney didn't take it well. "Just because you like him, you don't have to stop liking me."

"I haven't stopped liking you, Tier."

We were walking to school as usual, along the path where Uman had tricked us that time.

"You don't sit with me in class unless it's one Uman isn't in," she said. "You don't hang out with me after school. You don't message me or answer me when I message you."

"I *do* answer your messages."

"And if I call you, your phone goes straight to voice-mail." She clicks her tongue, exhales. "I mean, do you even go on Twitter any more?"

Truth was, I hadn't switched on my iPad in days, except for schoolwork, and I hardly looked at my phone. "I'm hanging out with you now, aren't I?" was all I could find to say.

"Hanging out? We're walking to school!" She shifted her bag from one shoulder to the other, roughly, like what she really wanted to do was swing it right at my head.

"You were the same when you started seeing Nathan," I told her. "For about a month, it was like I didn't exist."

"That's *so* not true."

This is going to sound mean, but I enjoyed the reversal of roles. The whole time I'd been friends with Tier, she had been the cute one, the pretty one, the popular one, the confident one, the one who called the shots in our friendship.

For once, it was so good not to be the needy one.

"You do realize that when he gets bored of you," Tierney said, "you'll be sobbing snot down my shoulder and expecting me to pick up the pieces."

"Hmm, would that be pieces of snot or pieces of shoulder?"

She looked at me. "Christ, you're even starting to talk like him."

Teachers noticed the change in me, too. Mr Brunt asked me to stay behind after tutor time for a quick word. Leaving the room with everyone else, Uman mimed a tightrope walker as he went through the doorway. I stifled a laugh but Brunt was sorting his papers and didn't notice. For Uman and me, the guy at the Hangingstones had become conflated (an Uman-word) with Jack Kerouac and the stripy-roof man. Symbols of individuality, non-conformity. Of madness to live.

"Now, I know this hasn't been your finest year, Lory," Mr Brunt said, adjusting the knot of his brown tie, the way that he does when he's nervous (i.e. talking to a girl). "Since Christmas, especially, your … ah, performance has deteriorated. You don't need me to tell you that."

So why are you telling me? Uman would've said it, but I just thought it.

We'd had a couple of quick words before – in December, and again before half-term and Easter as my marks dropped and the comments in my planner began to stack up. But this meeting felt more serious, more urgent.

Mum interrupts. "Why didn't I know about any of this?"

"I can't imagine," I say, looking at D.I. Ryan, not Mum.

"What does that mean?" Mum again.

"If you'd ever asked me about school, or actually looked

91

in my planner when you signed it, or bothered to come to a parents' evening—"

"This isn't helping," D.I. Ryan says. "Gloria, Mrs Ellis, this isn't why we're here."

Actually, it is, in a way. But she still doesn't get that. Neither of them do.

Back to Brunt. He wasn't playing the concerned uncle this time; he might've been talking to Callum Rudd or Jordan Mackay, who spend more time in isolation than they do in class.

But I'm a good girl, I wanted to say. Was that even true any more?

I don't mean my behaviour, but my work, my (lack of) enthusiasm. Year 10 had been a period of drifting, getting by on fifty per cent effort; since Uman came on the scene, I'd been making barely any effort at all. Just as I'd imagined a tsunami sweeping away the houses I could see from my bedroom window, so I'd sat in lessons imagining a plane crashing into the school.

"Miss Sprake tells me you missed English yesterday," Brunt said. "D.T. on Wednesday – another absence. What did you do, hide away somewhere? Or just walk off site?"

I offered him a shrug. Close to, he smelled so strongly of toast and coffee and shaving gel that I could picture him at home earlier, performing his morning routine. His gaze settled, as it always does, on my chin. Eye avoidance; boob avoidance. When he talks to Tierney, he stares at the window, the wall, the ceiling.

"You're turning up late for classes," he went on. "You're missing homework deadlines, and when you do hand in work it's way below your … ah, capabilities."

I sat across the desk from him, saying nothing. There was nothing to say. He hadn't asked for an explanation; he was simply laying out the evidence.

Then, he *did* ask me to explain.

"Is it the new lad?"

"Is what the new lad, sir?"

Like a phone with a poor signal, he started to break up. "The past week or two … since he … things have worsened, wouldn't you say? Your disengagement."

"You're saying it's Uman's fault?"

Mr Brunt leaned forward, elbows on the edge of the desk, fingers interlocked. "Lory, you seem to be … since Uman joined us, you appear to have fallen under … to be, ah, in his thrall."

In his thrall. Was that even a phrase?

"I'm capable of making my own decisions. Sir."

"Yes, yes, I'm sure you are. I'm just saying … just trying to get to the root, as it were."

We went round in circles for a few more minutes. I said the usual: yes, sir; no, sir; sorry, sir. I'll try harder from now on, sir. All the time, though, another response remained unspoken.

What's the point, sir?

Day after day, year after year, you go to school to learn

93

stuff to pass exams, and they give you bits of paper to say you've learnt all this stuff (most of which you'll end up forgetting or never needing to know), then these bits of paper get you into college or university so you can learn more stuff, to get more bits of paper, so you can use these bits of paper to get a job you don't want to do and won't enjoy, working day after day, year after year, to earn enough money to pay for a home you don't like (or which you do like but can't really afford), which looks just like every other home, in a town full of people just like you, living lives just like yours, where you live with a partner and have 2.0 children so you can raise them to do EXACTLY THE SAME with their lives, while you get older and older until you die.

And with your last breath, you whisper: *Is that it? Is that why we're here?*

Uman didn't make me think like that. He made me realize I already thought like that.

Uman didn't make me do what I did. He made me realize I wanted to do it.

Q8: Why do you think he lied to you?

On a Friday evening, after dinner, I was in my room when Mum called up the stairs.

"Lor, you have a visitor!"

He was in the hallway, wearing a bright pink hoodie with a picture of Barbie smoking a spliff. Uman Padeem was in our house. Talking to my mum.

"H-hey." I gripped the banister as I descended the last few stairs. I couldn't have said which bothered me the most: him meeting her or her meeting him.

"Oman was just telling me—"

"It's Uman," I said. "*Oomaan.*"

"Oh, sorry, Oman."

I exhaled. "It's *pronounced*—"

"That's quite all right, Mrs Ellis," Uman said.

"Call me Liz, please." Mum wore her plastic smile – an expression that said, *I'm not sure about this young man, but I'll try to be friendly,* with a hint of *Hmm, I wonder if this is Lor's boyfriend?*

"D'you want to come upstairs?" I said to Uman.

95

"Oman says you're working together on a History project."

I flicked a glance at him, then at Mum. "Yeah. We are."

The awkward silence probably lasted only a few seconds but felt longer, as if we were all waiting for someone to tell us what to do next.

"Right, I'll leave you to it," Mum said. "Help yourselves to biscuits."

"Thank you," Uman said, "but, being a vampire, I don't eat regular food."

Mum gave a strange little laugh. "Well ... very nice to meet you, Oman."

"What are you *doing* here?" We were up in my room. I'd shut the door and rounded on him the moment we were inside.

"I wanted to familiarize myself with your domestic circumstances."

"But how d'you even know where I live?"

"You pointed up the street towards your house that time I caught you following me," he said. "I just knocked on a few doors till I found the right one."

I covered my face with both hands. "I can't believe you were talking to my mum."

"She opened the door. What was I meant to do – mime at her?"

"And what was all that about being a vampire?"

"I blurt out stupid things when I'm nervous. And when

96

I'm not nervous, actually." He laughed, in a what-am-I-like? kind of way. "Aren't you going to invite me to sit down?"

We were standing in the middle of my bedroom, Uman taking care not to bash the light shade with his head. I gestured him towards the chair. "You might've let me know you were coming," I said, lowering myself onto the bed and sitting cross-legged at one end.

"Spontaneity. We like spontaneity, remember. Nice room, by the way."

Mine is the smallest of the three bedrooms, with a sloping ceiling, an alcove fitted with a clothes rail and shelves, and a multi-unit that trebles up as homework desk, dressing table and chest of drawers. The chair is second-hand, from Dad's office; you have to keep readjusting the height when you're sitting on it or you end up with your chin on the desk.

"Ivan's room is fifty times bigger," I said. "Rough estimate. And now he only uses it when he's home from uni for the holidays."

"Your long-haired, beardy brother."

"That's him." I smiled. "You'd get on well, you two." But I wasn't sure that was true. They were too similar.

He just nodded, non-committal.

Uman, in my bedroom. It was too strange. Good strange, though. "The look on Mum's face." I smiled and leaned back against the headboard.

"Am I hallucinating," he said, glancing at the ceiling, "or has the room got bigger?"

"It's the chair." I pointed. "There's a lever underneath."

"That's a shame, I was rather hoping it was the room." Uman jacked the seat so high his feet no longer reached the floor, then spun round so he was facing away from me. "Gloria?" he said, tapping the wall as if searching for a secret door. "*Gloria* – where did you go?"

It was dusk by the time he left. I snuck him out of the house without Mum or Dad realizing. Just beyond the foot of the drive, concealed by the conifer hedge, we said our goodbyes.

I thought he might kiss me. It was the first time I'd had that thought and I wasn't sure if I wanted him to or whether I was disappointed that he didn't.

We were standing beneath a streetlamp that turned our skin yellow. Moths zigzagged and spiralled above us in the hazy light like they were daring one another to settle on our heads.

"Let's meet up tomorrow," Uman said. "There's something I need to show you."

He refused to say what it was because it would spoil the surprise. Only after he'd gone did it occur to me to wonder why he'd said "need" instead of "want".

Saturday morning, he was waiting outside the supermarket on Leeds Road. He wore the pink Barbie hoodie again and sat on the back of a bench with his feet on the seat. He was reading the novel he'd borrowed from my room the previous evening. The title – *Being* – had caught his eye.

"Where are we going?" I asked.

Uman lowered the book at the sound of my voice. "I've often thought the same thing." He touched his chest. "That on the inside, I'm not all I seem from the outside."

"It's a good book, isn't it?"

"It's actually somewhere between very good and excellent." He folded the corner of the page to mark his place. I have a thing about that. "D'you have any others by him?" Uman asked.

"Yeah. I could even lend you some bookmarks."

It took him a moment to get the point. "Ah. I've always been a folder myself." Then, as if registering my expression, he added, "But this isn't my book, is it? Sorry."

"It might take thirty or forty years, but I'll probably forgive you."

He stowed the book in his holdall. "Shall we start this conversation again?"

"OK," I said. "Where are we going?"

"To my house." He coughed, just the once. "Now that our relationship has progressed from 'impending' to 'embryonic', it's time you knew the truth about me."

The house was in an area of Litchbury I'd never visited. It stood halfway along a terrace of grubby pebbledash walls and tiny front gardens, most of which were paved or overgrown, or strewn with litter and toys and, in one case, a partially dismantled motorbike. Another had a battered green sofa out front, which two small boys were using as a trampoline. Two of the homes were boarded up.

"This is a joke, right?" I asked.

Uman just swung open a gate and led me to the front door of No. 15. The paint, the colour of fake tan, was flaking in places and one of the glass panels was cracked. But the garden was well-tended, with a neatly mown strip of grass and pretty flowers lining the borders. Inside, a dog yapped like crazy as Uman slotted a key in the lock. I heard its paws scrabbling at the door.

"Don't worry about Fatima," he said. "She hardly ever bites."

Fatima was a Jack Russell. She bit me on the ankle the moment I went in.

"She gets excited by visitors," Uman said. "Don't you, Fats? Yes you *do*." He shut the front door behind us. "If she was a boy dog, she'd be humping your leg right now."

Instead, Fatima was standing guard, growling at me.

"Let her smell your hand – she'll be fine then. Go on, she won't bite you a second time."

Tentatively, I offered the dog my hand to sniff. She bit it. "*Uman!*"

"Let's go and find my grandmother. You can make friends with Fatima later."

I inspected the puncture wounds on my thumb. "Does your grandmother bite as well?"

Uman shook his head. "No teeth."

The hall was at the foot of a steep flight of stairs, with coat hooks and a shoe rack to one side and a frosted-glass door to the other. Uman pushed open the door, admitting a waft of warm air and television noise into the hallway, and led me through to a lounge that reeked of gas fire and cigarettes and sweet perfume. Still growling, Fatima accompanied us into the room.

An old woman sat in a flowery patterned armchair, watching a cookery programme. Her legs were sheathed in a green sleeping bag, like a cheap mermaid costume, and she wore a tartan blanket round her shoulders. A brown cigarette smouldered in an ashtray balanced on the armrest of her chair. Uman and I squeezed onto a sofa beneath the window. The curtains were drawn, but the thin fabric admitted a hazy amber light.

Without glancing in our direction, or even seeming to register us, Uman's grandmother said, *"Onlar pizza yapiyoruz."*

"What did she say?" I whispered to Uman.

"She says they're making pizza."

I looked at the TV. The two contestants were making omelettes.

"Ne tür bir aptal bir pizza tabani olarak yumurta kullanir?" the old woman said, turning to me with a fierce expression, as if it was my fault.

Uman translated. "What kind of fool uses eggs as a pizza base?"

"Doesn't she realize they're making omelettes?"

"Her eyesight's not so good," Uman said. "And she can't understand English."

"What language is she speaking?"

"Turkish. She's my mother's mother."

I shrugged off my jacket. The heat, along with the smoke and the stink of perfume, made it hard to breathe. I wondered if this explained Uman's cough.

"I'll introduce you," he said. Then, addressing the old woman, "Büyükanne, bu benim arkadaşim, Gloria."

Her gaze still fixed on me, she sucked hard at the cigarette then replaced it on the rim of the ashtray. Her eyes were very dark beneath arched black eyebrows that looked like they'd been shaved off and redrawn, clumsily, in thick pencil. Her frizzy grey hair might have been a wig.

On a smoky, outward breath, she said, "Eğer reçete toplamak için hatirladin mi?"

"She's asking if you remembered to collect your prescription," Uman said.

"My prescription?"

"She thinks you're my grandfather. He died five years ago."

The old woman's attention had drifted back to the TV. She shouted something at the screen – I think I picked out the word for "eggs" or "fools", I'm not sure which.

"Shall we go to my room?" Uman said.

"That sounds like a good idea." I tried not to look too relieved.

He spoke to his grandmother in Turkish again, but she flapped a hand at him. *Can't you see I'm trying to watch TV?* her gesture said.

Just then, the Jack Russell – who had been curled up on the rug by the old woman's feet – trotted over to the sofa and butted my knee with her hard snout.

"Hah!" Uman said. "Fatima *likes* you."

When he'd suggested we go to his room, I assumed he meant upstairs. But he led me across the lounge and into a cramped kitchen at the back of the house (quickly shutting the door to stop Fatima following us), then through to the back garden.

"Here we are." Uman nodded towards a tent, in camouflage brown and green, pitched on a short, narrow lawn. "My room."

"You sleep in your grandmother's garden? In a *tent?*"

"Yes, I do. And yes, I do."

"Isn't there a second bedroom?" I asked, indicating the house.

"I can't sleep indoors," Uman said, matter-of-factly.

"Why not?"

"In case of fire."

I let out a laugh. "How many times have you been asleep in a house that burnt down?"

"Once is enough," he said. Before I could think how to respond, he caught hold of my hand and led me towards the tent. "Come on, we can talk inside. Like the Bedouin."

We sat at either end of the rubber mat which served as Uman's bed. Even though we'd positioned ourselves beneath the apex, the top of my head brushed the canvas and Uman had to sit with a stoop. No wonder my tiny room hadn't bothered him. A sleeping bag, inside its stuff-sack, lay in a corner along with one of those inflatable pillows people use on planes, a heavy-duty torch, a pack of playing cards, two paperbacks and a National Geographic magazine. In another corner: a half-empty litre bottle of Pepsi, a Tupperware tub of crackers, a plastic knife and a jar of Nutella. Uman set the food down between us and we munched as we talked.

"I thought you were posh," I said, spitting crumbs. "I thought your parents were rich. I thought you had a tennis court in your garden?"

"I am. They were. I did."

Were. Did. "Your mum and dad…"

"Are dead. That's right." He took the knife from me and slathered another cracker with chocolate spread. "Hence the grandmaternal residence scenario."

"When did they … when was it?"

He spoke through a mouthful of food. "Few months ago."

"Jesus, Uman." I started to say how sorry I was, but he cut across me.

"Don't, please. I'm allergic to sympathy. It brings me out in a rash of self-pity."

I watched him finish the cracker. We'd left the flap open,

but it was still stuffy in there, and gloomy. The light had a greenish tinge and the tent smelled faintly of dog. Uman looked more uncomfortable than I'd ever seen him – literally, what with having to sit hunched up, but ill at ease, too. Like he'd rather talk about anything else. He wouldn't make eye contact. He *always* made eye contact – I'd never known anyone hold my gaze so directly.

"We can change the subject, if you like," I said.

He shook his head. "You deserve to know what you're getting into, here. Who you're getting into, I should say."

I smiled. "In our 'embryonic' relationship?"

"Precisely."

Uman reached for the Pepsi, took a swig, then passed the bottle to me. The drink was warm and flat, but I was thirsty enough not to mind.

A thought occurred to me. "So, if it was a few months ago—"

"Why did I only move in with my grandmother very recently?"

"Yeah."

"That's interesting," he said.

"What is?"

"You haven't asked how they died. I thought you would've done by now."

I hesitated. "I guess I thought you'd tell me when you were ready to." This wasn't true. I'd been on the point of asking, but had lost my nerve.

"Is that right?" Uman looked sceptical but also amused.

"No," I admitted. "I was afraid to."

"Afraid? Of what? Of upsetting me?"

"Actually, no, I'm afraid it's something horrible. Something really awful."

It was. More awful than I could've imagined. His father wasn't a hotshot lawyer, Uman told me; he was – had been – a businessman. An electronics entrepreneur. Over the years he'd made millions. But then the business went belly-up; whatever it was they made, someone else started making it cheaper and better. On top of that, he was being investigated for tax fraud. He was facing bankruptcy and a few years in jail.

"My father was due in court the morning after," Uman said.

The morning after the night he set fire to the house while his wife and sons were asleep; then, while they burned in their beds, he hanged himself in the garage.

"Sons?" I asked.

"I had a brother. Faisal. Eighteen months older. We were both home for half-term."

A brother. I studied him in the greenish light of the tent. "That's why you got upset that time in the park, when I talked about Ivan?"

"We despised each other, actually," Uman said. Then, with a shrug, "But, you know, he was my brother." He took another drink from the Pepsi bottle, although I got the impression it was to distract himself, to stop himself from

106

getting upset in front of me. "It was the smoke that killed them – Faisal and my mother. Asphyxiation. They weren't burned alive."

I didn't speak. Just watched his face, half-turned away from mine, like he'd spotted the bedding and reading materials in the corner of the tent and was puzzling out who they belonged to.

"At the inquest, the pathologist said they never woke up. They were still in their beds – what was left of them, after the fire was extinguished. He said my father had drugged them."

"What about you?" I asked.

"Whatever he gave us, I must have had less of it – or it didn't affect me as strongly."

I remembered the broken ankles. "You jumped out of the window," I said.

"The bedroom door was locked. He'd locked all of them."

Uman's room was on the top floor, in a converted attic, he explained. The worst of the fire hadn't reached it at that point, and he managed to escape before being overcome by the smoke. He'd had to stand on a chair to scramble through the skylight, slide down the roof and let himself drop from the guttering.

By the time the fire crews and police had arrived, Uman – unable to stand or walk – had crawled round the house to the steps up to the front door.

"I was trying to get back inside to save my mother and

brother. My father, too – I had no idea he was dangling from a roof beam in the garage." Uman's voice was steady, emotionless. I sensed it was a story he'd told before. "Of course, the front door would've been locked. And anyone still in the house was already dead by then."

They were his family, not mine, but I was the one with tears in my eyes.

"So, there you are," he said. "Now you know how I got my limp – and how my lungs got wrecked." Uman coughed, as if to demonstrate, triggering a choking fit.

I also knew why the teachers at Litchbury High had cut him so much slack. Trailing this tragedy behind him, Uman was more or less untouchable.

"The X-rays are spectacular," he croaked, once he'd eased his throat with Pepsi and was able to speak again. "The radiographer said I have the lungs of an eighty-year-old life-long smoker."

He finished the story. With his home destroyed and his immediate family wiped out, he returned to the boarding school once he was well enough to be discharged from hospital. But, a couple of months later, the next instalment of Uman's school fees was blocked by his father's bank. All of his accounts and assets had been frozen by the fraud investigation and whatever money remained would be used to pay off his tax and other debts. Uman had nothing except for a few hundred pounds in a savings account in his own name.

"The headmaster was very apologetic, very sympathetic – if

only there was *something* they could do to enable me to continue my education with them ... blah, blah *very* blah."

"Jesus, after what happened they threw you out?"

"That would be an alternative interpretation, yes."

D.I. Ryan breaks in. "Is that what he told you, Gloria?"

I look up, puzzled to see her there, to find myself in a police interview suite. I've been so wrapped up in that visit to Uman's grandmother's house. I nod. "That's what he told me."

"You know that wasn't why he left the school, don't you?"

"I do now, yeah."

"They offered him a scholarship on compassionate grounds," D.I. Ryan says. "Uman could have stayed at that school till he was eighteen, if—"

"I know. I know all of that."

"So he lied to you."

I don't respond, just look at her. She looks right back at me.

"Why d'you think he lied to you, Gloria?"

"Is it possible," I say, layering on the sarcasm as thickly as Uman had spread Nutella on those crackers, "that he lied to me because he didn't want me to know the truth?"

Q9: If you could have one wish, what would it be?

We hung out at Uman's grandmother's place for the rest of that day. Most of the time, we kept to the tent – talking, or listening to music on my iPod, or playing card games with bizarre rules that Uman changed whenever he was losing. We took Fatima for a walk round the streets and I helped Uman make a meal. Omelettes, as it happens. The old woman ate hers off a tray on her lap in front of the TV (BMX racing; she enjoyed the crashes, apparently) while we had ours at a picnic table on the tiny patio, with the dog lurking underneath for scraps. Fatima no longer bit me. Instead, she rested her chin on my knee and gazed up into my eyes.

Uman's grandmother was his only relation in this country, he told me. Given a choice of guardians, he'd picked her. "It was either this or live abroad with my dad's brother."

"Is she ... I mean she's ... the way she is." I laughed. "God, I sound like Mr Brunt."

"Is she a fit and proper person to be a fifteen-year-old boy's guardian?"

"Yeah, I guess that's what I was trying to say."

"To be frank," Uman said, "I'm not entirely confident she realizes I'm living here."

We tried not to find that funny.

"Who looked after her before you moved in?" I asked.

"I don't, really — look after her, I mean. A home help comes every day and the couple next door do the garden and get my grandmother's shopping for her."

I thought about that. "How come she lives like this when your parents were so rich?"

"She wouldn't touch their money," Uman said. "She hated my father. It didn't help that he wasn't Turkish, but she hated him anyway. My grandparents opposed the marriage, and when my mother went ahead with the wedding they pretty much cut off contact. Before this, I'd only met my grandmother at my grandfather's funeral."

It might've been Uman's idea, or mine; I really can't remember. But, in the evening, I messaged Mum to tell her I was still round at Tierney's and would it be OK if I stayed for a sleepover?

Have you eaten? she replied.

Yes.

That was it: my first night in a tent since our one and only family camping holiday when Ivan and I were still at primary school, and we all ended up in a B&B for the rest of the week after the campsite flooded on the third day.

Mum cuts in. "You shared a sleeping bag with him?"

"No," I tell her. "He fetched some blankets from the house."

After I've answered, I realize the oddness of her question: that the sleeping arrangements for that one night need explaining when Uman and I were "missing" together for fifteen days.

It was about one a.m. before we were tired enough to sleep. A breeze pressed gently on the sides of the tent and I heard music, faint and floaty, from a house along the street. I was starting to drift off when Uman asked a question. His breath was warm on the back of my neck.

"If you could have one wish," he whispered, "what would it be?"

I smiled into the darkness. "Can I really have one? Please tell me you're an actual genie."

"Is that your wish? You wish I was a genie?"

"Anyway, shouldn't it be three wishes?"

"One wish, that's the deal. My tent, my rules."

"OK, let me think." Eventually, I said, "I wish I could travel into the future to see how my life is going to turn out."

"Done. When we wake up in the morning it'll be eighty years into the future and you can find your ninety-five-year-old self and ask her what your life has been like. That is, her life."

"That would be so cool."

"Would it?" Uman asked. "If you knew everything in your life before it happened, there would never be any surprises."

"Isn't my wish supposed to be your command? Since when did genies quibble?"

"And what about free will?"

"What *about* free will?" I said.

"There might be thousands of future versions of Gloria Jade Ellis, each one turning out differently, depending on the choices you make during your life."

That stalled me for a moment. "Right, in which case I wish I could travel into the future to meet the oldest, happiest version of myself and ask what choices I should make to end up like her – oh, and could she please keep some stuff back so my life isn't entirely devoid of surprises."

"Good answer."

"Thank you."

"One problem, though."

"What's that?"

"That's your one wish used up," Uman said. "So you're now stranded in the future with no way back to live the life that made this old-woman version of you so happy."

I laughed. "Dammit, there's always a catch."

"It's what makes my job as a genie so interesting."

I rolled over beneath my blankets to face Uman. It was way too dark to see him properly – just a shadowy grey-black shape in the shadowy grey-black – but his breath was right there. A wheeze from his smoke-damaged lungs, a faint scent of egg, onion and toothpaste. His bangles clicked as he reached out to stroke my hair.

"What?" he asked. He sounded like he was smiling.

"Do you really believe that?" I asked. "That we can make thousands of different lives for ourselves?"

"Yeah, of course. Don't you?"

Was he still smiling? I couldn't tell. I pictured his face: the lopsided grin, the girly brown eyes, the too-big nose. Tierney is always telling me I think too much, but when I was with Uman I felt like I'd never be able to think enough. "I don't know," I said, at last. "I'm not sure how to make one life for myself, let alone a thousand."

"So, that was the Saturday," D.I. Ryan says. "Then you went off with him the next day."

"We went together."

"His idea? Or yours?"

"Our idea."

"It's actually quite difficult for two people to have the same idea simultaneously."

I don't bother to reply to that.

"Gloria, this is important."

"It might be important to you. But it isn't to me."

I can see all the things D.I. Ryan would like to say written on her face. But she leaves them unsaid. Instead, she says, "All right, let's try this – tell me what happened on the Sunday morning. Tell me how and why you and Uman went off together."

"You don't like me very much, do you?"

Mum chips in. "Can you blame her, the way you're acting? You might think you're all grown up now, but—"

"Look, we're all getting a bit tired and tetchy," D.I. Ryan says. "Shall we call a time-out?"

I tell her that sounds like a brilliant idea.

"And, Gloria, it's not a matter of liking or disliking. I'm just trying to establish the facts and sometimes that means asking you to talk about things you'd rather not." She pauses. "As it happens, though, I *do* like you. I wish I'd had your strength of character when I was fifteen."

I try to imagine what she was like when she was my age.

I can't, though. Any more than I could look at a picture of myself when I was a baby and find signs of the girl I have become.

Strength of character. Is that what I have? Uman thought so, and so does D.I. Ryan. But they've only seen what happens on the surface – the things I do, the things I say – and that's not where your character is. Uman knew me – knows me – better than anyone ever has, but even he never set foot inside my head or my heart. Never thought my thoughts or felt what I felt.

"Anyway, let's take a break," D.I. Ryan says. "Interview suspended, 3.47 pm."

When we resume, I tell her about the Sunday morning.

I woke up happy. Most of the night I'd been cold and uncomfortable and I'd had about four hours less sleep than

115

I'm used to. But I loved it. They have no idea how much, I say. And, before they ask — because I know they're dying to, both of them — I make it clear that nothing "happened" between me and Uman that night. He stayed in his sleeping bag and I stayed under my blankets. Fully dressed. We didn't even kiss.

"We *have* to do this again sometime," I said to Uman.

"What, wake up?"

"No, spend the night in a tent. Well, and wake up afterwards, obviously."

"Oh, OK." He yawned, stretched — flinging one arm across my face so that I had to nip his elbow to make him shift it. "How about tonight, then?" he said.

"Like I'd be allowed a sleepover on a school night. Even if they thought I was at Tier's."

"What if we pack up the tent and some gear and food, and just take off somewhere? To hell with permission. To hell with school tomorrow."

"Yeah, right."

Uman let the silence answer for him. We were side by side on our backs, gazing at the roof of the tent, its green-and-brown swirls diluted by the first flush of daylight. I rolled towards him, propped up on one elbow to study his expression.

"Are you serious?"

He just did his crooked-grin thing.

"Uman."

"Ms Inexcelsis, I am entirely serious to the point of utter seriousness."

116

I laughed. "But that's crazy! We can't just take off like that."

"What's stopping us?"

"It was Uman's idea, then?" D.I. Ryan says at this point. "You suggested sleeping in the tent again, but he was the one who—"

"No, it was both of us."

"But you just told us—"

"That's the thing: the moment he said it, I knew it was what I wanted as well."

"He planted the idea in your mind, though?" she says. "Of actually doing it."

I shake my head. "The idea was already there. He just showed it to me."

Mum does one of her tuts.

"Seriously, Mum, it was like the words were in my thoughts and Uman was just speaking them out loud for me. If it had been up to me, we'd have set off straightaway. It was only about eight a.m., but once he'd said it, I was ready to go right there and then."

"Why didn't you?" D.I. Ryan asks.

"Because—"

Unthinking spontaneity was the behaviour of an amoeba, according to Uman. We had to prepare, make a list of what we'd need. I'd have to sneak home and get my sleeping bag and ruck-sack, for a start. He began going through all the other things we'd have to do, but I cut in.

"You're saying we have to prepare to be spontaneous?"

"We do this properly, Gloria. We do it with panache and a certain degree of élan."

"But where are we going to buy élan on a Sunday?"

"And, of course, we do it with humour." Uman frowned. "That *was* humour wasn't it?"

We had a tickle fight just then. But there's no need for D.I. Ryan and Mum to know about it. Or that I won.

When we were done wrestling around the tent and Uman had finished the coughing fit it brought on, we fixed some breakfast from leftover crackers and Nutella and drew up a list. Several lists: camping gear, clothes, bedding, toiletries, food and "other kit". We helped ourselves to most of what we needed from his grandmother's house, or from mine. Sneaking in and out of my place was easy. Mum was out (on her bike, no doubt) and Dad shouted "hi" and "bye" from the dining room (the coffee-and-Sunday-papers ritual, no doubt), without even showing his face to see what I was doing or who I was with, or to ask how I was or where I was going.

Once we'd run out of free supplies, we hit a cashpoint to pay for the rest. Both savings accounts, I stress – not just mine – although it occurs to me that the police must already know this from the ATM records. They'll have seen the CCTV footage of us withdrawing the money, as well, and trailing in and out of the shops in Litchbury that morning.

By the time we returned to Uman's grandmother's, we had way more gear than we could fit into the rucksacks or physically carry. It took us a lot of experimentation and haggling about the difference between essential and non-essential items to realize it. We packed and repacked our rucksacks, attached and detached and reattached the camping equipment, set aside things we decided we really didn't need, only to decide that we really couldn't do without them.

"Do you even know how to use a compass?" I asked at one stage.

"Of course I do." Uman sounded indignant. "The Duke of Edinburgh handed me my Duke of Edinburgh Bronze Award in *person*, specifically because he'd heard how brilliant I was with a compass," he said. "*And* I can sail a boat."

"That'll come in handy, given how far inland we are."

"Anyway," he said, gesturing at my overflowing pack, "do you really need *three* changes of clothing?"

"Yes. I do."

"And the hair straighteners?"

"I don't have any hair straighteners. I have never *owned* a set of—"

"The full-length cheval mirror?" Uman interrupted. "The boxing gloves, the desktop PC, the ten-kilo sack of guinea-pig bedding, the English–Spanish dictionary, the complete set of Enid Blyton's Famous Five novels, the bridle and saddle for your Shetland pony, the Shetland pony, the ice skates, the bonsai kit and a Halloween pumpkin, complete with burning candle." He paused for breath. "And you have the *audacity* to suggest my compass is superfluous to requirements."

"I think you mean 'surplus'."

"Yes, I do. Thank you. I do mean 'surplus'. Damn, my whole argument falls apart."

"Does that mean I can take the pony?"

"Yes, *all right*, you can take the pony." He sighed. "I suppose we can always eat it if we run out of food."

Looking back, I realize just how careless I was about all of this. So caught up in the fun that the fact of what we were about to do – and the effect it would have on my parents – hadn't properly dawned on me. Not just then. It was way too crazy to be real. We were the mad people. We didn't yawn or say a commonplace thing. We were desirous of everything at the same time.

We were ready to burn, burn, burn.

Q10: Where shall we go?

"Where shall we go?" Uman asked.

"Oh, right, yeah. I suppose we should decide that."

"We need a destination. And a mode of transport. Any suggestions?"

"New York. By helicopter."

Uman nodded. "That was surprisingly straightforward."

He stood up, hoisted a rucksack on to his back and headed for the gate at the side of the house. Fatima, maybe thinking she was about to be taken for a walk, yapped loudly, ran round in a circle and bit her own tail.

Turning to look back, Uman said, "Gloria, you coming?"

"Slight snag – we don't have a helicopter."

"Bring me solutions, not problems," he said, pretending to be cross. He rejoined me at the picnic table. By now, Fatima was standing at the gate, looking puzzled by the fact that Uman was sitting down again. "Right," Uman said, "the cards shall decide."

"The cards?"

He pulled a deck of playing cards from a side pocket of his rucksack. "Transport options. I'm suggesting train or bus. Any others?"

I watched him shuffle, still not sure how the cards could decide anything. I said the first two things that came into my head. "Walking and, er, hitchhiking."

"Perfect, one for each suit. So, train is hearts, bus is diamonds, hitchhiking is spades and walking is clubs. Yeah?"

"I think hitchhiking should be hearts. They both begin with h."

Uman just looked at me.

"These are important decisions," I said. "I have a right to contribute to them."

"I seem to recall you were responsible for the helicopter fiasco."

"It's because I'm a girl, isn't it?"

He exhaled. "All right – hitchhiking is hearts, train is spades. Happy now?"

"Thank you."

Uman shuffled the cards again.

"Are we sure about diamonds for bus?" I asked.

"*Gloria.*"

"Sorry."

He held my gaze for a moment, both of us desperately trying not to laugh, then placed the deck on the table. "Cut," he said.

I cut the cards. Queen of Spades. Train.

* * *

At the station, we used the cards again to select our destination. Litchbury is at the end of a line that runs into Leeds and Bradford, so we nominated red for Bradford, black for Leeds. The cards said red. Then we turned eight cards over – one for each stop on that route; whichever place got the highest card, that was where we'd go.

"Shipley?" Uman said. He'd clearly never heard of the place.

"I think we should re-deal."

He shook his head. "You don't tamper with fate, Gloria."

We discussed the concept of fate on the journey: were we fated to travel by train to Shipley that morning, or was it just random chance? I said chance, Uman said fate.

"If you'd shuffled the cards differently," I said, "or if I'd cut them differently…"

"Ah, but we didn't. That's the point."

"What's the point?"

"Destiny. Pre-determination." Each syllable seemed to be jerked from his mouth by the jolting of the train. On the seats beside us, our rucksacks threatened to topple to the floor.

"But if I hadn't got you to switch hearts and spades," I said, "we'd have been hitchhiking now, and headed somewhere else, probably."

"Then that would have been our fate. But it wasn't."

"Hang on, though, I thought you believed in free will. That's what you said last night when we were talking about all my possible futures."

"Did I?"

"Yeah, you said our lives turn out according to the choices we make."

"Gloria, I am a tangled knot of complexity and contradiction. What can I say?"

"You could say: 'Yes, Gloria, you're right – it is random chance, and nothing whatsoever to do with fate, that we're on a train to Shipley'."

"Yes, but fate's a much better story."

I couldn't argue with that. We'd left Litchbury and were passing through rough pasture beneath a ridge of open moorland. The slopes shone so green in the sunshine they might have been spray-painted. Above them, the sky stretched wide and blue over everywhere we could go, everything we could do, like a blank screen waiting for us to type our own script.

None of it seemed real. And yet it was. We were actually doing it. Taking off.

I should've been more apprehensive about what we were getting into, or about landing ourselves in trouble, or what my "disappearance" would do to Mum and Dad, and to my brother. But it was only for one night, I told myself. How much harm could one night do? Anyway, I would message Mum to let her know I was OK; later, once we'd found somewhere to pitch the tent. *Gone camping with Uman*, I'd say. *See you tomorrow. Don't worry.* Or something. She *would* worry, of course. I was enjoying myself too much just then, though, to let myself think about that. Selfish, I know. Self-indulgent. Yet even now, with all that's taken place, I look back at that train ride and can't help the smiley joy that bubbles up inside me, as if it's happening all over again.

Outside Shipley station, Uman took one look and said, "We should've re-dealt."

"Actually, I know a good spot near here. If I can figure out the way."

I couldn't figure out the way. Not at first. I'd been there a few times with my family, but not for ages, and only by car. Nothing looked familiar. Then, after we'd wandered up and down a couple of busy, stinky roads, I saw a brown heritage sign for Salt's Mill, directing us through a modern business park to the town's Victorian quarter.

"They used to make wool here," I said as we approached the honey-coloured block of the restored mill, with its towering chimney. "But it's shops and cafés, now, and an art gallery."

"It's important for fugitives to find time for culture," Uman said. "For example, right after he shot JFK, Lee Harvey Oswald hid in a cinema."

"Fugitives. Is that what we are, then?"

"I like to think so. Not quite on Oswald's scale, obviously."

Culture wasn't why I'd brought us to Salt's Mill. (Although we did mooch around the bookshop, and look at the Hockney paintings, and share a scarily expensive slab of walnut cake.) The destination I had in mind lay further on, along the path that follows the canal just there.

"Drop Bear Woods," I said. "Mum and Dad used to take us there on 'family walks' – which was basically them walking while me and my brother grumbled about walking."

"Drop Bear?" Uman asked.

"When me and Ivan were little, Dad liked to scare us by saying wild bears lived in the trees – called drop bears because they hid in the branches and dropped on you as you walked underneath." I snarled, mimed bear paws.

"Aw, I bet you were sweet when you were little."

"I was." I let out an exaggerated sigh. "Where did all that sweetness go?"

Uman laughed. Then he swung his shoulder so his rucksack bashed against mine, nearly knocking me off balance. I did the same to him. We went on doing that for a while.

Ten minutes from Salt's Mill, we left the path and crossed the canal by one of the locks; the entrance to the woods was just there, beyond a small car park. It had been busy along the canal with walkers, cyclists, joggers, families on a Sunday afternoon stroll, but once we entered the trees, we had the tracks more or less to ourselves. A few dog walkers; that was all.

"There used to be a brilliant rope swing," I said. "I don't know if it's still here."

We found it. At least, I think so. It wasn't quite where I remembered it, and I had been sure it had an old tyre at the bottom, not a bit of broken-off branch; but even if it was a different rope from the one my brother and I used to swing on, it worked well enough.

"I haven't been on one of these in years," Uman said, dumping his rucksack at the base of the tree the rope was suspended from and launching himself with a loud *woo-hoo!* that sent a pair of wood pigeons clattering out of the branches above us.

We took turns, pushing each other harder and harder, swinging in wild loops, daring each other to dismount at ever-higher points. It was like being ten years old again. If Uman hadn't been wiped out by the mother of all coughing fits, we might've swung on that rope for hours. We sat under the tree while he recovered, eating the sandwiches we'd made at his grandmother's.

He massaged his ankles. "Take my advice, Gloria, don't ever drop from the roof of a burning building. Unless it's a bungalow, of course."

"I'll try to remember that."

I wasn't sure we should be joking about it, but if he was OK with it, then so was I.

I vaguely remembered hearing about the fire. Not that I read the newspapers or watch the TV news that often. But when Uman had told me what happened, it felt familiar. Sitting in Drop Bear Woods with him, though, I wondered why the story hadn't come up when I Googled him that time at school. Why his name hadn't produced a single link.

So I asked him straight out.

"Uman Padeem's not my original name," he said after a moment. "I changed it when I moved up here, so the media wouldn't find me."

They'd pestered him ever since the fire, he told me. Even though he was only fifteen and the court had ordered that his privacy should be protected, the story of that terrible night, and of Uman's survival, was too good for the journalists to leave alone.

"So what's your real name, then?" I asked.

"Legally, this is my real name, now," he said. "I left that other boy behind."

We stowed the rucksacks in undergrowth and tramped the woods looking for a site away from any of the trails.

Eventually, we found a clearing among thick scrub, where the ground was dryish and level. The only snag was, we got lost trying to find the place where we'd left our gear and, when we did find it, we got lost again retracing our steps to the clearing. By that time, dusk was settling. The tent was a pop-up, though, so it didn't take us long to pitch it. I say "us" but, really, Uman erected it by himself while I handed him stuff and made incredibly helpful comments like "Isn't that bit the wrong way up?" or "Have you noticed how the pegs look like kebab skewers?"

"You haven't camped in a while, have you?" Uman said.

We sat in the opening of the tent, eating biscuits and watching night fall and listening to the scurrying of unseen small animals that almost certainly weren't drop bears.

"You're very chilled about all this fugitivery," Uman said.

"Fugitivery. I'm not sure that's a word."

"Why not? It has letters and syllables. Anyway, you are. Chilled, I mean."

"Probably because you are. It's ... the way you are, it's as though this is a totally normal thing to be doing." Like Tierney giving up her seat for him, I thought. Or the usherette letting us into an 18-certificate movie. "What is it about you?" I asked.

"What is it about me, what?"

"The way you get people to do things."

"Confidence," he said, simply. "If you're totally sure of yourself, people trust in you."

"What if you're not sure of yourself?"

"Then it's even more important to act like you are."

"So it's not hypnosis, then?"

"No," he said. "And when I count to three, you'll forget you ever asked that question."

"What question?"

He smiled. Raised his water bottle. "To fugitivery."

"To fugitivery," I said, clunking my bottle against his. "You'll have to teach me how to put the tent up, though. I don't like being useless."

"You are not useless. These woods were your idea, remember – and they're perfect."

I liked him for saying that. For thinking it. It didn't occur

129

to me, at the time, that if I was asking for a pop-up tent lesson I'd already started to anticipate a second night on the run.

While he went off with a torch to find somewhere well away from the tent to *fertilize the woods*, as he called it, I switched on my phone for the first time since we'd set off.

It was just after ten p.m. I'd meant to message home before now, but it had gone clean out of my mind with all we'd been doing. There were texts and voicemails from Mum – several of them – and some from Tierney. My parents would almost certainly have found out by now that I hadn't been with Tierney at all. They'd be angry. Also, sick with worry. As for Tier – my best friend would know I'd used her as a cover story. We'd always told each other everything, but now she didn't have a clue where I was, or who with, or what I was doing. I stared at the inbox.

A part of me thought that if I read or listened to the messages it would spoil everything.

"*Spoil* everything?" Mum asks.

D.I. Ryan doesn't make her back off this time. They're both waiting for an answer.

I can't bring myself to look at Mum.

"I was enjoying myself with Uman," I said. "After those messages, I knew it wouldn't be fun any more. It would be serious."

"Did you open them?" Mum asks.

I nod. I tell her – tell them – how terrible I felt, once I had.

"But you didn't message back," D.I. Ryan says.

"No. I didn't."

"Why not? One text wouldn't have spoiled anything, would it? Just to let them know you were safe."

I could lie. Invent a reason why I left those messages unanswered. But I don't. I explain that Uman came back just then as I sat holding the phone.

"*Phones*," he said. "I should've realized."

I could barely make him out in the gloom. "Realized what?"

"They'll be able to trace us."

"My parents?"

"If they go to the police, yeah. Which they will do. *Inevitablement*."

I felt sick all of a sudden. Of course they would call the police and report me missing; how could I have been so stupid not to think of it? This went way beyond cross, anxious messages. This wasn't just a busted curfew.

"Have you messaged anyone?" Uman asked, sitting down beside me.

"Not yet, no."

"Right. That's good."

"But I should do. You know? They're really worried."

"We'll find a payphone. First thing tomorrow."

"Won't they be able to trace that as well?"

"We make the call, then" – he mimed running motions with his fingers – "skedaddle."

131

I couldn't help laughing. "Is that what skedaddling looks like?"

"It does. That's the internationally recognized sign for it."

Serious again, I said, "They'll be out of their minds if I leave it till morning."

"Message them now," Uman said, with a shrug, "and we'll have cops swarming all through these woods in no time, bellowing our names with loud-hailers. Is that what you want?"

I looked at him, his features spooky in the torchlight. No, it wasn't what I wanted. The phone was warm in my hand. Could we be traced that easily, that quickly? I had no idea.

Uman picked up the empty biscuit wrapper. "We should've made these last," he said. "We need to be more military about this whole operation. Rations, strategy, comms."

"Comms?"

"Communications."

He stood up, pulled something from his jacket. "This, for a start." It was his phone. Before I figured out what he was about to do, he gave an almighty swing and hurled it into the darkness. I heard it strike a tree some way off before crashing into undergrowth.

He gave a celebratory whoop.

"Give me yours," he said, a little breathless.

"Uman…"

"Gloria, we have to do this."

After a moment, I let him take the phone from me and send it spinning into the night.

Q11: What did you think you were doing?

D.I. Ryan:

Did you give him your phone, Gloria, or did he take it from you?

Gloria:

I don't know.

D.I. Ryan:

How can you not know something like that?

Gloria:

You wouldn't understand.

D.I. Ryan:

Try me. I'm not as thick as I look.

Gloria:

I just mean there's a difference between giving someone something and letting them take it.

D.I. Ryan:

It's an interesting distinction.

Gloria:

Also, seeing him get rid of his phone, throwing it into the

trees like that... (Shrugs) I don't know.

D.I. Ryan:

If he was prepared to throw away his phone, you felt you should do the same.

Gloria:

Yeah, kind of. It showed we were in it together, you know?

D.I. Ryan:

Yes, I can see why he—

Gloria:

(Shakes head) It wasn't just that.

D.I. Ryan:

What else, then?

Gloria:

I guess ... it made me see how easy it was to cut ourselves off from what we'd left behind.

D.I. Ryan:

You wanted to do that, did you? Cut yourself off.

Gloria:

Yeah. No. What I'm saying is it was easier to cut myself off than actually deal with it.

D.I. Ryan:

Deal with it. Like letting your mum know you were all right?

Gloria:

I know, I know. (Pauses) I'm sorry.

134

D.I. Ryan:

So, anyway, Uman asked for your phone and you gave it to him. Just like that.

Gloria:

Not "just like that", no. I mean, it was my first smart phone, a Christmas present from Mum and Dad. I'd only had it a few months and I knew they'd go ballistic if I lost it.

D.I. Ryan:

All the same, you gave it to him.

Gloria:

Well, yeah, he didn't have to snatch it from me or prise it from my fingers or anything. Even as he took it, though, I wasn't sure I was doing the right thing. But it was too late by then.

D.I. Ryan:

He threw it into the trees.

Gloria:

Yeah. Then he held up his hand for a high five.

D.I. Ryan:

And you high-fived him?

Gloria:

Yeah. (Nods) Yeah, I did.

D.I. Ryan:

(Pauses) OK, let's move on from the business with the phones. I'd like you to tell us a bit more about that day, Gloria. The decision to go off with him and why you didn't leave a note.

Gloria:

Like I keep saying, I didn't go off with him. We went together.

D.I. Ryan:

OK, so ... you went off, the two of you. No note or message – you just went.

Gloria:

(Nods)

D.I. Ryan:

For the recording, please.

Gloria:

No. We didn't leave a note.

D.I. Ryan:

Why not? Was that Uman's idea, too?

Gloria:

No. We didn't even talk about a note. We were just ... taking off, you know? That was the whole point.

D.I. Ryan:

What was the whole point?

Gloria:

Who leaves a note to say they're going on the run? Anyway, I didn't even think we were going on the run or anything like that. Not then. Not that morning.

D.I. Ryan:

What did you think you were doing?

Gloria:

I don't know. I don't know. I just enjoyed being with Uman

136

so much I didn't want it to stop. Sleeping in the tent and everything. (Pauses) I thought it would be a laugh.

Mrs Ellis:

A laugh.

Gloria:

Yeah, taking off somewhere, just the two of us. Skipping school. I thought it was only for a couple of days. Sunday, Sunday night, Monday. We'd be back home by the Monday evening.

D.I. Ryan:

That was the plan, was it? Just a day or two.

Gloria:

Yes. No, not really. We never even talked about how long for. I just … assumed.

D.I. Ryan:

You weren't intending to stay away as long as you did. Is that right? Neither of you.

Gloria:

No.

D.I. Ryan:

But your parents wouldn't have known that, would they?

Gloria:

(No response)

D.I. Ryan:

You don't come home on the Sunday, you're missing overnight. They call Tierney's parents and discover you were never even there the night before. Then, Monday morning, there's a call from the school asking why you aren't in lessons.

Gloria:

(No response)

D.I. Ryan:

You can imagine what they went through in those twenty-four hours, can't you?

Gloria:

(Quietly) Yes.

Mrs Ellis:

We didn't have a clue where you were, Lor, or who you were with. Even if you were still alive.

Gloria:

I know and I'm really sorry. I am. But ... I was with Uman. It wasn't like some guy had dragged me into a car and driven off with me.

Mrs Ellis:

For all we knew, that might've been exactly what happened. And, even once the police said you'd gone off with that lad, it hardly put our minds at rest. Not after what he'd done—

D.I. Ryan:

OK, Mrs Ellis. Let's not—

Gloria:

It wasn't like that. *He* wasn't like that. I don't care what you say he did before, you're totally wrong about Uman.

Q12: Are you serious about this?

I slept badly. Being in a tent in Drop Bear Woods was different to sleeping in his grandmother's garden. For one thing, we were fugitives now. For another, the creaks, scuffles and sighs of dead-of-night woodland are more disturbing than the breeze rustling a suburban hedge, or a cat yowling, or the occasional swoosh of a car. Town should be scarier because towns have people in them, and people are way more dangerous than any creature you might meet in an English wood. But I was spooked that night. By where we were, but also by what we were doing.

Uman acted like the hurling of our phones into the trees had been liberating – setting us free. During the night, though, I didn't feel liberated. I felt cut off. Guilty, too. If I'd had a bad night, what must Mum and Dad's have been like?

I'd more or less decided to tell Uman I was going home.

I woke early. Phoneless, I had no idea what time it was, but when I unzipped the flap carefully, so as not to wake Uman, and poked my head out, a smoky just-after-dawn light seeped through the woods, turning the trees into charcoal sketches. All was quiet, except for the songs of unseen birds. Tired and just-woken grumpy as I was, the effect was calming.

A movement caught my eye. A few metres away, a family of rabbits loped about the clearing: two adults, browsing, and four young, play-fighting. I held my breath, kept dead still. For a moment, they carried on, oblivious to my presence, then one of the adults spotted me and all six scampered into the bracken, vanishing so quickly and so totally that I might've imagined them. Thirty seconds, a minute? But those rabbits were the most magical thing I'd ever seen.

I waited in the opening of the tent in the hope they'd come back. They didn't.

Never mind. I was still smiling inside at the sight of them. At how beautiful the woods looked, now that the darkness had been erased by the breaking of a new day.

I found somewhere to pee. By the time I returned, Uman had pegged the "apron" (his word) of the groundsheet in front of the tent and was setting out a breakfast of crackers, Nutella and a carton of orange juice we'd left outside overnight so it would be chilled. To judge by his puffy eyes, he'd slept as poorly as I had. But his grin when he saw me lit up his features.

"Is this the life, Ms Inexcelsis?" he said, gesturing at the woods. "Or is this the life?"

As we sat and ate, I told him about the rabbits.

It wasn't until we'd cleared away the breakfast things and

brushed our teeth and washed our faces as best we could with some of our remaining drinking water that I said, "Uman, I wish you hadn't thrown our phones away."

He nodded. He had a smear of toothpaste in the corner of his mouth and his fringe was spiked with damp. "I know. It was a bit rash, wasn't it?"

His response surprised me. I'd expected him to justify what he had done.

"We could try to find them," he said, gazing in the direction in which he'd flung them.

"Shall I come out with the needle-in-a-haystack cliché," I said, "or do you want to?"

Uman spread his hands wide, hung his head. "Sorry. It's what I do: I act on impulse and worry about the consequences later."

"You *worry* about *consequences?*"

"Actually no, you're right. I just do the thing, whatever the thing is."

Looking back, I can see how childlike it is to behave like that. You have the urge to draw on the wallpaper? Just do it. You want to push your kid sister over in the paddling pool? Just do it. You fancy eating an entire two-litre tub of ice cream? Just do it. To hell with what happens afterwards. At the time, though, I saw it differently. Uman's impulsiveness. It reminded me of how I used to be. Made me long to be like that again.

"A free spirit," I said.

"What's that?"

"Oh, just something Mum said about me and my brother one time on holiday. *You two, you're a pair of free spirits floating on the breeze.* I was only about eight so I had no idea what she meant, but the phrase stuck in my mind. It made me think of a dandelion clock – you know, the seed-head thing – being carried away on the wind like a fairy."

"If ever we buy a boat," Uman said, "we should call it that: *Free Spirit.*"

Buy a boat. Right. I smiled but kept the thought to myself.

I slotted my toothbrush back in the toiletry bag, pulled out the deodorant and reached under my top to give each armpit a blast. A shower would've been good. Better still, a soak in a hot bath, followed by a looong sleep. In a soft, warm bed. All the same, it was pleasant, standing there in the woods, dazed with tiredness, breathing in the fresh air.

Difference, that's what it was. It was the first morning of its kind in my entire life.

"We'll find a payphone, if you like," Uman said. He'd dragged his rucksack out of the tent and was repacking it. "Let your folks know you're alive and well."

I took a breath, then another. "Actually, Uman ... I was thinking of going home."

"Oh. OK." He paused, as if frozen in a game of musical statues. Coughed a couple of times. He did that when he was stressed, I'd noticed. The damage to his lungs was genuine, but sometimes the cough was a kind of nervous tic. He resumed packing. "We can do that, sure. Just head back to Shipley and hop on a train." He might've been talking to the rucksack. "With a bit of luck, you'll be at school in time for register."

"You're disappointed in me, aren't you?"

"No, I'm not."

"Yes you are – I can hear it in your voice," I said. "You can't even look at me."

He stopped fiddling with the rucksack and stared directly at me. "Was it the crackers?" Uman indicated the spot where we'd had breakfast. "Me having more than my fair share – that's the real reason you want to go back, isn't it?" He frowned. "Or maybe the snoring?"

"You don't snore," I said.

"No, but you do. I'm wondering if you're leaving from a sense of embarrassment."

"I do *not*—"

"Gloria, I *am* disappointed," Uman said. "But not with you." He shrugged. "I'm just disappointed this is coming to an end before we gave it a chance."

I wasn't sure if he meant the adventure or us.

"How long did you think we'd be away?" I asked. "A few days? A *week*?"

"I don't know. Until we felt like stopping, I guess. Why, how long were you expecting?"

I told him I hadn't given it any thought. Which was true. I hadn't really considered any of it: what we were doing, why we were doing it, how long we'd be gone, where we'd go. The fact that we'd be missed, that people would worry about us and come looking for us.

"It is crazy, isn't it?" I said.

Uman nodded. "Yes. It is."

"Good crazy or bad crazy?"

"Both, I'd say." Then, "Come on, I know it doesn't matter any more, but let me show you how to disassemble and pack away a pop-up tent."

Working together, we took longer than if Uman had done it by himself; but it was fun, in a slapstick kind of way, especially when the tent sprang back open and whacked him in the face, or when we broke off to play Throw Tent Pegs at a Tree to see who'd be the first to get one to stick in the trunk like a knife-thrower's knife. (Neither of us managed it.)

One or two people were on the canal towpath as we headed back. A jogger, his face shiny-purple; a woman walking six different breeds of dog. Smoke writhed from the chimney of a red-and-green houseboat moored near the lock. *Annabelle*. Not *Free Spirit*. I wondered what it would be like to live on a houseboat, travelling from place to place, casting off whenever you felt like it and chugging to somewhere new. Dad had lived in a caravan for a bit during his trying-to-crack-the-American-music-business phase and said it was the best time of his life.

Another glorious day in the making. Still not quite into June, and spring was doing a fair impersonation of summer.

144

"I'll walk with you to the station," Uman said.

"What d'you mean?"

"See you off. Say goodbye and all that."

I stopped. He took another step or two, then came to a halt as well, half-turned to look back at me. *What?*, his expression said. Puzzled, not irritated. We were close to Salt's Mill; Uman was framed by the arch of the bridge that took the road over the canal just there.

"Aren't you coming back to Litchbury?" I asked.

He looked a little sheepish. "No. Sorry."

"What are you—?"

But I knew exactly what he would be doing. He'd be going off with his rucksack and his tent – somewhere, any-where. He'd be doing this, giving this a chance. Without me.

I cried, then. I was tired. So tired and so overwhelmed by everything. Why did it have to be so complicated?

By the time I'd finished and he had released me from a long, tight hug and I'd dried my face on my cuff, I had changed my mind about going home. I wanted to go with him after all.

"Please," I said. "If you still want me to, I mean."

"Are you serious about this?" Uman asked, quietly.

"Yes." I nodded. Laughed. "Yeah, I absolutely am."

"He played that situation very well, wouldn't you say?" D.I. Ryan asks.

I don't give her any kind of answer at all.

* * *

145

Where next, that was the issue. We couldn't stay put, Uman reckoned, in case they'd picked up a signal from one of our phones before we hoiked them.

"You'll have been reported missing by now," he said.

You, not we. Of course. Uman's grandmother barely realized he lived with her, so she wasn't likely to wonder where he was. No one else would, either. He didn't have anyone else. As for school, his attendance had been so erratic I doubted they'd raise the alarm right away. Most likely, the school would contact his "family" first of all. His grandmother, in other words. Good luck with that conversation, I thought.

"The police won't be searching for you for days, will they?" I said. "I mean, if you were doing this on your own they wouldn't even know you were missing."

"I suspect your analysis is correct."

"So, you'd be better off without me."

"Oh, well: a) no, and b) no."

"What *a* and *b*? I only said one thing."

"Point *a*, I wouldn't be better off without you because this fugitivery malarkey – and, indeed, my life in general – is much more fun with you around. And point *b*, what the hell is the use of being on the run if no one's coming after you?"

We were sitting in a scuzzy bus shelter, sharing a can of Red Bull we'd bought at a petrol station on the main road, a short walk from Salt's Mill. We weren't waiting for a bus; it was just somewhere to sit. A girl about our age, in school uniform, stood at the other end of the shelter, texting, nodding

146

along to whatever was playing through her earpieces.

"Do you mean that?" I asked.

"Gloria, hide-and-seek with no seeker is like a raspberry roulade minus the raspberries."

"No, that your life is more fun with me around."

Uman had raised the can to his mouth; he lowered it without drinking. "Yes," he said, matter-of-factly. "I meant that too."

We sat in silence while I figured out whether to be pleased or embarrassed. The morning rush hour was under way. None of the drivers paid us any attention; to them, we were just two kids at a bus stop. How could the start of our day be so extraordinary while theirs was so same-old, same-old? *Look at us!* I wanted to yell. *Look at what we're doing!*

Before the silence became awkward, I said, "Raspberry roulade minus the raspberries?"

"I know: an infinite number of similes and that's the best I can come up with."

We drank Red Bull. The shelter vibrated against my back as a lorry rumbled by.

"We should put some distance between us and Litchbury — between us and here," Uman said. He made a zigzag motion with his hand. "Dodge and weave. Throw them off the scent."

"What, wade along a river for a few kilometres to lose the tracker dogs?" I said.

"If this was a movie, it would certainly be an option."

We had a "window" before they picked up our trail, he

147

reckoned. OK, so I was officially missing – for maybe eight or ten hours – but teenagers stropped out on their parents all the time. The investigation wouldn't kick into gear until this morning, when my absence overnight was followed by a no-show at school. Even once they'd broadcast an appeal, though, it would take time for witnesses to come forward; then the police had to sort out the genuine sightings from the rest. It would take longer still to trawl through the CCTV at Litchbury Station to figure out which train we'd caught. Then they'd have to work out where we'd got off.

"For the time being," Uman said, "they have absolutely no idea where we are."

"How do you know all this?"

"From crime novels, mostly. And TV dramas."

"Right." The thought of Mum and Dad surfaced again. This was no TV drama. "I have to find a payphone," I said.

"Yeah, we will. We'll find one."

We'd kept an eye out for one since leaving the woods, but there'd been nothing at Salt's Mill or along the main road. The guy who served us at the petrol station was no help. ("Who uses a phone box these days?") It even occurred to me to ask the schoolgirl in the shelter if I could borrow her phone. I never got the chance, though.

A bus drew up at the stop just then, its doors clattering open with a pneumatic hiss.

"Come on," Uman said, grabbing my hand. "Let's get on."

* * *

The bus might've been headed anywhere for all we cared. We were on the move again, that was the thing. We were dodging. Weaving.

"Two tickets, please," Uman said, placing a ten-pound note in the tray.

The driver gave him a look. "A destination would be helpful, pal."

"Regrettably, I am unable to furnish you with that information."

I cut in, asking for two day-riders, and bundled Uman inside the bus. We stowed our rucksacks in the luggage bay under the stairs and made for the top deck.

"Well done," I whispered as we sat down. "That driver won't forget us in a hurry."

"Ah, good point."

"'I am unable to furnish you with that information.' Jesus."

Uman indicated the tickets in my hand. "What's a 'day-rider', anyway?"

"Seriously? Have you never been on a bus before?"

"I believe our chauffeur may have overtaken one once."

I laughed. "You are such a snob."

Uman looked pleased with himself. Then his expression changed. "What if this bus is going to Litchbury? That would be a complete and utter catastrophe."

It wasn't going to Litchbury. The road signs said the

149

bus was headed for Bradford city centre. Cities were good, according to Uman. Cities had transport links to other cities. They had payphones, too. But Uman wasn't thinking about that right then.

"A few hours from now," he said, "we could be anywhere in the country."

We were in such a hurry that morning. Move, move, move. Putting as much distance – as many dodges and weaves – between ourselves and Litchbury as we could, as soon as possible. It wasn't just Uman. I'd woken in the woods, ready to go home, yet once I'd changed my mind it was as if the thought of quitting had never entered my head, and now I couldn't hit the road fast enough. Or maybe (and this is more likely) I knew, not so deep in my unconscious, that if I didn't throw myself into the fugitivery thing – if I didn't really go for it – the doubts and guilt would leak back in and I wouldn't do it at all.

So there we were. In Bradford. Scurrying from place to place, almost as if we were being chased along the streets by a posse of vigilantes.

We got off at the bus-and-train interchange (called Interchange, which Uman thought *supremely imaginative*) and merged with the morning hordes. First thing we did was hit the shops to stock up on rations and buy a map of the country on which to plot Operation Escape.

Then we changed our appearance.

"Clothes," I said.

150

"What about them?"

"When people go missing, the police issue a description of what they were wearing."

"Yes. Yesyesyes. Gloria, you have a whiff of genius about you."

We'd drawn a chunk of cash in Litchbury but couldn't risk using our cards again for fear of being traced, so we had to make our money last. A charity shop, then. We found one and kitted ourselves out in second-hand sets of clothes and snuck into some public toilets to change. I'd chosen an emo look: black top, black denim jacket (too big), grey-and-black stripy leggings. As for Uman, he'd gone for a purple zip-up hoodie, pale green T-shirt and orange cords.

"Nice one," I said. "Very low profile."

"I've always had a thing for secondary colours."

"Your mind doesn't quite work like other people's, does it?"

He grinned. "You noticed?"

Our own clothes we bagged up and left on the door-step of a different charity shop, apart from the spare sets, which we hadn't worn yet, and my fake pilot's jacket, which I couldn't bear to lose. I buried it in the bottom of my now crammed-to-bursting rucksack.

D.I. Ryan interjects. "Did you dye your hair that morning, as well?"

"Yep. Right after."

"Whose idea was that?"

"We drew cards. Highest dyes, lowest cuts. Uman drew a three, I drew a nine."

We bought scissors and dye and returned to the toilets, shutting ourselves inside the more spacious disabled cubicle. By the time we were done, my light-brown hair was carroty red (the blonde came later, I tell D.I. Ryan) and Uman's long tresses had been trimmed to a stubbly crew cut. Cutting his hair for him had been nice, intimate; but it broke my heart to see all that lovely silky hair swirl away with one flush.

"Hey," I said, running my fingers over his scalp, "you *are* a boy after all."

"Does that mean you'd be prepared to kiss me, now?" Uman asked.

"I was before, actually. Given the chance."

So we did. Right there, in the public toilets: our first kiss.

Back at Interchange, wearing our charity clothes and startling new hairstyles.

It was time to make that call.

I went into a phone booth while Uman waited a little way off, watching me. My palms were clammy, my breathing too fast. Had I even used a payphone before? Not that I could remember. It took me a moment to figure out what to do, where to put the coins.

I dialled almost all of the number of the home landline before hanging up. Clumsily, banging the phone too hard in its cradle so that it popped out and swung on the end of the cord and I had to replace it properly.

Outside, Uman was doing his tightrope walker impression along the kerb. I frowned through the glass at him to stop, but he kept right on.

On a regular morning, Mum and Dad would already have been at work by that time. But this wasn't a regular morning. With me missing, they'd have stayed at home, wouldn't they? Waiting for the phone to ring. I imagined one of them – Mum, probably – grabbing the handset as soon as it did and saying my name before I'd even had a chance to speak.

Gloria, is that you? Oh, thank God – where the hell are you?

I couldn't face it. Couldn't face actually talking to her. Telling her I was fine, I was safe, but I wasn't coming home yet. Couldn't face *explaining myself*. The hundred questions she'd have for me. Or the sound of what I was doing to her – to them – echoed in Mum's tone of voice. In her tears.

All the same, I couldn't leave that booth with the call unmade. They had to know.

I retrieved the coins, picked up the handset. Dialled again. Only this time, I called the "office" phone in Dad's study in the loft conversion. They'd hear it ringing – just about – from two floors below (I pictured them in the living room, or kitchen) but, if I was quick, there was no way either of them could reach the phone in time to pick up before I'd finished my message. Unless Dad was sitting at his desk.

He wasn't.

"Hey, it's me. I'm OK and nothing's happened. Nothing bad. I'm just … not coming home for a bit, that's all." Then, after a pause, "Sorry."

I hung up. Pressed my hands against the sides of the booth to stop myself from trembling.

Q13: Well, were you?

With the call made, the message left – our location traceable (for all we knew) – it was time to skedaddle. Time, once more, to consult the Cards of Destiny, as we'd decided to call them. *Pink-and-purple stripes*, I told myself as I rejoined Uman outside the booth.

"You speak to them?" he asked.

"Voicemail." I repeated what I'd said in the message.

He gave my arm a rub. "You OK?"

I nodded. "Yeah, I'm good. I'm good."

"That's your 'good' face? All I can say is, I wouldn't like to see your—"

"Don't, Uman. Please."

"OK. Sorry."

I pushed my newly dyed red hair out of my eyes. "Let's do the thing with the cards."

In a quiet corner of the station concourse, we shuffled the pack. We cut. The cards said "train". We cut again and they said "west".

155

By mid-morning we were in Manchester.

Not that we spent long there, because another straight cut – "stay" or "move on" – told us to move on, and a deal picked "south-west". Uman opened the map of the UK and drew a line with his finger while I noted down the place names along the route. We dealt again.

"Church Stretton," he said, as if practising a phrase in a foreign language. "Heard of it?"

"Nuh-uh."

"That bit of the map is very green. And remote."

"Green is good," I said. "Remote is good. And, look, there's a train station."

By that afternoon, we had well and truly skedaddled – leaving Manchester and Bradford and Shipley far behind – and were hiking into the hills where England begins its slow climb to the Welsh mountains.

Litchbury was two hundred kilometres away, give or take. It felt like a thousand.

As for the message I'd left on Dad's answering machine, that call might've been several days ago, not several hours.

"I was a coward," I said. "I should've spoken to them."

"What matters is, you told them what they needed to know."

"They'll be so worried, though. So mad at me."

"They'll be *so relieved* to have heard your voice," he said, drawing me into a hug. I let myself believe him. Let myself be hugged a little longer.

We made camp at the bottom of a steep-sided valley, a couple of hours' walk from Church Stretton. For the last hour we hadn't seen any people at all. Just sheep. Hundreds of sheep strewn around the slopes like torn-off scraps of cloud that had fallen from the sky and become snagged in the gorse. I heard them bleating outside the tent that night.

Our second night as fugitives.

Snuggling up to Uman, I whispered, "Do I really snore?" But he was already asleep.

We spent almost a week in the Stretton Hills. I've always thought of myself as a town girl – never been fussed about the countryside or getting back to nature and all that – but those six days hiking and camping with Uman were just the happiest time.

Each night we pitched the tent somewhere different. Dodging and weaving. It was fun breaking and remaking camp, going walkabout, searching for ever more obscure hideaways. There were plenty to choose from; once you leave Church Stretton and head into the hills the hamlets and farmsteads are few and far between. These we skirted round. We avoided roads and lanes, sticking to tracks and footpaths, or just striking out over open moorland where the heather was shin-deep and meadow pipits and whinchats scattered ahead of us like children playing tag. The only people we encountered were ramblers and off-road cyclists, a horse rider or two, and an occasional farm worker, none of whom showed any particular interest in us. A wave, a hello, a cheery smile. That was all. Sometimes a walker paused to ask directions or to comment on the weather, and one time a whiskery old guy loading feed into a trough nodded at Uman's clothes and said he hoped "all them bright colours" didn't startle the sheep.

Apart from that, we had the land to ourselves. Just us, the sheep and the birds. At night, we'd hear the scuffling of what might have been foxes or badgers foraging near the tent.

To plot our bearings, we used Uman's compass and a local OS map we'd bought at the tourist information centre in Church Stretton the day we arrived off the train. Although we continually moved on, we made sure to stay within range of the town so we could sneak back every couple of days to buy food and drink. I say "we" but only one of us would go on a food run. Even with radically altered appearances, two teenagers together – a dark-skinned guy with a white girl – might arouse curiosity in a small town.

We were news, by then. On our third day in the area, I'd flicked through a paper to see if we were in there. We were. Main story on page 5: *Concern grows for runaway teens*, with side-by-side headshots of Uman and me (mine was a hideous school photo, which made me look like my lips had been glued shut). I read the article right there in the supermarket.

"*Police are increasingly concerned for the safety of two 15-year-olds who appear to have run away together,*" it began, before giving details of the last "*confirmed sighting*" – by the driver of a bus from Shipley to Bradford. Good. It meant we hadn't been traced beyond Bradford yet. The story mentioned my phone message, then gave our descriptions (*before* the clothes-and-hair makeover) and a quote from the head of Litchbury High, calling me "*bright, gifted and popular*" and a "*valued member of the school's community*". Not much about Uman. He was new to the school, had a "*troubled background*" (no details), and had "*exerted an influence over Gloria in the short time they have been friends*". Then, a quote from Mum. "*Gloria, sweetheart, please get in touch. We love and miss you so much and want you back with us, where you belong. You're not in any trouble – we just want you to come home.*"

I put the newspaper back on the rack and shut myself in the toilets for a bit so no one would see me crying. When I'd composed myself, I bought food and drink and hiked back to the tent.

I told Uman about the article. When I said what they'd written about him he nodded, like he'd been expecting something of the sort. "It didn't say anything else about me?"

"No."

Another nod. "So I'm the bad guy, then."

He said it like he was joking, or as if he wasn't bothered; but I could tell it upset him.

"Uman, they don't know you. Not like I do." I smoothed my palm over his short hair. I'd loved his hair when it was long, but since it had been shorn off I was addicted to stroking it. "They don't know us."

We unpacked the shopping in silence. I thought he was slipping into another low mood, like that time he shut down on me for a bit when I was showing him around Litchbury. But as he stowed away the last of the food he asked if I was OK. Like I was the one who'd gone quiet.

"Me? Yeah, I'm fine. Why wouldn't I be?"

"The quote from your mother."

Uman was right; it had been turning over in my mind. The thought of what they were going through, Mum and Dad. Seeing her name in the paper – my name, my picture – made it all so real, so full-on. People all over the country were reading about us. Looking for us.

"D'you think they've been on TV?" I asked. "You know, making an appeal?"

"Your parents? Probably."

I pictured them flanked by police officers, in front of a bank of microphones, camera crews, photographers, answering one question after another. Trying to keep it together. They'd be holding hands, blinking into the flashguns like a pair of startled deer.

"Shit, Uman."

"D'you want to phone her?"

"I can't, can I?"

"If you really want to, though."

I shook my head. "We'd have to move on if I did. And I like it round here. Anyway, I already called once – so they know I've not been abducted or anything like that."

Uman studied my face.

A thought struck me. "My *brother*. He might've come home from uni because of me."

He took my hand, pressing it between his. "If this is getting too off-the-scale serious, just say the word and we can pack up and walk right into the nearest police station."

I could see he meant it. He really did. "But why, though?" I was almost pleading.

"Why what?"

"Why should we? Why can't we just take off like this if we want to?"

"Because we're fifteen," he said.

"So?"

"So, until we're adults we belong to other people."

"Belong. I don't *belong* to Mum and Dad. I don't belong to anyone."

Uman shrugged. "It's the way things are, though. Parents, teachers, police – they make the rules. Not us. We just do as we're told."

"You don't believe that," I said. "You wouldn't be here in this tent if you did."

"No, I don't. And no, I wouldn't."

"Then why are you suggesting we quit?"

"I'm not. I'm just saying I will quit if that's what you want."

"You'd do that?"

"Gloria, I wanted to make you happy. For us to be happy,

doing this. If you're not happy, then what's the point?"

"But I am happy." I half-laughed, half-cried. "That's *exactly* the point."

We snuck into Church Stretton that evening and treated ourselves to fish and chips. I bought them while Uman waited on a bench in a moonlit churchyard. Our first hot meal since we'd become fugitives. It was the best food I've ever eaten.

We settled into a routine. First thing in the morning, we'd spread the sleeping bags to air while we had breakfast, then pack up and head off to a new site. We'd pick a likely spot on the map – several kilometres away, ideally – then check out the lie of the land when we got there. After setting up camp, we'd have lunch. In the afternoons, we went walk-about to gather materials to decorate our campsite. Twigs, berries, leaves, tufts of moss, pine cones, feathers, bits of sheep wool (a sheep's skull, once), snail shells, gorse petals, sprigs of heather – to be fashioned into a kind of art instal-lation (all very pagan), which we left the next morning to mark the spot where we'd stayed. Not that anyone would know who'd done it.

We are leaving beautiful mysteries in our wake, as Uman put it.

It reminded me of making dens with my brother when we were little. Ivan would build the den – in the garden at home, or on holiday – and I'd painstakingly decorate it. With Uman, there wasn't a boy–girl division of jobs. And I felt more adult, not less, while we made camp and prettified it – so I'm not sure why childhood memories of my brother came to mind just then. It was the adventure, maybe. I associate my younger self with adventurousness and my adventures, back then, would've involved Ivan – with me, the kid sister, running in his slipstream. A couple of times, at least, Mum or Dad had to track down our den and shoo us out of there for teatime or bathtime or bedtime, and we'd receive a telling off for hiding ourselves away like that.

"Did you and your brother ever go camping?" I asked Uman one time.

"No," he said, matter-of-factly. End of subject.

Anyway, I loved creating those decorative … shrines, I guess you'd call them. Those beautiful mysteries. Uman always included a circle of pebbles in honour of our hike to the Twelve Disciples back in the Days of Then, as we referred to them. This was Now, the time before going on the run was Then, and the days before we met were Before Then.

"What about the time *after* our fugitivery?" I asked when we were deciding these matters.

He thought for a moment. "Let's name them the Days of Next."

"The Days of Next." I smiled. "Yeah, I like it. Before Then, Then, Now, Next."

In the evenings, we ate tea ("supper", according to Uman) and played cards or listened to music on my iPod (until it ran out of charge), or played Twenty Questions. Last thing, we'd take turns to tell stories: true ones from our childhood, or made-up tales of ghosts and demons. One night, we acted out scenes from favourite episodes of *Friends*, with Uman as Chandler, Joey and Ross, and me playing Rachel, Monica and Phoebe. Uman's Ross was so funny I almost wet myself.

When it rained, which it did one day that week, we pulled on waterproofs and stuck to the same routine. As for washing clothes, we rinsed them in a stream (we always camped near running water) and hung them to dry on the lines that fixed the tent to the ground. *We* washed in streams, too, as best we could. One time, we came upon a waterfall where a brook spilled from a rocky overhang about three metres high. Uman and I didn't even discuss it. We just swapped glances, set down our rucksacks, stripped off, and soaped ourselves from head to toe beneath the *freezing* water, gasping and squealing with the shock. By the time we'd finished we were bright pink and shivering and too teeth-chattery to talk, but it felt so *good* to be properly clean again.

I see Mum and D.I. Ryan exchanging looks. While I'm recalling the exhilaration of taking an outdoor shower, they're picturing me and Uman naked under the water together ... and how casual we were about it. They're imagining, I'm sure, all those intimate nights in a small tent.

"Go on," I tell the detective. "Ask me. You know you want to."

"Ask you what, Gloria?"

"If we were having sex."

She flicks another glance at Mum, then back at me. "Well, were you?"

"What if we were?"

"You're fifteen," Mum says.

"Yeah, both of us."

"What difference does that make? You're still underage, Lor."

Mum looks upset, so I bite back what I was about to say and go with something else. "We got undressed and washed under a waterfall in the middle of nowhere." Speaking calmly. Softly. "Wasn't there a time when you might've done something like that?"

She doesn't answer.

We're all quiet for a moment. I expect D.I. Ryan to press me on the did-we-didn't-we-have-sex thing now that I've opened the door for her.

"If you liked it around there so much," she asks instead, "why did you move on?"

We wouldn't have done, I tell her. If things had worked out differently, we'd have stayed in the Stretton Hills for weeks. Months. It's a lovely area. It suited us as a hideout. I'd never had so much exercise and fresh air and I felt great. I'm not usually a sound sleeper, but those nights in the tent I slept well and woke refreshed every morning. Invigorated.

"I don't ever want to sleep in a bed or live in a house again," I told Uman.

"Let's not, then," he said.

Easy as that. All things were possible for us in those days and I couldn't imagine them coming to an end. Of course, deep down, I knew they would – somehow, sometime. But, for the moment, we lived in the Days of Now and let ourselves believe the Days of Next were no more than a wisp of cloud on a distant horizon. Literally over the hills and far away.

Six nights, though. That's all we had there.

On the day it happened, we woke early, as usual. We spread our bedding and washed at a nearby stream, then fixed ourselves some breakfast. The art installation had been mussed up a bit by the breeze during the night, so Uman and I spent a few minutes tidying it. It featured a dead crow that we'd come across the previous afternoon – curiously undamaged, so perfectly intact it might have been asleep. Its bluish black wings shimmering, it lay on a flat stone surrounded by twelve pebbles at the centre of a display of ferns and heather, arranged so that the bird seemed to be floating on a raft on a green-and-purple sea. A mythical creature on its voyage to the afterlife.

It was this which drew attention to us.

A Monday morning; the previous day had marked the end of our first week. Uman and I had been discussing it – how the time seemed to have passed so quickly, and yet that first night in Drop Bear Woods already felt like a distant memory.

"I don't feel fifteen any more," I said as we cleared breakfast and bagged the rubbish.

"I know what you mean," Uman said. Then, "Actually, I'm not sure I do know."

"This. Being here, with you – this past week, it's like I'm twenty years old or something. Like we're university students on a gap-year trip."

Uman sealed the remaining crackers in their Tupperware box. "If you keep ageing at that rate, in two months' time you'll be about seventy."

"No, listen." He could be annoying like that; joking when I was trying to be serious. "I just want to do so much with my life, and it's as if I've started already. Right now."

"Right now." Uman nodded. "That's a good place to live your life."

I studied his expression to see if he was making fun of me again. He wasn't. "It's what *you* do, isn't it?" *Since the fire,* I left unsaid. "It's one of the things I really like about you."

"Just run through all the others for me."

"*Uman.*"

"OK, OK – serious." He screwed the lid back on the Nutella and passed it to me for stowing in my rucksack. "D'you know what my father used to say?"

"What?"

"Live as the river does, never standing still or turning back but forever flowing onwards. If you should reach a desert, transform yourself into cloud and float across it, then fall as rain on the other side to become a river once more." He shrugged. "It's an old Arabic proverb."

167

"It's beautiful."

"He was full of crap, actually." He said it without spite or bitterness towards the man who'd killed his mother and brother and, very nearly, Uman himself. "My father lived his life for money and possessions – the more he had, the more he wanted."

"Was he always like that?"

"Not when he first came to this country, no. It was an adventure, a new life – that's what my mother says. Said." He paused. "But Dad had to prove himself, to have some measure of his success. The immigrant done good, you know? It wasn't enough just to 'live as the river does'. He had to become the biggest, most powerful river he possibly could."

We were gathering the sleeping bags from where we'd spread them to freshen up in the morning air. I was conscious of hanging on his words. Uman rarely talked about his dad – even when we told tales from our childhoods, he kept his father at the margins.

"Funny, isn't it?" he said, with something that wasn't quite a laugh. "If he'd had his way, I'd be dead. And here I am, quoting the advice he gave me about how to live."

He coughed two or three times. Bad ones. The coughing had been less frequent in the days we'd spent in the hills. Uman's limp had improved, too, despite all the walking; although he had taken to sitting with his bare feet in a stream after each hike.

"You OK?" I asked, and he nodded.

We started to dismantle the tent. I imagined his dad as a young man, leaving his homeland for a new life in a strange country. His dreams and hopes. Had it been the same for my folks when they quit England and travelled halfway round the world to America, years before I was born? Before their rivers reached the edge of the desert. Before they stopped and turned back.

"We don't have to become them," I said.

"What?" Uman looked up from what he was doing, tugging pegs from the ground.

"Our parents. We don't have to live the way they did. Or think like they do."

"No. I know that."

"They've had their turn," I said. "It's ours now." As soon as the words were out, their insensitivity struck me – the fact that his parents were both dead, their "turn" quite literally over.

But Uman just flashed me a grin. "Well said, Ms Inexcelsis."

We were folding up the groundsheet when we heard the crunch, crunch of boots on the stony track that followed the course of the stream. Usually, we camped well away from footpaths but, there, the options had been limited, short of pitching the tent on a steep slope. It was still early; surprisingly early for someone to be walking in such a remote spot.

Uman and I looked at each other. No words passed between us but we knew the drill. *Be friendly. Act naturally. Watch what you say.*

The guy appeared from behind a spur of rock. He was almost as colourful as Uman: red fleece jacket, blue trousers; the orange laces in his boots were practically fluorescent. In one hand he held a green plastic sack by the scruff of the neck, in the other he carried what I'd mistaken at first sight for a ski-pole walking stick but was, I now saw, a litter-grabber.

"Morning!" he called, as bright and cheery as his clothing.

"Hi!" I called back.

Uman, for some reason, saluted him. I hoped he wasn't in one of those moods.

The track missed our pitch by about thirty metres and it looked as if the guy might pass by with no more than a greeting. No such luck. I saw him register the dead-crow art installation, then pause and leave the path to take a closer look.

"This is rather smashing, isn't it?" he said.

I returned his smile. "Thank you."

What I could see of his hair beneath a blue peaked cap was mostly grey; his wispy beard, too. His teeth were too white, too neat.

"We call it Dead Bird with Flora," Uman told him.

So he *was* in one of those moods. I widened my eyes at him, willing him to be normal – that is, most people's version of normal, as opposed to his own interpretation. The guy seemed unfazed, though. He'd set the plastic sack down and had removed his cap, wiping his brow with the cuff of his fleece. His hair stuck up in a silvery quiff.

170

"I'm a countryside warden," he said, indicating the sack. "Volunteer."

"What's in there, then?" Uman asked. "An enemy parachutist?"

The old guy looked at him.

"D'you want us to clear this up?" I cut in quickly, meaning the art installation.

"No, no, not at all. Just ... well, don't go uprooting any more heather, will you?"

"Oh, OK. Sorry."

He pointed to the ferns. "Now, the *bracken*, rip up all you like. Too much of that bloody stuff – kills everything else, given the chance." He made a swiping motion with the litter-grabber. "Last weekend, ten of us were up here, beating the living daylights out of it."

"Sounds like enormous fun," Uman said.

The guy fixed him another look. "So," he said, "what brings you two young pups here?"

Young pups? I answered before Uman could. "Just hiking around, camping and that." I conjured up my best smile. "It's so beautiful in these hills, isn't it?"

"It is. It is indeed." He put his cap back on. Picked up the litter sack. *Good*, I thought, *he's moving on*. Then, "Tell me to mind my beeswax," he said, "but shouldn't you both be in school?"

"Yeah, but this is for the Duke of Edinburgh," I said. "You know, the award thing. We were given permission to skip a day."

"By the Duke of Edinburgh himself," Uman said. *Jesus.*

The old guy just nodded. No hint of a smile. "Which school d'you go to? My grandson is about your age. You might know him."

"Oh, we don't live round here," I said. "We've come down from Manchester."

Another nod. He adjusted his grip on the sack. While we'd been talking, his gaze had been drawn repeatedly to my red hair. He was staring again now. In disguising my appearance, had I just succeeded in making myself look like a girl who had disguised her appearance?

"Well, I should be off." He looked at Uman, then at me. "Nice chatting to you."

"Yeah, and you," I said. "Have a good day. And sorry about the heather."

After a couple of steps towards the footpath, he turned and said, "By the way, you do know you're not supposed to camp here? This is all National Trust land hereabouts. Nature conservation and all that. Actually, it's a designated Site of Special Scientific Interest." I told him we hadn't realized and he said, "If you're planning on staying any longer, I'd suggest you go to an official campsite before one of the Rangers gets wind of you."

"Thank you for that information, sir," Uman said. "We'll certainly bear it in mind."

"You can be such a dickhead sometimes," I said, once we were alone again.

172

"Double bluff," Uman said. "If we were really a pair of runaway teenagers, we wouldn't have drawn attention to ourselves by displaying such brazen impudence."

"We?"

"He liked our artwork, though. In my experience, people with artistic appreciation very seldom report fugitives to the authorities. In fact, I can't think of a single example."

And so on. It was pointless arguing with him when he was like this. We finished breaking camp and repacking our gear. Usually, this was when we would open out the map to identify a likely location for the next night. That morning, I suggested we quit the Stretton Hills altogether.

"That guy sussed us, I know it."

I expected Uman to contradict me. But he said, "I think so, too."

"Right, we move on."

"Whoa there, Gloria, we have fifty-two consultants to consult; fifty-four, including the Jokers." He produced the cards from his rucksack. "One doesn't talk to Destiny, one listens."

"We can't cut for this, Uman. It's too important."

He shuffled, offered me the pack. "Red, we stay; black, we move on."

I refused to cut.

So he did. It came up black.

"There," he said. "Destiny hath spoken."

Q14: Where's your happy place?

We separated. Uman's idea.

Even if there was a mobile signal up there and litter-grabber guy had called the police, it was unlikely they'd follow it up immediately, what with all the other tip-offs they must've had from every part of the country. The time-wasters and cranks, the cases of mistaken identity. We didn't expect a SWAT team to ambush us at any moment or a police helicopter to swoop over the brow of a hill. We figured we had time to hike to Church Stretton and get the first train or bus out before they'd be on to us. The alternative was to pull out the compass and walk due west into Wales for a few days. But we wanted to put as much distance behind us as fast as possible.

"There is a third option," Uman said.

"What's that?"

"We run after that guy and kill him, then bury him in a shallow grave."

I smacked my forehead with my palm. "Why didn't I think of that?"

We discussed potential murder weapons; skewering him with his own litter-grabber would be the most appropriate method, we decided.

"Instead of burying him, we should chop him up and feed him to the sheep," I said.

"Theoretically brilliant," Uman said. "Alas, I doubt that my Swiss Army knife is up to the job … and, I might be mistaken, but aren't sheep herbivorous?"

"Damn. It shouldn't be that complicated to dispose of a volunteer countryside warden."

As we reached the town Uman suggested we travel separately, just for that day, using different types of transport. One of us dodging, the other weaving. If the police did get round to investigating the guy's call, they'd be checking CCTV for two teenagers travelling together. "We can meet up again later," he said, "once we're well away from here."

"Meet up where?"

"At an agreed rendezvous point."

"Oh, good," I said, "I'm glad we've sorted that out."

"Just out of interest," I ask D.I. Ryan, "did the litter-grabber guy call the police about us?"

"Not that I'm aware of, no."

"Seriously? So we could have stayed down there?"

The detective nods. "At that point, we thought you were in London."

* * *

175

Bristol. I can't even remember how I got there – that is, the route the Cards of Destiny selected for me – except that it involved two buses, then a train, and took an entire lifetime. Four buses, in fact, because I got on the wrong one and had to catch another back to where I'd gone off course. When I told Uman, he called it a "stroke of genius – weavery of the highest order". His route had been more straightforward, if indirect – by train from Church Stretton to Cardiff, then another train back into England. By the time I found him under the departures board at Bristol Temple Meads station, he'd been waiting nearly two and a half hours.

I've never seen anyone look so pleased to see me in all my life.

We hit a coffee shop in the station, bought two supersize hot chocolates with all the trimmings and took them over to a corner table, sitting with our backs to the other customers. We swapped the stories of our journeys. It was odd, after more than a week of doing everything together (apart from food runs) to have something to tell each other about our day.

"I felt as if someone was going to recognize me at any moment," I said.

Uman said it had been the same for him. "There was a guy who got off the train at Cardiff – I was convinced he was an undercover cop. It was quite thrilling, actually."

"I know. How weird is that?"

I didn't admit to Uman that, on my own, I wasn't half

as confident – in myself, but also in the whole fugitivery malarkey – as I was when we were together. The worst part of travelling separately, though, was being phoneless and unable to keep in contact. That and the thought of something going wrong. Of one of us being caught. Of having him taken from me or of being taken from him. I wasn't ready for the Days of Next.

"What would you have done if I hadn't turned up?" I asked.

Uman shrugged. "I'd have waited till you did."

"But suppose I didn't."

"You did, though."

"Yeah, but—"

"Gloria, I'd have waited for you under that departures board until I grew so old my heart stopped beating and I fell down dead; until my rotting corpse oozed foul-smelling fluids across the concourse; until my remains were swept up and the floor swabbed with disinfectant by a cleaner in a high-visibility jerkin."

I told him I guessed that showed an acceptable level of commitment to our burgeoning relationship. (We were "burgeoning" by then. We'd moved on from "impending" and "embryonic".)

Where now? That was the other thing we discussed.

"Let's go somewhere special," Uman said.

"In what way, special?"

"Special to us. I mean, special to you or special to me."

177

"A happy place?" I suggested.

"Exactly and precisely that. So where's your happy place?"

"Am I only allowed one?"

"No, you're right, we must make lists. I'm a boy and boys make lists, don't they? It's what I have to do, now my hair's short."

We didn't make lists of our happy places, as it happens. We drew lots.

I tore a blank page from the pad where we kept score in our card games and Uman cut it into strips with the scissors tool on his knife. Three strips each. I took an age but he'd written his in a few seconds, folded each one and dropped them into an empty cup. No peeking, we'd agreed. I actually wrote "NO PEEKING!!!" on one of my strips because I just knew Uman was sneaking a look. Sure enough, he raised his hands in apology. He cut me another strip.

"No hurry, Gloria," he said. "We can always pitch our tent here in Starbucks tonight."

"Don't be so impatient."

"I'm not impatient, I'm desirous of everything at the same time."

"And don't quote Kerouac at me when I'm trying to think."

I was tempted to write "Stretton Hills" on all three slips, just to see his face if one of mine was pulled out. It was my happiest of happy places by a mile. We couldn't go

178

back there, though. *If you hadn't been such a dick with that guy,* I thought, *we wouldn't even need to do this.* But I left it unsaid. I couldn't be cross with Uman for long. To be honest, I was very happy just sitting there with him, reunited after half a day apart; just being on the run together.

"You know, I'd be happy wherever we go," I said.

"That's sweet," Uman said. Then, flicking a chocolate-soaked mini-marshmallow at me, "But, so help me, I will start the mother of all food fights if you don't fill those slips in now."

"All right, all right – God, you're like my mum, nagging me to do my homework."

"Shit, *homework.*" He made a face like the figure in Munch's "Scream". "We forgot to arrange a forwarding address for the school to send us our assignments."

That cracked me up, it really did.

I finished my slips and added them to Uman's in the cup. He used a stirrer to swizzle them about, then placed a hand over my eyes while I picked one out. I handed it to him for the ceremonial unfolding and announcement.

"Drum roll, please," he said.

I drummed my index fingers on the table edge.

"Lady and gentleman, I can reveal that the next destination on" – he lowered his voice to a whisper – "the Uman-and-Gloria fugitive roadshow is … Bryher! Where the—?"

"It's pronounced 'briar'. Silent h," I said. "We went there a lot on holiday when Ivan and me were kids. It's one of the Scilly Isles."

"Aren't they somewhere near Scotland?"

"They're off the tip of Cornwall, actually." I shook my head. Tutted. "Thirty thousand a year in school fees and you don't know one end of the country from the other."

Uman looked at the slip of paper again. "Bryher," he said, as if the word was a spoonful of ice cream and he was trying to guess the flavour. His eyes lit up. "Right, that's settled then."

No matter how often we made decisions on a whim – the turn of a card, a lucky dip – I couldn't quite get over how ridiculously easy it was to live your life that way. How ridiculously brilliant it was. I felt a soppy grin spread across my face at the thought of going back to Bryher for the first time since I was about ten years old. My happy place. My happier past self.

As we gathered our belongings and hauled our rucksacks on to our backs, I asked Uman, "What were your happy places, then?"

"Kyoto, Niagara Falls from the Canadian side and the mountains of Andalusia."

I laughed. "Yeah, right."

He rummaged in the cup and pulled out his three slips and showed me what he'd written. Sure enough: "Kyoto", "Niagara Falls (from the Canadian side)", "the mountains of Andalusia".

"Uman, how in the world would we have paid the air fares? How would we ever have got on a plane, for that matter? We don't even have our passports with us!"

"Ms Inexcelsis, trust me – we'd have found a way."

We changed our appearance again in Bristol. If the litter-grabber guy had reported us, the police would have new descriptions: my red hair, Uman's crew cut. Our clothes. Well, Uman's mainly. My black gear was pretty neutral, and I hardly wore my spares because Mum would've figured out what was missing from my wardrobe by then. Uman, though, looked like a children's TV presenter on acid. Reluctantly, he binned that outfit and chose a less garish one from a charity shop (brown hoodie, khaki combats). He also bought a big woolly Rastafarian-style hat, in the red, yellow and green stripes of the Ethiopian flag.

"I can't be *completely* unobtrusive," he said. "It runs contrary to my nature."

As for me, I dyed my hair blonde. Punk blonde, not Barbie-doll blonde.

Our other problem was money. Funds were dwindling, what with all the food and other stuff we'd bought, and the train and bus fares we'd paid.

We did the math. We did the math again and it still didn't add up too well.

To reach Bryher we'd have to travel down to Penzance, then catch a ferry to St Mary's, the main island in the Scillies, then another boat. Flying wasn't an option. Too expensive and, anyway, you probably had to provide names and

I.D. even for a domestic flight. The rail fare from Bristol to Penzance would leave enough cash for a few days' worth of food or the cost of the ferry tickets, but not both. Even if we took the cheaper option of making our way down to Cornwall by coach, we'd still be short. And hitchhiking would make us vulnerable to suspicion.

"Maybe we should go somewhere else," I said.

"Gloria, we've discussed this before. We drew lots. We are puppets and Destiny is the puppeteer."

"I don't suppose Destiny could lend us a couple of hundred quid, could she?"

"Sarcasm. In certain circumstances it can be a highly amusing form of humour."

"What about taking a chance on a cashpoint?"

Uman thought for a moment. Somehow, he managed to look cool in that Rasta hat. "If they're monitoring our cards," he said, "how quickly could they trace us?"

"I don't know, you're the one who watches TV crime dramas."

He ignored this remark. "All right, we hit an ATM and immediately skedaddle the hell out of here by the speediest means at our disposal. Does that sound like a plan?"

It sounded like a plan. It was late afternoon, though; the next train to Penzance would get there after dark and the coach even later, at midnight. Both rubbish times to be hiking out of an unfamiliar town to find a suitable site to camp and then erect our tent in the pitch black.

"We need another plan that sounds like a plan until we can implement the first plan that sounds like a plan," Uman said.

"How about we stay in Bristol tonight – I don't know, camp in a park or something – then, first thing tomorrow, we draw out some cash and catch the train to Pee-Zed."

"Pee-Zed. Is that what the locals call Penzance, *dorn thar in Carnwooorl?*"

"Was that supposed to be a Cornish accent?"

"Not necessarily."

I looked at him. "So, my plan – does it sound like a plan?"

"It does sound like a plan." Uman clapped his hands. "Let's go find a park."

As city-centre parks go, it was OK. There are worse places to sleep rough, for sure. It had a ruined church and a riverside walk, neat lawns and pretty flowerbeds. More usefully, it also had an area of trees and bushes where, once dusk fell and the park emptied, we could sneak in and hide till morning. It was too overgrown in there to pitch the tent, so we simply crawled into the densest part, spread the mats as best we could and laid our sleeping bags on top. If it rained, we hoped the shrubbery and canopy of trees above would shelter us. The main thing was, we were well concealed from police or security patrols, or any *undesirables*, as Uman called them, who might hang out in the park after nightfall.

It didn't rain. I slept badly, though. It wasn't the noise of

183

the city (although the quiet spell between Bristol shutting down and re-opening seemed way too short) or the cold (in fact, it was quite mild). What disturbed me most was the strangeness of trying to sleep with fresh air on my face after so many nights tucked inside our tent. Even when I buried my head in my sleeping bag I still felt … exposed, I guess. Endangered. *Don't be scared*, I told myself. But you can't convince yourself not to be scared, even if you're not sure what's scaring you.

I must've dozed off eventually because I dreamt that a fox was biting my face.

The early morning traffic woke me. I groaned, rolled towards Uman. The open-air thing had bothered him, too, by the look of it: he'd pulled the Rasta hat right down so that it covered his entire head, like a bank robber's balaclava minus the eye- and mouth-holes.

I kissed the place where I thought his lips might be. "You taste woolly."

"Mmmng."

"How can you breathe?"

"I can't," came the muffled reply. "Anyway, I'm still asleep."

"You look like a talking tea cosy."

Uman faked a snore.

"I had a nightmare that a fox was eating me," I said.

"All right, you win. I'm awake." He pushed the hat back off his face, leaving tufts of red wool snagged in his stubble.

The daylight made him squint. He looked as tired as I felt. Gazing up at me, he said, "Hey, I'd forgotten you were blonde now."

"Does it suit me?"

"You look like that woman – what's her name? From the sixties."

"Twiggy? The model?"

"No, Myra Hindley. The one who murdered all those kids."

I yanked the hat back down over his face. Hard.

After freshening up in some public toilets, we made our way back to Temple Meads station and bought tickets for the next train to Penzance. The remaining cash would last us two or three days, we reckoned. Four if we rationed our food. Then that would be it.

"Are we rationing yet?" I asked, eyeing the detritus of our breakfast donuts and coffee.

Uman licked his fingers and dried them on a paper napkin. He still had scrags of wool on his chin. "Come on. Time to visit our dear old friend, Mr ATM."

We had no choice. No money meant no more fugitivery.

The train left in twenty minutes. The plan was to use a machine we had spotted a few streets away – not one in the station itself (more dodging-and-weaving) – and draw as much cash as we could on both of our cards, then scoot back to the station and *vamoose* with his wallet and my purse fat with the funds for all the food we could eat for a month and one-way tickets to the Scilly Isles. To Bryher. To whatever lay ahead of us in the next stage of the Days of Now.

"Here goes," Uman said, at the cashpoint, flexing his fingers as if he was about to crack open a safe. He grinned at me. But I could tell he was trying to laugh off his nervousness.

I felt sick.

What did we expect: flashing lights and an ear-piercing alarm the moment he inserted his card and tapped in the digits?

Uman inserted the card. Tapped in the digits. No problem.

He shot me another smile. This was going to work. He selected £200. We waited for the chuntering of notes being counted, the whirr of the slot opening, the money shuffling into the tray, the beeps reminding Uman to take the cash and retrieve his card.

None of that happened.

"'Card retained,'" he said.

He didn't need to: I could read the words myself. Uman swore. A lot. Loudly. I thought he was going to punch the screen, but as quickly as his temper had flared, it dissipated. He simply leaned forward and rested his forehead against the ATM, his breath condensing on the glass.

"Let me try mine. I mean, you never know, yeah?"

"OK," he said, flatly, after a moment.

We both suspected what would happen this time. It did. Both cards gone. No cash.

We just stood there, staring at the screen, as if it might all have been a horrible mistake, as if the message might erase itself, as if the ATM might suddenly clunk into action and dispense the money after all. Neither of us spoke. Neither of us said the words that were running through my head and, I'm sure, Uman's as well.

We'd given ourselves away. For nothing.

Someone else was waiting to use the ATM. We moved out of their way. Uman pulled me into a hug, kissed the side of my face – aiming for the cheek, I think, but landing on the ear. He smelled of a night spent sleeping rough in a city park, but I didn't mind one bit. "Right," he said, his breath warm against my skin. "That's settled, then."

"We quit?" I said. I could barely get the words out.

He un-hugged me, placed a hand on each of my shoulders and looked me square in the face. "No, no, no, Ms Inexcelsis – I have two tickets to Penzance in one pocket and a pack of playing cards in the other." He frowned, nodded towards the rucksacks propped against the wall. "Actually, the cards are in my rucksack – but you get my general point."

"Dramatic licence," I said.

"Precisely. Dramatic licence. You see, this is why I love you."

"Shall we take a break there?" D.I. Ryan says. "Get a stretch of our legs?"

I just look at her.

"We could order in some pizza, if you like."

187

I'm about to say we only just had lunch, but I glance at the clock on the wall and see that it's 18:35. Actually, it could be midnight for all I know.

"I think we should call it a day." This is Mum. She's holding my hand. How long has she been holding my hand? From the detective's expression, she'd prefer to carry on; but then Mum says, "Look at her – she's wrung out."

D.I. Ryan sits back in her chair. Nods. "Sure. We can do that. Gloria?"

Instinctively, I want to object. Who are they to decide whether I'm OK to go on? But Mum's right, I'm dropping. A moment ago I was gabbling away and now I can barely hold my head up straight or keep my eyes open. It's not just that, though; it's the way she said it. *Look at her – she's wrung out.* The way she held – is holding – my hand, her thumb stroking my knuckles like I've grazed them and she's making them better.

Like she's on my side.

"Yeah," I say. "I'd like to stop."

"Interview suspended, 18:36." D.I. Ryan doesn't do a great job of keeping the impatience out of her voice. She clicks off the recording machine. "Grab some food and a good night's rest and we'll go again in the morning. Nine o'clock."

"Thank you," Mum says.

The detective exhales. Smiles at me, softens her voice. "You're doing really well."

I rub my eyes and discover that my face is wet with tears.

"Where is he?" I ask. Pleading. "What's happened to him?"

But D.I. Ryan doesn't have an answer for me.

Q15: How can you still believe that?

We don't go home. There are too many reporters, too many cameras. Instead, the police have arranged for us to stay in a smart hotel. They sneak us out of the station the back way, me and Mum ducking out of sight on the rear seat of an unmarked car. No blankets over our heads, though. Which is a pity because I've always wondered what that would be like. We enter the hotel through a service door. A detective constable ("D.C. Washington," he says, "not to be confused with Washington, D.C.") escorts us upstairs and tells Mum the telephone extension of a room along the corridor, where *a couple of uniforms* will be on duty overnight, if we need them.

"We had our wedding reception here," Mum says.

D.C. Washington seems to find this information unremarkable. "Order whatever you like on room service," he says. "We're picking up the tab."

If I was Uman, I'd ask for a hundred orchids, two kilos of Belgian chocolate and enough pink champagne to fill the

bath. But I'm not. I'm so spaced – and all of this is so sur-
real – I barely remember to mumble a "thank you" to the
cop as Mum ushers me through the door.

Dad is already in the room, which surprises me but, at
the same time, seems perfectly natural. He's sitting at the
foot of the double bed, watching the news. As we come in he
clicks off the TV. Stands up abruptly, like we've caught him
doing something he shouldn't.

"Hey," he says. "You made it." You'd think we'd travelled
a thousand miles to get here.

I gesture at the television. "Was that about me?"

Dad looks at the blank screen, then back again. "Not
unless you're the president of the United States, no."

I don't know whether to believe him. He looks as if he's
about to hug me but isn't sure of the etiquette for welcoming
his daughter to a "safe room" at a hotel after a day's questioning by the police. For some reason, one of his shirt sleeves is
rolled up and the other isn't.

Mum rubs my back. "Long day," she says.

"How did it go?" Dad asks, addressing me. He looks
afraid of the answer.

Even though I've been home a day or two, I haven't
adjusted to him. He seems smaller than he was before all
of this. Quieter. He hasn't shaved today. Dad never fails to
shave, even at weekends. Only in photos from way back –
pre-kids – have I seen him stubbly.

I shrug. "OK, I guess. I mean, I've no idea."

191

"The girl done good." This is Mum. She's rubbing my back again.

We're all just standing here. Hesitant, self-conscious. It reminds me of the time Uman turned up at the house and came into my bedroom. There's a single bed as well as the double, so I figure we're sharing. Maybe they think I'll run off again if I have a room to myself.

"I brought some clothes for you." Dad points to a holdall by the wardrobe.

"Anything that actually goes together?"

I've made him smile. "I wouldn't have thought so," he says.

I see Mum's expression. "What, I'm not allowed a sense of humour any more?" I ask.

She doesn't reply. She puts her bag down, goes over to the tea-making area and shakes the kettle to see if it has any water in it. She remains at the counter with her back to us, holding the kettle, but not replacing it on its stand or taking it over to the basin to fill it up either.

Dad realizes before I do that she's crying.

"Liz, sweetheart." He moves towards her, but she shrugs off his attempted hug.

"Can you give us a moment?" Mum wipes her face on her cuff, roughly, like she's cross with herself. I think she's talking to me but she means Dad. "Lor and I need to debrief."

Debrief. Do we?

"OK," Dad says. But his tone of voice says it's not OK, really.

"I need to talk to her without you jumping in," she says, turning back towards us. Her face is blotchy, shiny. "Without it turning into a…" She waves a hand in the air. She doesn't say what it might turn into. "A few minutes, Kev, that's all. Please."

"You loved him," Mum says once Dad has left the room. She's referring to Uman. "In all the time you were gone, that never even occurred to me."

"What, you thought I'd just—?"

"I thought he'd taken you. Tricked you, anyway. Manipulated you. And by the time you realized what he was up to, it was too late. But you actually *loved* that boy."

"Yeah." The word comes out croaky.

Mum's eyes are still sparkly from when she was crying just now. "When he said it, by the cash machine – when he said he loved you – was it the first time a boy told you that?"

I nod. I expect her to say you shouldn't always believe it when a boy tells you he loves you. Or that we're too young to be in love – that, when you're fifteen years old, what you think of as love is nothing of the sort. Or that Uman is absolutely the wrong person to fall in love with. *For Christ's sake, you hardly even knew him.* She doesn't say any of it, though.

She says, "The other thing I hadn't realized, till today, was just how much you hated us."

Us. Her and Dad. "I didn't. I don't."

"Sounded like it, Lor, the things you said to D.I. Ryan."

193

"I don't hate you, Mum."

"You must do, to run off like that – to let us think the worst possible things. D'you have any idea at all how worried we were? Did you even care?"

"I phoned."

"A message. One bloody message, then nothing for nearly two weeks."

"I know, I know. And I'm really sorry. But when I was with Uman I ... I just wanted to be with him so much more than I wanted to be at home, or at school, or any of that."

Any of that. I want to snatch the words back as soon as I've said them.

Mum looks at me for the longest time. She seems old, suddenly. Weary. We're sitting facing each other – me at the foot of the single bed, Mum in the chair by the desk. She made herself a cup of tea after Dad went, but it has sat untouched beside her while we've been talking. This room is too purple. Burgundy carpet, mauve walls, maroon curtains. Even the flowers in the two paintings on the wall are lilacs, I think. Lilac-coloured, anyway. The room should smell of blackcurrants, but it smells of lemon-scented air freshener.

"God," I say. "That must have sounded so selfish."

"Maybe when you have kids..." She lets the sentence trail off. Then, with a half-shake of the head, "I sent your father away so we wouldn't do this." Squabble, she must mean.

As we've talked I've been sipping at a can of Lilt from the mini-bar and working my way through a Toblerone. She watches me break off another triangle of chocolate and slot it in my mouth. At home, in the time before, Mum would've told me not to spoil my tea but here, now, she just looks disapproving; as if I shouldn't have an appetite, in the circumstances.

"Bryher," she says. "D'you know, when the police asked me where I thought the two of you might've gone, that didn't even come close to making it onto the list."

"Why not?"

"I don't know. Perhaps because I find it so hard to make a connection between the girl you were back then, on those holidays, and the one you are now."

"Sorry for growing up, Mum. I didn't do it on purpose."

She sighs. "Lor, I'm trying to understand. Trying to see how it was for you." Mum jogs the cup with her elbow and some of the tea slops onto the desk. She doesn't appear to notice. With something close to a laugh, she says, "I'm not doing a very good job of it, am I?"

"Sometimes, in there today, it was like you were the cop and she was my mum."

Even though she tries to mask it, I can see how much that hurts her. "They shouldn't even be questioning you yet," she says, quickly. "You should spend some time at home, with us. I need to spend time with you – not sitting in a police station for God knows how many hours, watching you being interviewed."

"Thanks for making her stop," I say. "I thought she was going to just carry on right through the night."

195

"Yes, well, I could see you were pooped. You're a child. She needs to remember that."

Child. I let that go. "It's not me they're bothered about, really. It's Uman."

"My point exactly. If you need to speak to anyone, after what you've been through, it's a counsellor, not a detective inspector."

"I haven't been through anything, Mum. Seriously."

She looks exasperated. "How can you still believe that?"

"He's not what they think."

"And that other time, before – I suppose the police got that wrong as well, did they?"

"Oh, so this is you 'trying to understand'."

"Lor, chicken, the state you were in when they found you."

She hasn't called me "chicken" since I was about eight. They didn't find me. And the state I was in by the end wasn't down to Uman. Not really. As for that other girl ... but I don't have the energy to argue any more. I'm done with explaining myself for today. Anyway, I'll have to go through all of this tomorrow with D.I. Ryan: the final days of our fugitivery. What happened. What he did. How it finished.

"I need a shower," I say, getting up from the bed. "I stink of police station."

Dad's back. They stop talking the moment I step out of the bathroom and both turn to look at me. I'm wearing one of the (way too big, amazingly soft) white dressing gowns that come with the room, a towel turbaned on my head. My skin is tingly and I must look very pink. I thought a shower might wake me up but, if anything, I feel more tired. I presume Mum has been giving Dad the edited highlights of my day with D.I. Ryan. From the way he asks about the shower – the user-friendliness of the controls, water strength, temperature – I'm guessing she has also warned him to go easy on me. To talk about anything but my interview. Which is fine by me.

"Where did you go?" I ask.

"Just out in the corridor," Dad says. "I didn't risk the bar in case any reporters were in there." Then, to Mum, "I'm not sure they've changed the carpets since our wedding bash."

I try to picture them back then, in the ballroom downstairs. The *banqueting suite*. I've seen the photos, obviously, and the video, but looking at them, now, after all that's happened in the past couple of weeks, I can't match these versions of Mum and Dad to their frilly-frocked, sharp-suited, twenty-something selves, taking to the dance floor with confetti still in their hair. That night, they couldn't have dreamt they'd be staying in the same hotel nearly twenty years later.

Not like this.

I feel bad for talking to Mum the way I did earlier. Bad that Dad had to stand in the corridor like a kid sent out of the classroom. Seeing them both, trying so hard to make sense of all this – to love me, to do the right thing, to *be there* for me –

197

I know they don't deserve my resentment. But, even as I think it, I resent them for making me feel bad for resenting them. And I hate myself for it.

They wanted me back. Well, I'm back. This is me, now. This is who I am.

We order food from the room-service menu. While we're waiting for it, I dry my hair.

I catch Mum observing me in the mirror. "You should dye it back to its natural colour," she says, over the noise of the dryer. "Just while the blonde grows out."

"They don't do 'mousey brown' hair dye, Mum."

"I think blonde suits you." This is Dad.

Mum gives him a look as if to say, *You might as well go back out in the corridor if that's the best you can do.* The hair bothered them when we were reunited. Yesterday, was it? Or the day before. I'm losing track already. They didn't say anything, but I could tell. To them, my blondeness was a sign of my "otherness" – the daughter who went away and came back a stranger.

"Ivan texted while you were in the shower," Mum says, changing the subject. "He's coming home at the weekend, once he's finished his assessments."

The ones my brother has to pass to progress to the second year of his degree, and which my disappearance could have (might still have) jeopardized. Apparently, he wrote one essay on the train from London, when he came up to Litchbury to sit alongside Mum and Dad at a televised press conference, pleading for my safe return.

"He put a P.S. for you as well, sending his love."

Mum is my message taker. I haven't had a chance to replace the phone Uman threw away, and the police are still holding on to my iPad and laptop – trawled through during their investigation for clues to my disappearance, or for evidence against Uman.

"Love," I say. "That would be, 'Say hey to G', then."

Mum laughs. "Actually, that's exactly what he said. Word for word."

When I came back, he phoned home and told me he was a "legend" at uni, thanks to me. The other students call him Glo-Bro, he said. He sounded drunk. I half-expected him to have a go at me over my *stupid disappearing act*. But he didn't. He said he'd shaved off his beard (he promised to send me a link to the pictures on Tumblr). What he also said was, "I hope the folks aren't giving you too much grief, girl."

I wish it was the weekend. I wish he was here now.

It crosses my mind to call Tierney from the phone in our room. But how could I, with Mum and Dad eavesdropping? I snuck a call to her yesterday, on the home landline, but it went straight to voicemail. Just hearing the recording of her singsong, mock-ditzy voice set me off. The message I left was mostly sobs and sniffs, with "sorry" and "missed you" and "really need to talk to you" thrown in, and not much that made sense. Tier is my best friend from way back and I feel I walked out on her almost as much as I walked out on Mum and Dad. We'd never kept secrets from each other and yet she knew nothing about the most exciting, most outrageous, most meaningful thing I've ever done.

She hadn't returned the call by the time the police whisked me away.

I switch off the dryer and frisk my hair, trying not to remember Uman helping me to dye it in the washrooms at Bristol Temple Meads. His fingers massaging my scalp.

If I don't change the colour I'll think of him every time I look in the mirror.

I try to calculate how many hours it is since I saw him, but I'm too tired to focus.

When the food comes, we eat round the coffee table: Mum and Dad on chairs, me at the foot of the single bed. I'm still in the bathrobe. I catch Mum glancing at my unshaven legs. The room smells of tuna and melted cheese, chilli and chips, beer and Pepsi Max.

There's more silence than conversation. The sounds of three people eating.

Most of my food is gone by the time Dad says, "We were thinking – me and Mum – that maybe we could ... after all this business with the police is over, and Ivan's home, we should go away on holiday, perhaps? Somewhere nice." He takes a slug of beer. "The four of us."

"I've just been on holiday." It's meant as a joke but comes out wrong.

They let it go. Dad thumbs the neck of his beer bottle, like

200

it's a microphone and he can't figure out if it's switched on. "New York, maybe. You've always wanted to go to New York."

New York. The effort it takes not to break down altogether and just let them hold me is almost more than I can manage.

"What about school?" I say. "Or your work?"

"Do you *want* to go back to school just yet?" Mum asks.

God, the thought of it. "No. I couldn't face it."

"Well," Dad says, "I can't face going back to work. Neither of us can."

"You've been off all this time?"

"Obviously."

Of course, obviously. "Dad, I'm really—"

"Don't waste your sympathy on him," Mum says. "I was so worried about you I cut my training schedule down to fifty kilometres a day."

It's a nanosecond before we realize she's joking. I almost swallow my tonsils and Dad snorts beer out of his nose. Then, just as we're recovering, he asks Mum how she plans to get her bike on the plane to New York and that sets us all off again.

When we're done laughing, another silence settles. A better kind of silence, though.

We finish the food. At least, I do; they leave half of theirs. Mum refills her wine glass.

"Think about it," she says, meaning New York. "You don't have to decide right now."

I watch her tidy up the remains of the meal, the plates and everything, loading it all onto the tray. Neat, efficient hands; a notch of concentration between her eyebrows, as if the placing of the items on the tray is a puzzle with only one solution and she's determined to crack it.

"When you're out on your bike," I say, "do you ever think about just … keeping going?"

She pauses in what she's doing. "What d'you mean?"

"I guess, just – riding off and not coming back."

"No." Mum sounds shocked at the suggestion. She shoots a glance at Dad, then back at me. "No, I've never thought of doing that."

"I don't mean for real – literally riding off. But as a fantasy. Like, *I wonder what would happen if I just kept riding in a straight line instead of turning for home?*"

She finishes loading the tray. Sits and stares at it for a moment. Still gazing at the tray rather than me, she asks (gently, cautiously), "What's this about, Lor?"

Dad cuts in before I can reply. "Is that how it was for you? With th— with Uman."

That boy, he nearly said. The boy he believes abducted or duped me; who must have seduced or, worst of all, raped me. How hard was it for Dad to speak his name?

"Kind of." Neither of them seems to know how to respond. So, in the awkwardness that follows, I push another question out there. "What happened to you guys in America?"

"What happened to us?" Dad asks.

"You both just took off, *living the dream*. Where did those two people go? The 'Liz' and 'Kev' you'd been when you left England. What happened to them? Why did they come back?"

"I was twenty-seven years old. Your mum was twenty-three." He pauses. "You're fifteen."

I look at him. "You didn't answer my question."

"We'd had our adventure, Lor." This is Mum. "Our fling, or whatever you want to call it. We'd met each other and fallen in love and we were ready to do the settling-down thing."

"Happy ever after."

Dad says, "There are different kinds of happiness. Different … intensities."

"Are you happy being an accountant?" I ask. Then, to Mum, "Being a receptionist?"

"Don't criticize our choices." Mum's tone is even, but her lips are drawn thin. "Please don't tell us how we should have lived our lives."

"Then don't tell me how I should live mine."

"Christ, you're still a child."

"Liz," Dad says. He reaches for her hand and she lets him hold it. There are tears in her eyes. She blinks them away. Turning his attention to me, he says, "No, I don't wake up every morning with joy in my heart at the thought of another day's accountancy. Yes, I'd much rather be doing something more exciting."

"Like music."

"Like music, yes."

"So why didn't you? Why don't you?"

"Because I'm not good enough. I never was." His matter-of-factness is like the thud of a slammed door. "When you're young, you imagine anything is possible. You're happy to take your chances with life and see how things work out. You take risks, do wild and crazy things. You live *the dream*." He shrugs. "Then you grow up."

I shake my head. "When you say 'grow up', d'you really mean 'give up'?"

"She's discovered Jack Kerouac," Mum says.

Dad frowns. "Is he the lad in Year 10, with the ginger hair?"

"No," I say, "he's—"

"Lor, I know who Jack Kerouac is," he says, laughing. "I read *On the Road* years before you were even born. Read it in California, as it happens."

"Tell Dad the quote," Mum says.

I don't tell him the quote.

"Something about people who are crazy to live, who never yawn or—"

"Stop making fun of me, Mum."

"Honey, I'm not making fun of you. Really, I'm not."

"D'you know how Kerouac died?" Dad asks. When I don't respond, he says, "Drank himself to death by the time he was my age. He wasn't a romantic hero, he was an alcoholic."

I sit there and scowl. Pathetic, but it's what I feel like doing just now.

Dad finishes his beer. Mum stands up and takes the tray

out into the corridor. I hear something topple as she sets it down. She comes back in, pulls the door shut and locks it.

"Lor," she says, picking up her wine, "when you're old enough to leave home you can live however you choose. Hook up with whoever you like. Spend your entire life travelling from place to place, with your rucksack and tent. Paint your tent in pink-and-purple stripes."

"Yeah, but first there's school to finish," I say, laying it on thick with the weary voice. "Then uni, then all that student debt to pay off and, oh, OK, I might as well just get a crap job and rent a scuzzy flat till I've got myself straight – and then, yay! I can go off and do something really exciting with my life. Assuming I'm not married with kids and a mortgage by then."

"When you put it like that," Mum says with a smile, "it does sound bloody boring."

I'm still too cross to find that amusing.

Dad, looking confused, asks, "Why would anyone want a pink-and-purple tent?"

The voices wake me.

I feel as if I've been asleep for ages. When I open my eyes a couple of the lamps are still on and I see from the digital alarm clock on the bedside table that it's 21:50. Which I think is nearly midnight, till I redo the math and realize it's only ten to ten. I've been in bed for less than an hour. I sit up. The TV is still on – muted, with subtitles flicking across the screen – and the book Mum was reading is lying open, face-down, on the chair where she'd been sitting when I turned in for an early night. But neither of them is in the room.

Voices again. From outside in the corridor.

Still in the dressing gown, I slip out of bed and cross the room. The door is closed, but I hear people talking just the other side of it. Mum, then a man whose voice I vaguely recognize but don't place. The sound is muffled enough that I can't quite piece together what's being said.

I open the door.

My appearance shuts them up. Mum and Dad are standing with a tall, fair-haired guy in a creased grey suit and a tie that looks like a stripe of fluorescent green paint down the front of his shirt. Journalist? No, I remember him: he's a cop. He visited the house after I came home; he'd been more or less living with Mum and Dad while I was missing.

"Oh, hey, Gloria." He musters up a smile that doesn't hide the fact that he really wishes I hadn't shown my face just then. "Paul Coker. Family Liaison. We met yesterday."

"Yeah, I know."

Mum and Dad seem as uncomfortable as he does. "Paul just came by to see if everything was OK," Mum says. She rubs my arm. "Sorry, sweetie, we didn't want to wake you."

I look at her, then at Dad, who is staring at the carpet. Then I look at the cop again. "It's about Uman, isn't it? Something's happened – that's why you're here."

The cop nods. "Yes." He clears his throat, starts again. "Yes, I'm afraid it is."

Q16: Are you sure you're ready to continue, Gloria?

D.I. Ryan:

Interview resumes 9.07 a.m., 15th of June, Litchbury police station. Same persons present: myself, Detective Inspector Katharine Ryan; Miss Gloria Jade Ellis; Mrs Elizabeth Mary Ellis.

Are you sure you're ready to continue, Gloria?

Gloria:

Yeah.

D.I. Ryan:

OK. (Rustling sound) I'm showing the interviewee an evidence bag containing a plain brown hoodie-style polyester-cotton top, size large. Label, River Island. The item is stained with blood and sand and is water-damaged. Gloria, do you recognize this hoodie?

Gloria:

Can I take it out of the bag?

D.I. Ryan:

Put these on. I am handing the interviewee a pair of

207

non-contaminant gloves.

(Delay) The interviewee is examining the garment.

Gloria:

(Cries)

D.I. Ryan:

Do you recognize it?

Gloria:

(Nods)

D.I. Ryan:

For the recording, please.

Gloria:

Yes. It's Uman's. The one he bought in the... (Cries) Sorry. In the charity shop in Bristol.

D.I. Ryan:

You're sure it's his?

Gloria:

Look. (Indicates the garment) He did this on some barbed wire.

D.I. Ryan:

The interviewee is showing me a jagged rip, approximately 3cm long, on the reverse of the left sleeve, just below the elbow.

Gloria:

And there's the blood.

D.I. Ryan:

That happened while you were with him?

Gloria:

(Nods) Yeah. (Cries) It's definitely Uman's hoodie.

D.I. Ryan:

OK. Thank you, Gloria. I am returning the item to the evidence bag.

Mrs Ellis:

Do you want to stop a moment, Lor?

Gloria:

(Shakes head) Was there anything else of his on the beach?

D.I. Ryan:

No. (Pauses) Just the boat.

We're awaiting the owner's confirmation to I.D. the vessel, as well as a full forensic examination. But, at this stage, I have to say that all the indications suggest—

Gloria:

He could have made it ashore, though. Couldn't he?

D.I. Ryan:

Our preliminary findings suggest the boat was badly damaged *before* it beached.

Gloria:

But you don't know for certain.

D.I. Ryan:

I realize this is tough to take, Gloria, but the very real probability is that Uman—

Gloria:

Probability. That's all it is. A probability. You haven't

found him, have you?

D.I. Ryan:

No. No, we haven't.

Gloria:

Well, then.

Mrs Ellis:

Have there been any ... sightings of Uman? On land?

D.I. Ryan:

(Shakes head) None have been reported. Realistically, we're not expecting any at this stage.

Gloria:

So, why are we here? I mean, how can you arrest him or charge him with anything if he's—

D.I. Ryan:

Until we have confirmation... Gloria, I appreciate that talking about all of this is going to be even harder for you, today – even more upsetting – after this latest development. But the—

Gloria:

Development.

D.I. Ryan:

But the fact is, whether Uman's still alive or ... not, and regardless of any offences he may or may not have committed, we need to know what went on in those last days you were together. Where you were, what you did. How it ended. All that's changed is that yesterday we were trying to trace a suspect and today we're looking for a missing boy who we presume to be dead.

Gloria:

(Cries)

Mrs Ellis:

She barely slept last night, after hearing about this.

D.I. Ryan:

I'm sure. I'm sure. (Pauses) Do you want to take ten minutes?

Gloria:

(Shakes head)

D.I. Ryan:

Believe me, Gloria, if I could avoid putting you through all of this, I would. But you're quite possibly the last person to see Uman alive. That makes you a really important witness. And we have a duty to establish, as best we can, what happened and what led up to it. How and why we have a wrecked boat and a boy's hoodie washed up on a beach. And no boy.

Mrs Ellis:

You put my daughter through a very long, very hard day yesterday.

D.I. Ryan:

I know, Mrs Ellis.

Mrs Ellis:

And she's suffered a real shock with this news. You just have to look at her to see that.

D.I. Ryan:

I understand. Of course I do. You're her mother, it's only natural that you—

Mrs Ellis:

You've been so good to us through all this, D.I. Ryan, and I don't want to fall out with you now, but don't you *dare* patronize me.

Gloria:

Mum, it's OK. Seriously. She's just doing her job.

D.I. Ryan:

Look, the fact is, if we don't do this now, today, we'll only have to—

Gloria:

Let's do it now, then. Get it over with.

D.I. Ryan:

Liz?

Mrs Ellis:

It's Lor's call. But the moment she wants to stop...

D.I. Ryan:

We stop. Absolutely. (To Gloria) Deal?

Gloria:

(Nods) OK.

D.I. Ryan:

Good. Thank you. That's good. Let's make a start, then, shall we?

Gloria:

(Shrugs) Yeah.

D.I. Ryan:

OK. So, when we wrapped up yesterday, the ATM had swallowed your cards but you'd already bought your train tickets, so you decided to head down to Penzance anyway. Is that right?

Gloria:

It wasn't us who decided – we cut the pack.

D.I. Ryan:

Right. Of course. (Pauses) Anyway, you're on the train.

Gloria:

We sat in different carriages. After the ATM, we didn't know how soon you'd be on to us. Uman thought other people on the train would be less likely to notice us if we didn't sit together.

D.I. Ryan:

Dodging and weaving.

Gloria:

We were calling it "dweaving" by then.

D.I. Ryan:

Not "wodging"?

Gloria:

That was my suggestion, actually. But Uman said (Puts on posh voice), "Wodging carries a whiff of vulgarity." (Cries) Sorry. (Pauses) Sorry. I'm OK.

D.I. Ryan:

Sure?

213

Gloria:

(Nods)

D.I. Ryan:

So, what time did you arrive in Penzance?

Gloria:

You must know that already. Off the CCTV.

D.I. Ryan:

Nope. We never traced you beyond Bristol, as it happens. Not for definite.

Gloria:

(Shakes head and mutters inaudibly) We got there about 2 pm, I think. Something like that.

D.I. Ryan:

And were you still intending to go to the Scilly Isles despite having so little money left?

Gloria:

We'd cut the pack again by then. The cards still said "Bryher".

D.I. Ryan:

These cards had an uncanny knack of choosing the options you wanted to pick in the first place.

Gloria:

"Fate is a handshake between Free Will and Random Chance." I came up with that one, not Uman.

D.I. Ryan:

(Pauses) So, go on. Bryher.

Gloria:

> Actually, we did fix that one. We were so determined to make it over to Bryher, we did best of three. Best of five, in the end.

D.I. Ryan:

> All right, you're in Penzance. Short of money. Something like sixty kilometres of sea between you and Bryher. The cards say "Yes" – but how? What happens next, Gloria?

Q17: Could we swim there?

That was when it all started to turn to shit.

First thing to go wrong (second, including the ATM): there's only one crossing a day to the Scilly Isles – and we'd missed it. Which meant spending the afternoon, the evening, the whole night in Penzance. No big deal, really, except that having set our hearts on Bryher – my happy place – we were impatient to get there. Once we reached the island, everything would be OK, just as it had been in the Stretton Hills. Bryher was a magical realm of golden beaches, clear blue skies and all-day sunshine, I told Uman. I'd filled his head with tales of idyllic family holidays when I was a child, my brother and me roaming the island from dawn to dusk, barefoot and brown-limbed. Those *free spirits* Mum spoke of, drifting on the gentlest sea breeze. If it had ever rained in those summers, if there'd been family quarrels, I'd erased it from my memory.

It rained that day, in Penzance. That was the next thing to go wrong. After mostly warm, dry days since we'd gone on the run, the weather turned against us.

"We are young," Uman said. "We are weatherproof."

"We are."

We were huddled in a shelter on the seafront, watching the slate-grey sea send wave after wave crashing in a beery froth onto the shore. Killing time. Conserving what was left of our money. Avoiding shops and cafés, and the busier parts of a Cornish town where a dark-skinned guy in a Rasta hat and a fake-blonde girl might draw attention. On a wet, blustery afternoon, we had the front to ourselves, apart from a dog-walker in head-to-toe Gore-Tex and a few gulls flapping about.

We played game after game of Twenty Questions (despite Uman's annoying habit of choosing the most obscure things for me to guess: cherry blossom, tungsten, Bert Monkey from the Noddy books). Or we talked about Bryher and our plan to get there. Not that we had a plan.

"Could we swim there?" Uman asked.

"Uman, the ferry takes two and a half hours."

"What's that in breaststroke?"

"Exactly halfway between too far and drowned."

"Actually, I'm a very good swimmer."

"OK," I said, "so you could manage sixty kilometres?"

Uman thought for a moment. "I've done twenty lengths of a fifty-metre pool."

"You had an Olympic-size pool at your school?"

"Yes, of course. But I was referring to the one at my house."

Later, after the rain had eased off and while it was still light, we strolled down to the harbour. Casual as you like, just a pair of backpackers mooching around. A few people were out and about – visitors, like us, as well as workers in yellow oilskins or high-vis jackets. The air reeked of fish and salt, engine oil and bird poo. The ferry had returned from the Scillies by then and was moored at the end of an old stone quay, ready to depart again in the morning. It was smaller than I remembered but impressive, even so, alongside the fishing boats and pleasure cruisers that bobbed and creaked against their ropes. When I was little, waiting there with Mum, Dad and Ivan to board the ferry, I used to imagine crossing from one side of the harbour to the other by clambering from boat to boat.

The idea still appealed to me. I bet Uman would've done it if I'd suggested it.

But we were there on a mission, not to have fun. We reconnoitred – looking for a way to sneak onto the ferry. Not there and then (cleaners were on board, by the look of it, and men were winching crates of supplies onto the upper deck). But later, in the night, we would return. That was the plan we'd settled on: to make the voyage to the Scilly Isles as stowaways.

"We will get caught," I said. "You do know that."

Uman shook his head. "It'll be like those times we cut class and just walked out of school – it's the last thing they'll be prepared for."

"There'll be night-time patrols down here. Men with dogs. CCTV cameras."

"Dogs with CCTV cameras."

"Uman, I'm being serious."

"This is Penzance harbour, not Heathrow Airport."

"Anyway, they'll have raised the ramp." I pointed out the height from the quayside to the upper deck, the gap between the dock and the side of the ship. "How do we get on board, with our rucksacks? Even without our rucksacks?"

"Can I remind you, we're only doing Plan B because the cards chose it over Plan A. And because you objected to Plan C."

Plan A was to plead with a fisherman to take us across in his boat. Plan C had been to buy replica guns and hijack the ferry.

Uman would have denied it, but I think we were resigned to the fact that we had reached the end of the road with our fugitivery. That we expected to be caught trying to stow away. But that it was better to finish like this – recklessly, daringly – than play hide-and-seek in Cornwall for two or three days till the last of the money was gone.

It rained again that evening. In need of somewhere dry to hole up for a few hours before putting Plan B into action, we went to the cinema. The film was the latest Hobbit-y thing. Not my kind of movie, or Uman's, but it was very long, which suited our purposes just fine.

"What is a hobbit, exactly?" Uman asked as we queued to buy tickets.

"A cross between a horse and a rabbit," I said.

A boy in front of us – about twelve years old – turned and, as if addressing two kids half his age, told us, "A hobbit is a small humanoid creature who lives in a hole."

"Oh, I think I used to go out with one of those," Uman said.

The young lad gave him a withering look. "I very much doubt it."

We cracked up. "Let's adopt him," Uman whispered in my ear as the boy turned away.

Uman detested the film. One hundred and sixty minutes of his life he would never get back, and so on. "Like all fantasy films, it's escapist nonsense hidden by a smokescreen of CGI."

"You don't like escapism?" I said, trying not to laugh.

"No. I don't."

"So what have we been doing for the last ten days?"

"This isn't an escape from reality," Uman said. "This is our reality."

Was it? I guessed it was, if we chose it to be. But who gets to choose their own reality, really? And for how long, even if they do? It occurred to me, just then, that we were like small children covering our eyes with our hands and imagining that other people couldn't see us. Or that the rest of the world would leave us alone.

"The real reality is still out there," I said to Uman. "It doesn't go away."

"I never said it did," he replied.

We returned to an alleyway where we'd stashed our rucksacks behind an industrial-size rubbish bin. They were still there, protected from the rain by their waterproof covers.

"Stowaway time?" Uman said.

"Stowaway time."

Butterflies in the tummy time. We would pull off an amazing stunt ... or be arrested. The prospect of all this coming to an end was too upsetting. I closed my mind to it. Stopped myself from blurting out that we should just hike off into the countryside, pitch the tent, and extend our adventure – our reality – for as long as possible. We could always steal food once the money ran out, couldn't we? I didn't say any of that.

I simply took hold of his hand and said, "I love you, Uman Padeem."

"That's fortuitous because I love you too, Gloria Jade Ellis."

We'd both said "I love you" a lot since Uman's declaration by the cash machine in Bristol. As if we'd discovered a fantastic new flavour of ice cream and couldn't resist scooping another spoonful whenever we felt like it. I'd never been in love before. Or been loved. But already I knew more about being in love than anyone who had ever lived.

These latest *I love yous* sounded more like goodbyes,

though. Like neither of us was too sure when we'd get the chance to say it to each other again after Plan B had failed.

We headed along a pedestrianized street in the direction of the harbour. The wet ground was slick with a sheen of reflected lights. The bars and pubs had already emptied out by then, but a few stragglers were still making their way home or on the hunt for fast food. Shouts and laughter echoed along the street. A siren sounded somewhere.

I saw them before Uman did.

Three guys coming the other way; maybe eighteen years old. They'd been drinking, you could tell. Uman had just asked me to name my top three films of all time and I'd got as far as, "One, *Juno*; two, *Little Miss Sunshine*..." They were ten metres away. The middle one looked at me, then at Uman; nudged his mates and said something I couldn't hear. But I knew. Like in school, when a fight is about to break out – the threat of violence leaks into the air and leaves a sour taste in your throat even before the first punch has been thrown.

"Hey, Paki," the middle one said. "Nice hat, *maaan*."

The other two laughed. The guys' shirts were translucent with damp, pasted to their skin, each one buttoned right up to the collar. Red shirt, yellow shirt, green shirt. Like a set of traffic lights. I don't know why that thought occurred to me just then.

"I'm talking to *you*." The middle one again. Ginger hair, cropped short and quiffed with gel; he was shorter and skinnier than his mates – kind of stringy, almost literally

222

bouncing with unspent energy. The other two (twins?) looked like they'd been sculpted out of dough and had their faces painted pink.

Side by side, the three of them blocked our way.

"And your third film?" Uman asked me, as if oblivious to them.

I slowed to a halt, tugging on his hand to make him stop too or, I swear, he would've just walked right into Ginger.

"Are we a deaf Paki?" the guy said. "Or a no-speakie-English Paki?"

Please, Uman, I thought, just for once, don't be a smart-arse.

"Oh, I'm sorry, were you addressing me?" Uman said, breezily, laying on the poshness. I groaned inside. "If so, then I'm afraid you've erred in your assumption of my ethnicity."

Jesus Christ. "Uman," I hissed, squeezing his hand to shut him up.

"I've *what*?" Ginger said.

"Is it my accent that confuses you?" Uman asked. "Or my mode of discourse?"

Ginger hoiked up a mouthful of phlegm and spat on the ground between Uman's feet.

"You see, my forebears hail from Turkey and various parts of Arabia and I was born in the UK," Uman went on. "So, by no categorization could I be Pakistani." Then, smiling like it was all an amusing misunderstanding, "Unless you used 'Paki' as an indiscriminate pejorative."

223

Ginger stared at him, flanked by his mates. His face was shiny with damp, his nipples distinctly visible through the rain-soaked yellow shirt.

"Please," I said, my voice shaky, strange-sounding, "we aren't doing you any—"

The sound of the fist connecting with Uman's face seemed to happen before the guy had swung his arm. A wet smack, like he'd thrown a tomato at a wall.

Uman looked as surprised by it as I was. I don't know if the blow was hard enough to have knocked him down anyway or whether the weight of the rucksack on his back unbalanced him. Whatever, he was on the ground like an upturned beetle. As he rolled over, struggling to free his arms from the shoulder straps, Ginger stepped round him and landed a kick in his ribs. Uman's grunt sounded more animal than human.

I screamed then, I think. *No!* or *Stop it!* or *Leave him alone!* Something like that. I tried to get between them, but one of the Dough Boys grabbed my arm and yanked me out of the way.

Uman was on all fours, with one arm free, and gloopy, bloody strings of snot drooling from his nose and mouth. Ginger kicked him again, full in the face, snapping Uman's head back and sending his Rasta hat flying.

"He's only fifteen!" I yelled.

Dough Boy One was still holding on to me and I half-pulled us both to the ground trying to free myself. I thought

Ginger was going to kick Uman again – just go on kicking his head like a football – but he'd bent over him instead and was jabbing and groping at him, like he wanted to pull his jacket off … or as if he was stabbing him in the chest.

"Nooo!" I was shrieking, demented, my shoulder nearly wrenched out of its socket.

Did he have a knife? I couldn't see – just those hands, the rapid flashes of white. I heard someone else shouting, then – saw more people gathering round Uman – and, for a moment, I thought a whole mob was going to join in the attack. But it was two thirtysomething couples, and the men were right there, in front of Ginger. They looked like rugby players.

"Come on, then!" Ginger shouted. "You want some as well? You *want* some?"

They stood their ground. "I'm ready when you are, son," the bigger of the two men said, not raising his voice at all. Behind them, one woman was bending over Uman and the other was using her phone, letting Ginger know she was calling the police.

Dough Boy One loosened his hold of me. "Leave it, Craig," the other one said.

"Come on, there's only two of them."

They were pulling him away. "*Leave* it."

They must have gone then. I don't know. I was on my knees beside Uman, helping to untangle him from his rucksack, sobbing, saying his name over and over again.

"It's OK, love." I felt a hand on my shoulder. "The ambulance is on its way."

I'd been in the waiting area for a couple of hours when a nurse came to tell me I could see him. He wasn't in the best shape for a conversation, she explained, but I could have five minutes.

"Is he going to be all right?"

"He has concussion, so we're keeping him in overnight to monitor that," she said. "And he's broken his nose and might've cracked a rib or two as well." She made it sound as if Uman had inflicted these injuries on himself. She looked Chinese; pretty, smaller than me. A mole on the bridge of her nose resembled a chocolate chip. "Apart from that, it's just cuts and bruises."

She pronounced it *bruces*. "I saw the guy stabbing him," I said. I caught myself miming Ginger's hand actions and instantly let my arms drop to my sides.

I'd said the same to the paramedics when the ambulance arrived; screamed it at them — "He's been stabbed, he's been stabbed!" But there were no knife wounds; the blood down the front of his hoodie had come from his face, they told me. To begin with, I didn't believe them — they hadn't examined him properly, they were humouring me, the hysterical girl. Even now, at the hospital, I had to hear it again from the Chinese nurse.

"No," she said. "He wasn't stabbed."

226

"I was afraid he…" But I couldn't get the words out.

She smiled. "Come on, I'll take you to him."

A curtain had been drawn around Uman's bed. The head of the bed had been raised a little and, what with the pillows, he was halfway between sitting up and lying down. His top lip was four times the size of the bottom one and six different shades of red, apart from a "zip" of white stitches. His nose looked like a fat purple leech feeding on the middle of his face. They'd stuffed each nostril with cotton swabs. Two black eyes were already forming.

Uman was gazing blankly in the direction of the foot of the bed when I slipped through the gap in the curtain. It took him a moment to register it was me at his bedside.

"Hey," I said, reaching for the hand that wasn't attached to the IV.

He half-turned his head towards me and gave a sleepy grimace that I figured was the closest he could get to a smile. "Hey, Ms Inexcelsis," he croaked. At least, I think that's what he said. Mostly it was S-sounds and wheezing and pink-tinted spit.

I stood there and cried for a bit. Uman squeezed my hand, his eyes never leaving mine.

"I thought you were going to die," I managed to say, at last.

"Not me." *Dot nee.* Then something completely incomprehensible.

"Uman, are you speaking Danish?"

He laughed, then immediately winced and clutched at his side. His cracked ribs.

"Sorry, sorry," I said.

When he'd recovered, he whispered, "I dub oo, Doria."

I nodded. Grinned. "I dub oo doo, Ubab."

D.I. Ryan asks if the local police questioned me at the scene of the fight, or later, at the hospital.

"It wasn't a fight," I say. "Uman got beaten up."

"Did they speak to you?"

I nod. "At A&E, yeah."

"And you … told them what?"

I take her through the lies I handed the young police-woman, with her face full of freckles and such bad eczema on her fingers it was almost painful to watch her grip the pen as she made notes. I'd been sitting in a corner of the waiting area, both rucksacks propped next to me. When I spotted the WPC approaching the inquiry desk, I moved to another row so she wouldn't realize the packs and camping gear were anything to do with me. I'd just settled myself into the seat as the receptionist pointed the cop in my direction.

She led me to a consulting room across the corridor. It smelled of antiseptic. They hadn't managed to interview my friend yet, the cop told me. At least, they'd tried to but couldn't make sense of what he was saying. Not even his name.

"He doesn't have any I.D. on him," she said.

I tried not to stare at her chapped knuckles. "His name's

Fernando," I told her. Same name I'd given to the para-medics. "He's Spanish. From Andalusia."

"Surname?"

"I can't remember." When she fixed me a sceptical look, I added, "He's an exchange student – he's only been staying with us a couple of days. Martinez, I think." I offered a shrug of apology. "Begins with an M, anyway. Or an N."

I spun her the rest of it. A fleshed-out version of what I'd said to the woman on the desk when Uman was admitted. I'm not sure why I lied. Maybe I'd become so used to a life of deceit while we had been on the run that it was instinctive to throw in another dodge, another weave. Or maybe I just didn't want it to end like this. Or at all. During the long wait at A&E, I had been fine-tuning the story. The one in which Fernando, who was staying with my family on a school exchange, joined us on a week's holiday down there in Cornwall. No, it was half-term, up north. We'd been to the cinema (the Savoy, to see the latest Hobbit-y thing – yes, just me and Fernando) and, as we were walking down the street afterwards... I described what happened. Described Ginger – "Craig, they called him" – and the two Dough Boys.

My dad was on his way to the hospital, I told her. No, I couldn't recall the name of the holiday cottage or the address, but it was somewhere near the train station. My name? I gave her the name of one of my cousins. And her address in Cumbria. Risky, but it was nearly two a.m. by then and I didn't reckon the police would be checking it out just yet.

"This WPC didn't ask for your I.D.?" D.I. Ryan says.

"No."

She tuts, shakes her head. Then, after a pause, "You could've just given up at this point. They were keeping Uman in overnight and it was only a matter of time before the medical staff or the police put two and two together." She looks at me. "You'd more or less resigned yourself to getting caught if you tried to sneak onto the ferry – and, besides, Uman was in no fit state to go anywhere. So why not just call it quits? Right there in the hospital."

I don't answer.

"Come on, Gloria."

"I couldn't quit for both of us."

"What d'you mean?" D.I. Ryan asks.

"I had to speak to Uman first. I had to know he wanted to quit."

"You'd agreed this with him, had you?"

"I had to talk to him," I repeat. "If he said he'd had enough, then we'd stop. Give up."

"And if he said he wanted to go on?"

I shrug. "Then we'd go on."

The WPC said the police would be back in the morning to speak to Fernando. She told me to go back to the holiday cottage with my dad, when he arrived, and get some sleep. In the meantime, she needed a way of contacting me. I should have anticipated that. With no time to think, I gave her the number of the mobile phone we'd thrown away in Drop Bear Woods.

I spent what was left of the night in the waiting area at A&E.

They weren't happy about it, given my age; if I was determined to stay ("I am, absolutely – I'm not leaving him"), I should have an adult with me. At the very least, they wanted to speak to my parents. My dad was on his way to the hospital, I told the woman at the desk. Not long after, there was a change of shift and a different receptionist came on duty. They forgot about me after that. Too busy. There'd been a big crash on the A30 or something and all the staff in A&E were acting out an episode of *Casualty* for the next couple of hours. A teenage girl curled up on a seat at the back of a crowded waiting area was the least of their concerns.

I snuck away once to look in on Uman, but he was asleep. Upsetting as it was to see him in that state, I stayed and watched over him as long as I dared.

Held his hand. Stroked his hair. Whispered to him.

I don't know what I was thinking. To be honest, I'm not sure I was thinking at all by then. I was too tired, too stunned by what had happened. *What next* didn't even enter my head. All I wanted was to be with Uman – be near him, anyway – and wait for him to wake up.

At some point, I must have dozed off myself.

Someone's hand was on my shoulder, gently shaking me. *It's OK, love, the ambulance is on its way.* For a moment, I was back

231

in the street, bent over Uman, with one of the women trying to comfort me... Or, no, I'd fallen asleep at Uman's bedside and a nurse or doctor or the police were trying to wake me. Or I was just dreaming.

Another shake, less gentle. "Doria."

I jerked, blinked my eyes open. Where was I? In the waiting area, slumped forward on the seat, my head resting on one of the rucksacks. As I sat up there was the sound of my cheek unpeeling from the rough fabric like a strip of ripped-off Sellotape.

A voice was whispering to me. It was too bright, my eyes were too gummy, unfocused.

"Hey," the whispery voice said.

I found him, then. His bashed-up face loomed in front of mine.

"Uman?"

He raised a finger to his lips. Beckoned me to get up. Said something that might have been, "We've got a ferry to catch."

Q18: Why are you still here?

We walked right out of that hospital. No one challenged us, or called us back, or ran after us. The doors slid open and we stepped into the greyish light of a new day. Neither of us spoke until we'd left the hospital grounds and were following a road sign-posted for the town centre.

"How you feeling?" I asked.

"Od a scale ob one do ded? Dought boint bibe."

"Nought point five," I said. "That's roughly point five better than you look."

"Danks."

"You're welcome. Good to see you, by the way."

"You doo." Uman swore. Either that or he was telling me he'd just seen a bucket. He stopped walking and gingerly plucked the cotton swabs from his nose. "That's better," he said.

I pulled a tissue from my pocket and handed it to him. "You're leaking."

According to the clock on the wall, it was eight a.m. when we left A&E. The ferry was due to sail in an hour and a quarter. We didn't even discuss how we hoped to get on board; we just aimed for the harbour, so glad to be reunited that nothing else mattered. His limp was worse, his lungs too, but what really slowed him down was the pain in his cracked ribs. Each step brought a wince and a hiss of breath as the weight of his rucksack shifted.

Luckily, the hospital wasn't far from the town centre. After a few minutes, the road gave way to a pedestrianized street and I recognized where we were. The blue frontage of the cinema was just a hundred metres ahead, and beyond that lay the place where Uman had been attacked. Even in daylight, with the bustle of people heading to work and some of the shopkeepers raising shutters and setting out displays, the street scared me. As if Ginger Craig and the Dough Boys might still be there, lying in wait for us.

"We can go a different way, if you like," I said.

Uman shook his head. He didn't look bothered at all. When we reached the spot where it had happened, he paused to study the ground for bloodstains – disappointed, it seemed, not to find some, or any sign of what had taken place there. The rain overnight had erased everything. No, not quite everything. Two halves of a blue plastic bangle lay a little way apart, like brackets with the words in between deleted.

"I could've won that fight," he said. "If the other guy hadn't beaten me up."

He was talking normally, now, apart from a lisp due to his damaged lip.

234

"Taking the piss out of him wasn't such a good idea, was it?" I said.

"He would've done it anyway. Guys like that, they're looking for a fight – and I just happened to be there, wearing the wrong skin colour and a silly hat."

"Yeah, but—"

"Gloria, it's what I do. He has his fists and feet, I have my words – my devastating wit and, frankly, genius-level intelligence. And you know what? In those few seconds before he hit me, I really, *really* enjoyed showing him how stupid he was."

"Can I say 'yeah, but' again?"

"No, you can't. And my final point is, my injuries will heal – but he's going to remain a stupid, violent, racist *bastard* for the rest of his life." One or two passers-by glanced at him. Uman pressed the tissue against his nose, which had sprung a fresh leak. He held the tissue for me to see. "Look, the bloodstains have formed the exact pattern of the Indonesian archipelago."

At the harbour, a queue had already formed on the quayside and the first of the passengers were boarding the ferry. The system was the same as I remembered from family holidays. You lined up at a Portakabin window to exchange your ticket for a boarding pass before continuing onto a loading area, where two guys stowed your luggage in a metal container. Then you walked up the ramp and handed

235

your pass to a steward as you stepped onto the deck.

Easy. If you had a ticket to begin with.

Dad always let me and my brother hold the boarding passes; two each. The first time, I cried when the steward took them off me and she smiled and let me keep them.

"I suspect we've missed our opportunity to stow away in the dead of night," Uman said.

"Never lets you down, does it? That genius-level intelligence of yours."

"What if we create a diversion?" He coughed, spat a mixture of blood and saliva onto the ground. "Set fire to one of the boats in the harbour and, while everyone's distracted—"

"Uman, I know he kicked you in the head, but there must be *some* brain function left."

"Fair point, actually. I think I'm still concussed. How many fingers are you holding up?"

"I'm not holding any fingers up."

He shook his head. "God, it's worse than I thought."

"Can we stay focused here?" I said, trying not to laugh.

"OK … I got mugged and the guy beat me up and stole our tickets."

"No, they'll just check on the computer to see if we've made a booking."

We fell quiet and watched what was going on. The quay was wide enough that there'd be no problem bypassing the queue, the Portakabin window and even the luggage guys; but without boarding passes we'd never make it past the stewards at the top of the ramp. Maybe Uman's diversion tactic wasn't such a crazy idea after all.

"I'll go and buy some matches and a can of paraffin," I said.

As I spoke the words a solution came to me. I didn't think it had a hope in hell of working … but twenty minutes later, we were on board the ferry.

"Whoa, hold on a sec," D.I. Ryan says. "Can we back up a little, here?"

I play dumb. "Oh, right, you want to know how we did it?"

She laughs. "That would be good, yes."

I tell her what she wants to know. How I fished some coins from my pocket and bought a coffee from a kiosk near the harbour entrance. (I hadn't told Uman what I was up to, just that he should wait where he was.) How I joined the check-in queue, not drinking the coffee. How, as I neared the head of the line, I removed the plastic lid. At the Portakabin window, I tell D.I. Ryan, I stood the cup on the ledge and pre-tended to search my jacket for the ticket while the woman at the desk waited with an air of patient boredom. She snapped out of it, though, when my elbow caught the cup and sent coffee all over her desk, her lap, her computer keyboard.

I couldn't apologize enough, I really couldn't. I even tried to help her mop up. And, would you believe it, I'd just real-ized my boyfriend must have had the tickets all along. I'd go get them from him and rejoin the queue, I told the woman.

Who was still cleaning up and checking her PC was working and trying not to get *too* cross with a customer about the state of her skirt. I apologized again. To her, to the family behind me who were waiting to check in.

Then I stepped away from the window and walked back along the dock to Uman.

"What was that all about?" he asked.

"That was all about these," I said, showing him the two boarding passes I'd snaffled from the desk while the woman was surfacing from the coffee tsunami.

It was a while after we set sail before we stopped grinning at each other, before we stopped high-fiving, before I stopped saying I couldn't believe we'd got away with it, before Uman stopped telling me I was the most brilliantly cunning dweaver in the history of dweaving.

Before we stopped taking turns to say things like, "Hah, we are *so* going to Bryher!"

The only tricky moment had come when we'd flashed our stolen passes and one of the stewards – alarmed by Uman's bashed-up state – was all set to radio the on-board medic to come and examine him. But Uman had lost none of his skill in out-insisting people. He'd just left the hospital, as it happened, and they'd given him the all-clear to travel over to the islands.

"I have an appointment to see a GP when we get to St Mary's," he assured her.

"OK, well, you make sure you do," the steward said. Then, gesturing at his face, "What happened, anyway?"

"Oh, my horse pitched me head first over a hedge. Damn fox got clean away."

That earned him a long, hard look, but finally she waved us aboard.

"You just can't help yourself, can you?" I muttered, once we were out of earshot.

"It certainly seems that way," Uman whispered back.

We both burst out laughing.

On a chilly, damp morning, almost all of the other passengers were inside. But we stood on the upper deck, at the stern, watching Land's End drift by. Gulls followed, zigzagging in the air above the ship's wake, shrieking at one another. Or at us, maybe. Like they'd missed the boat and were yelling at us to slow down so they could catch up and hop aboard. Cooking smells reached us from the café on the deck below. Bacon, specifically.

"Let's celebrate with a slap-up breakfast," Uman said, the breeze snatching his words.

I kissed an undamaged part of his face. "Will you be able to eat it?"

"You can mush it up for me. Be good practice for when we're old."

It wasn't until we'd loaded the tray with food and reached the till that Uman discovered his wallet was missing from his jacket. That, far from stabbing him while he was lying

239

semi-conscious on the ground, Ginger Craig had been robbing him. And that, between us, we had a crumpled five-pound note from the back pocket of my jeans and £6.74 in coins.

"How much is the boat trip from St Mary's to Bryher?" Uman whispered.

"I'm not sure."

He nodded. Apologized to the girl on the check-out and told her we weren't hungry after all. Then he set the tray down and we went back up on deck.

As a young girl, I'd always arrived at Bryher in a state of the-holiday-starts-here excitement. That's how I remember it, anyway. At Church Quay, Ivan and I would be first off the boat, skittering down onto the beach while Mum and Dad grappled with luggage and greeted the snowy-haired owner of the cottage we always rented. As they loaded his trailer for the quad-bike ride up the sandy track to "our" cove, my brother and I would already be turning up our first cowrie shell or cuttlefish bone or crab claw of a two-week holiday that, for us, stretched ahead into infinity. It was always, always sunny.

"You reckoned Bryher might have been designed by Enid Blyton," I say to Mum.

She smiles a happy-sad smile. "We had some lovely holidays there, didn't we?"

"I wanted Uman to see it the way I did. To fall in love with it."

240

The sky above Church Bay was overcast as we disembarked that day. After paying the fare for the short hop from St Mary's we had just over three pounds left. We were hungry. Uman's nose wouldn't stop bleeding and his vision was blurred, he said. His head ached and, if he breathed too deeply, the pain in his ribs brought tears to his eyes. All the same, my mood lifted as one of the boat crew ushered us ashore and swung our packs onto the quay. Even in the dull light, the long arc of the beach glistened and the gorse on Watch Hill was as vibrantly yellow as I remembered, beckoning us to race to the top, as my brother and I had done so many times. A residue of childhood joy bubbled up, despite everything.

Against all the odds, Uman and I had set foot on the island, my happy place.

I squeezed his hand. "Come on, let's find a spot to pitch the tent."

There's an official campsite in a field beneath Watch Hill, before the land rises again to the rugged finger of headland at the top of the island. When the drawing of lots picked Bryher, I'd imagined Uman and I would camp there. But, with no way of paying the daily fee, we'd just have to fly-pitch somewhere and sneak into the official site now and then to use the showers.

"Bryher's only five and a half kilometres long, with seventy-odd people living here," I told Uman. "Just two roads – well, lanes – and no vehicles, apart from tractors and quad bikes. Oh, and a Land Rover at the hotel at the bottom of the island, to carry all the posh folk and their luggage to and from the boat. We used to treat ourselves to a meal there once every holiday."

"The Land Rover?" Uman asked.

"No, the hotel."

We were following the lane that runs down the centre of the island, past the straggle of houses, their gardens lush with brightly coloured flowers and shrubs and the occasional palm tree. I told Uman some of the island's history – how they were mostly fisherfolk in the old days, how they also used to grow daffodils here and ship them over to the mainland.

"But it's mostly tourism, now – holiday cottages and boat trips to see the seals," I said. Then, laughing, "Sorry, I'm banging on a bit, aren't I? It's just, it's all coming back. The stuff Mum and Dad read out to us from guidebooks that me and Ivan thought was so *boring*." I laughed again. "God, I'm turning into my parents."

"I could do with a rest, actually," Uman said. He'd been wheezing most of the way.

We'd reached the brow of a hill, where the lane curves towards the bottom of the island. The grocery was just there and a shop selling arts and crafts. We sat outside, Uman needing my help to remove his rucksack and giving a small grunt as he lowered himself onto the bench.

"Is it much further?" he asked. We'd only walked a few hundred metres.

"Another five minutes, that's all. There are some disused

daffodil fields beneath Samson Hill," I said, pointing along the road. "We'll be out of sight down there."

He nodded. "Sorry to be so useless."

He had nothing to apologize for, I told him, stroking the back of his neck. His hair was growing back, shaggy and uneven. Uman hadn't worn the Rasta hat for long, but he already looked odd without it. It had been left behind when the ambulance came and was no longer there the next morning. People still gave him funny glances – on the boat from St Mary's a young boy had stared at him the whole time – but it was his battered face that drew attention now, rather than strange headgear. Other passengers, the crew, the folk we'd passed walking up from the quay, looked at him like he was a yob.

"This is my favourite view on the whole island," I said.

Scattered with wildflowers, the meadows sloped down to a kidney-shaped lagoon and a ragged line of dunes. Beyond them, the Atlantic was studded with uninhabited rocky islands, some as big as castles while others barely broke the surface. Waves crashed against the rocks, sending up great clouds of spume. On a sunny day, the whole scene would have been glazed with gold.

I gave Uman a sidelong look, trying to read his expression. Willing him to appear happy.

"You can't quite see it from here, but there's a beach just over those dunes," I said. "Me and Ivan made a sand octopus there when I was about six. A huge one. We used shells for the suckers on its tentacles and seaweed for the hair."

"Octopuses don't have hair."

"Ours did. I wanted to build a mermaid but Ivan insisted on an octopus. The hair was part of the deal to keep his kid sister from blubbing, or stropping off to Mum and Dad."

Uman just nodded. Shifted into a more comfortable position on the bench.

"I can see why you wanted to come here," he said, neutrally. I couldn't tell if he was being polite or whether he was simply too unwell to muster enthusiasm for anything just then.

"Would you sooner be in the mountains of Andalusia?" I asked, putting a smile into my voice. Teasing him. "Or gazing out over the Niagara Falls or the temples of Kyoto?"

"Bryher'll do for now." He coughed, winced. "One … step at a time … and all that."

"That steward was right," I said. "You really *should* see a doctor."

"Lie down and sleep is what I should do."

"Seriously, Uman, you might have a bleed on the brain or something."

"Not possible. Every millilitre of blood in my body is concentrated in my nostrils." A couple of drips splashed onto his trouser leg as if by way of demonstration.

I shook my head. "I can't believe how stupid we've been, coming here when you're like this. I shouldn't have let you walk out of that hospital."

"We're here, that's the only thing that matters," he said. "OK, it's not Andalusia, but we're together. That's the *other* only thing that matters." I laughed, so pleased to hear him being more like his usual self. We sat in silence, just taking in the view. Then Uman said, "I wish we still had a phone. I could show you some YouTube clips of guys walking El Caminito del Rey."

"El what?"

"The Path of the King. It's this long walkway, high up along the side of El Chorro gorge. A metre wide and fixed to the cliff wall by metal posts – except you can see in the YouTube clips that most of the saftey rail has gone and there are loads of holes in the concrete. Some sections are missing altogether and the guys have to walk along the supporting girder." He was so animated, it was as if he was up there on that path as he spoke. "We're talking a hundred metres high, in places."

"Seriously? You're allowed to walk along it?"

"Well, no, it was closed for years. Quite a few people died." He dabs at his nose. "But it wasn't hard to climb over the barricades if you really wanted to – loads of guys did. It was one of the ultimate death-defying challenges, to walk El Caminito del Rey."

"While filming yourself," I said.

"Of course. What's the point in doing anything if you don't post a clip on the internet?" He was being ironic. I think. "This one guy, he walks the whole length of the path with a hand-held camera, not even one of those things you strap to your head." He laughed. "I tell you, your stomach flips just watching."

"So, that's why Andalusia is one of your 'happy places', yeah?"

"We went. To El Chorro." *We*. Uman, his parents and brother, I assumed. Their last ever holiday, perhaps. "We only walked as far as the point where the path was blocked off, but you could see it up ahead, snaking along the side of the gorge. Thoroughly stupendous."

I looked at him. "And, what, you'd like to go back there and walk it?"

"Yeah, that's exactly what I'd like to do. I mean, they've reopened it now and it's been repaired … but it still looks pretty damn scary. You could still die."

"I should tell you," I say to D.I. Ryan, "I committed a crime at this point."

"In addition to the one where you stole boarding passes for a free ride on a ferry?"

I ignore this remark. I explain how I left Uman resting on the bench and went into the grocery shop, browsed the aisles while the young woman on the counter was busy with other customers, then paid twenty-five p or something for a packet of painkillers and went back outside. Once we were a safe distance along the lane, I turned out the various pockets of my fake-leather, fake pilot's jacket to show him all the stuff I'd nicked.

246

Biscuits, two cans of Diet Coke, a bottle of water, a tin of rice pudding, two Snickers bars, a big bag of Doritos (under my top), a packet of sliced ham and two bread rolls.

As I displayed them, Uman nodded, staring intently at each item as if I was a magician producing rabbits and coloured streamers and he was trying to figure out the trick.

"The Doritos," he said, when I'd finished. "Didn't they have any barbecue flavour?"

We made camp in the corner of a narrow field overrun with grass and weeds but still furrowed from where rows of daffodils had once grown. Our pitch was hidden from the lane and any paths and tracks, nestled in the angle of two high, overgrown windbreak hedges and shielded on the other side by the gorse-thick lower slopes of Samson Hill.

As soon as we'd set ourselves up, Uman went into some kind of relapse.

He hardly left the tent for the next forty-eight hours, apart from stumbling outside to pee. Most of the time, he buried himself in his sleeping bag and slept.

Some of it was physical – his ribs, his face, his headaches; I'm not saying he didn't need to rest, to allow his body to heal. But his withdrawal was psychological, too. Whether it was a delayed reaction to getting beaten up or the fact that we were stranded on a small, quiet island with hardly any money and too little to eat, I don't know. Maybe Bryher had been so full of promise, but also so seemingly unattainable, that the reality of being there was an anticlimax. Whatever the reasons, we barely spoke over those two days. At least, he barely responded when I spoke to him. Sometimes, I wondered if he was actually asleep inside that bag or simply pretending to be.

Talk to me. How many times did I say that? *Please, Uman, just let me in.* Nothing. It was as if Uman had unplugged. As if he'd given up on himself, on me, on our fugitivery. On everything.

The contrast with his mood when he'd been talking about El Caminito del Rey couldn't have been starker. I thought he'd had some kind of death wish, wanting to walk that path, yet he'd sounded so full of life. Like life was only worth living if it was worth risking. It fitted with how he had been on the moor above Litchbury that time, watching the tightrope walker cross the quarry at the Hangingstones. Exhilarated by seeing someone flirt with death, putting his mortality – literally – on the line, but in a way that was life-affirming, not life-renouncing. It was the same when he mocked Ginger Craig; like he actually wanted the guy to give him a kicking, if only to prove Uman's aliveness to himself through fear and pain and the rush of adrenaline.

Now, it was almost as if living was too much bother. As if he just wished he was dead.

"D'you think it all stemmed from the fire?" Mum asks, when D.I. Ryan calls a loo break. We're standing in the corridor outside the interview room, our voices echoing.

"His mum and brother dying, his dad taking his own life. For Uman – for any teenager – to lose his family like that, to be the only one not to die that night ... well."

Survivor guilt, she means. I shrug. "I asked him about that one time."

"What did he say?"

"What's this, Mum? You sound like you almost care about him." I try to sound teasing, not snide. I like the fact that Mum is showing an interest in Uman rather than just blaming him.

"I care about *you*," she says. "And you obviously cared – *care* – for Uman."

I nod. Start to speak but have to stop. I want to ask if she believes he's dead but I can't bring myself to say it.

Anyway, I'm afraid of her reply.

Instead, I answer her question. "He said the worst of it wasn't 'why me?' or 'why them?' but 'what does life even mean if it can be snuffed out so easily?' Uman was still trying to figure it out." I pause at the door to the loo; Mum has hung back by the snack machine, searching her purse for change. "Actually," I say, "I think he half-believed he was indestructible – that if he'd got out of that burning building alive, he could survive anything."

I went out quite a bit. I hated leaving Uman alone in that state, but staying in the tent for hours on end with someone who's blanking you was more than I could handle.

I didn't know what to say or do. I didn't know how to help. What to think.

Although I'd seen glimpses of Uman's capacity to be down, he'd never been anywhere near this low or for this long. Not with me. I recalled all those days he'd failed to show at school and wondered if he had been like that, then. *Please be yourself again*, I caught myself wishing. But, of course, he was being himself. This was part of Uman, too. If you love someone – and I did, I do – you have to love all of him, the down as well as the up.

It's hard, though, when he shuts himself off from you.

So I distracted myself by hiking around the island. It takes an hour to walk the length of Bryher, from Rushy Bay to the rocky headland at the northernmost tip. Longer if you follow the coastal paths and beaches. There wasn't a part of the island I hadn't explored as a child, and I revisited them all again, desperately hoping Uman would have come out of hibernation by the time I returned to the tent. When I tired of walking, I headed for a beach; skimmed stones, searched for unusual shells, or just sat and watched the waves and the seabirds and the coming and going of the boats. I must have cut an odd, solitary figure to the locals and holidaymakers. If they smiled and said hello, I did the same; mostly, I avoided them whenever possible.

Water was easy enough to get hold of. I salvaged plastic bottles from a recycling bin and refilled them at the wash-basins in the public toilets by Church Quay or from the standpipe at the official campsite. Hunger was a constant drag, though. I didn't have the nerve to steal again in case I got caught. And we'd finished the stuff I'd shoplifted before, apart from the biscuits; for about twenty-four hours they were all we ate. In the end, I returned to the shop and blew most of our remaining money on bread. It was our second afternoon there. Or maybe the third. On the way back to the tent, I swung by a cottage I'd passed earlier and helped myself to a jar of home-made honey from a stand by the garden gate. I hadn't planned to pay for it but my conscience won out. I rummaged in my pocket for the last few coins and dropped them in the honesty box.

That was it. We had no money whatsoever.

The bread and honey were delicious, even without butter. I made Uman eat as well. I wanted us to sit outside – it was dry and there were scraps of blue sky – but it was as much as I could do to coax him into a sitting position inside the tent. With the sleeping bag pulled up to his armpits, he reminded me of his Turkish grandmother in her smoky, overheated living room.

I could've given him his share of the bread and taken mine outside. But I sat and ate with him – grateful that, for once, he wasn't asleep or hiding inside his bedding.

I opened the flaps as wide as they'd go to at least let in some light and air. Even so, it was dingy in there and the tent reeked of body odour and stale sweat and unwashed clothes. I didn't speak. I'd learnt not to. I just sat cross-legged beside him and ate, slowly, to make it last, although it was all I could do not to bolt it down. It was cramped; our knees and elbows bumped. I heard him chewing, swallowing, heard the snuffle of each breath, so close it was hard to distinguish between his breathing and mine.

I'd never felt more lonely in my life.

"Uman—" I began.

At the same moment, he turned to me and said, "Why are you still here?"

"He wanted you to go away?" D.I. Ryan asks.

I shake my head. "He couldn't understand why I hadn't left him."

Q19: What did you think would happen?

Uman told me about the other time. The girl before me. The real reason why he'd had to leave his boarding school.

This was after he'd asked why I was still there and I'd said, "Because I love you."

I shouldn't, he said. He wasn't worthy of it after the way he'd shut me out. His moods – *deep, dark troughs*, he called them – made him unlovable; knowing this side of him, why would I want to hang around for the next one? I deserved better. "How can I make you happy when I'm still figuring out how to be happy myself?"

"You do make me happy."

Having withdrawn for so long, Uman finally re-emerged that afternoon, in the stinky, gloomy tent. We talked for ages. *He* talked, mostly. The shutdowns – the troughs – had begun after the fire. Sometimes they'd last an hour or two, sometimes a whole day, sometimes longer. He would retreat to his bed. Or just take off somewhere – go missing for a while.

"You've done this before?" I said. "Gone on the run?"

"Never for this long – but, yeah."

"By yourself, though."

Uman shook his head. "One time, there was someone else."

That was when he told me about Dominique. She was in the year below. They'd become friends through the school drama society and she'd developed a crush on Uman. A serious one. "They called her my groupie," he said. "Not that I did anything to encourage her."

"No?" I teased.

"No. Gloria, you only have to catch their eye or smile at them or talk to them."

"Tell me about it. I can't move at school without tripping over one of my groupies."

Uman laughed. It had been so long since he'd laughed I had forgotten how it sounded. I noticed he didn't wince, or hold his ribs. The bread was all gone and we were passing the half-empty jar between us, spooning honey into our mouths. My fingers and lips were sticky. I knew I would never eat honey again without thinking of Uman in that tent.

"Anyway, one evening, I could feel I was about to hit another trough," he said.

Shutting himself in his room and hiding under the duvet wasn't an option. He'd tried it two or three times already and they had simply unlocked his door, roused him out of bed and packed him off to the school counsellor for more therapy.

"All I wanted was to be alone – just sink into my deep,

dark place until I was ready to come out again. But they wouldn't let me."

So, he slung a few things in a bag and took off into the grounds ("we're talking twelve square kilometres"), hiding out in an underground air-raid shelter dating from the school's use as an army base in World War II. There were several shelters around the site, each long since boarded up. But, taking a short cut on a cross-country run a few months earlier, he had come across one where the boards had rotted and worked loose. That time, he'd done no more than peer inside.

This time, he crawled right in.

"Dominique followed me. She must've seen me leave. Or been stalking me, more likely."

Uman had barely scrambled into the shelter when he heard her voice, asking to come in.

"And you let her?"

"She said if I didn't she'd go and tell them where I was." He shrugged. "Anyway, you've seen what I'm like when I go into shutdown. I just wanted to lie down and not wake up. I didn't have the energy to argue or make her go away."

So Dominique joined him – stretched out beside him on a single mat, with an unzipped sleeping bag spread over them. Thirty-six hours they spent in there, surviving on water, crackers and sleep. Uman lay with his back to her the whole time and reckoned they didn't exchange more than twenty words. It wasn't hard to believe, having seen the way he'd been with me.

"She seemed content for us just to be together," Uman said. "Then, when I surfaced again and we went back to school, Dominique told them I'd tricked her into going to the air-raid shelter with me, that I'd held her hostage in there, that I'd threatened her with my Swiss army knife, that I'd made her *do things* with me."

"*Uman*. Why would she say all of that?"

"Because I told her I didn't love her or even think of her in that way. Because I said she shouldn't hang around me any more – that she creeped me out. And because, when she tried to stop me from leaving the shelter, when she tried to kiss me … I shoved her away. Harder than I meant to." Uman looked at me, as if trying to gauge my reaction. "They saw the bruises from where she fell. They found the knife in my pocket. They'd seen the way I'd been since the fire. There was only one side of that story they were going to believe."

The school hushed it up as best they could, he said; Dominique's parents reluctantly agreed not to press charges, in the circumstances (Uman's tragic bereavement). Not too long after that he moved to the north of England to live with his grandmother, changed his name to Uman Padeem and started at Litchbury High.

"Why are you telling me this?" I asked when Uman had finished. "Why now?"

"Because when this is all over, you'll hear about it. I wanted you to hear it from me, first. The truth of it."

256

When this is all over. My head was spinning so much with the rest of what he'd told me that the significance of Uman's remark didn't register at the time.

It was the next morning before he felt ready to leave the tent and see some of the island with me.

Things were awkward between us. On Uman's part, he was ashamed of having blanked me over those two or three days, I think, and embarrassed that I'd seen him in that state. As for me, I had to adjust to this version of him. I had to re-learn how to be with him. Also, if I'm honest, I was upset that he'd taken so long to open up to me about what happened before. I *believed* him. It didn't cross my mind to doubt his side of the story; but when we'd supposedly shared everything, it hurt that he'd kept back something so important.

Did it bother me that he'd hurt that other girl, even if he hadn't meant to? Yes. Even when I'd heard the reason, it still bothered me.

Bothered him, too, I could tell. That he'd done it. But also that I knew about it and might think less of him as a result.

It rained that morning. We went out anyway, our water-proofs rustling. I think we were both hoping the fresh air and exercise would help us click back into place.

Uman wasn't up to a circuit of the island just yet, so I took him on a short walk up the track to Great Par, where I'd seen a pair of oystercatchers along the shoreline the previous day.

They were there again and we sat and watched them from the rocks at one end of the cove. I named other birds for him: sanderlings, terns, a pair of shags flying low over the water, a huge black-backed gull that landed quite close to us. I told Uman about the time one had swooped to snatch a Jammie Dodger from my hand on another of Bryher's beaches, and how Ivan had given chase, leaping in the air to try to grab the biscuit back even when the gull was way too high.

"D'you think it's the same bird?" Uman asked.

"I'm not sure they live that long." The gull tilted its head to one side, as if listening to us. "Although it does look very similar, now you mention it."

The gull flew off and Uman said he guessed it would remain one of life's innumerable unsolved mysteries. As he watched the bird go I studied Uman's face: my first proper look at it in daylight since his shutdown. His eyes were watering in the breeze.

"You're starting to heal up," I said.

"I can still only breathe through one nostril."

"Headache?"

"No, thanks, I've just had one."

I couldn't work out if he was back to his usual self or trying to be back to his usual self.

The rain worsened. Neither of us wanted to return to the tent and we couldn't sit in the island's only café without buying anything. So we took shelter in the community centre. It was unlocked, unstaffed; a collection tin sat on a table in

258

the entrance, with the admission charges handwritten on a card beside it. We went in anyway. The only people in there were an oldish couple playing chess; they looked up, said hello and commented on the weather. If they were curious about Uman's bruising, or his bloodstained hoodie, or why we weren't in school, they were too polite to say so. There were shelves of books, a table-tennis table, pool table, board games, a skittles set. The walls were arranged with black-and-white photos from Bryher's past: a lifeboat setting out to sea, men mending fishing nets, women carrying huge baskets loaded with sheaves of daffodils, that sort of thing.

Uman's ribs were still too sore for ping pong or skittles, but he could manage pool if he didn't bend too low over the table. After a couple of frames, though, we switched to Scrabble.

Over the following days, the weather improved – along with Uman's health. His physical health, anyway. We acted as if we were on holiday: going for hikes, lazing on beaches, swimming in the sea. But, to me, rather than the start of a holiday it felt like the end, when the prospect of going home hangs over you. I didn't ask whether Uman felt the same way in case he told me he did.

D.I. Ryan cuts in. "How did you eat?"

I don't answer.

"Gloria? By this point, you had no money—"

"We scavenged round the back of the posh hotel. In the bins behind the kitchens." Mum tuts. In her worst nightmares

259

about my eating habits, she can't have dreamt of me doing that. "I thought they'd throw out loads of food," I said. "But they didn't. Stale bread, mostly."

Mum says, "You must've been so hungry, both of you."

"Absolutely bloody starving."

"Why didn't you just steal from the shop again?" This is D.I. Ryan.

I raise my eyebrows at her. "Are you suggesting we should have done?"

She laughs. "It did sound like that, didn't it?" Then, serious again, "But...?"

"I wouldn't do it. Wouldn't let Uman do it either."

"But you'd as good as stolen the fares for the ferry by boarding without tickets and you'd nicked from the shop once already. Why stop there?"

"That's exactly what Uman said."

"And what did you say?"

"I didn't want it to be like that. I didn't want us to be like that." I shrug. "It was one of the things we quarrelled about towards the end."

D.I. Ryan looks at me. "One of the things?"

It was all wrapped up in the same thing, really, I tell her. I don't know what I'd been expecting when we went on the run together – an "adventure", I guess, but nothing much more specific than that. For a while, that's what it had been. By the time we were on Bryher, though, it had become something else. Closer to an ordeal.

260

Having our cards swallowed by the ATM, Uman getting beaten up and robbed, his big shutdown, the lack of food, being so hungry all the time ... it was as if our luck was running out. We couldn't use the showers or laundry room at the official campsite because a warden had challenged us the first time we tried to and we didn't dare go back. We stank. Our clothes stank. The tent stank, and was damp and muddy from all the rain we'd had. Any of these things on their own might have been bearable, but coming one after the other, they sapped my morale. While I'd got a buzz out of those boarding passes and the shoplifting, it wasn't long before guilt kicked in. I felt ashamed of myself. Another low point.

"I don't mind being a fugitive," I told Uman, "but I don't want to be a thief."

"What did you think would happen? We were bound to run out of money eventually."

"I didn't think. Not about that."

"So what do you suggest – we starve?"

No, of course we couldn't just let ourselves starve. But the alternatives were to steal food from the shop again or give ourselves up. Even though most of the fun had leaked out of our fugitivery, I wasn't ready to go back to what I'd come to think of as my old life. The Time Before. Wasn't anywhere near ready to face Mum and Dad, Tierney, school, the police, the media and all of that – the consequences of what we'd done. An avalanche that would engulf us the moment we stopped being on the run. Most of all, though – and despite

261

everything – I wasn't ready to stop being with Uman, just the two of us.

So we made believe we were on holiday. Acted like nothing was wrong, as if we could carry on indefinitely, living on stale bread and water. If Uman tried to discuss money, or food, or the big question, What Next?, I refused to go there. Or I went there and we bickered. In the end, he stopped talking about it. I think we were both in denial by that stage.

One blustery morning, we went to the small cove overlooked by the cottage where I used to stay on holidays. I'd spent hundreds of hours of my childhood there – paddling, beachcombing, scrambling on rocks, skimming stones, building sandcastles, flying kites, eating ice creams or having sand-encrusted picnics. My happy days. Somewhere along the way, our family had forgotten how to be like that. Or I had. As Uman and I played noughts and crosses with sticks in the wet sand, I gazed along the windswept curve of the beach and it was as if the place was haunted by the ghosts of those other times. My seven-year-old self, kneeling near the water's edge, a red plastic spade in hand, scouring out a channel to direct the incoming waves into the hole I'd dug with my brother, then fetching pretty shells to decorate the rim of our "lagoon".

The pictures seemed so real I couldn't quite believe they were only memories.

"Your turn," Uman said, indicating the noughts-and-crosses grid.

"D'you think people leave impressions of themselves in a place?" I asked.

"After they've died, you mean?"

I scored a cross in a square. "No, after they've been somewhere." I told him about the flashback images of my childhood. "It's happened a few times while we've been on Bryher. Like the island is covered with traces of me from the past."

"Maybe it is." Uman made a nought, won the game.

"Wouldn't it be weird if we left millions of shadows of ourselves wherever we went?"

He seemed to give it some thought. "Or what if there are millions of shadows of us in all the places in the world we haven't been to yet," he said, "just waiting for us to make them real?"

I frowned. "How would that work?"

"Oh, and your idea *does* work?"

"Yeah. I mean, if you walk along this beach," I gesture at the wet sand, "you're going to leave a trail of footprints behind you – but you can't leave footprints *ahead* of you."

"Not literally, no." He'd scuffed out the game and was marking the grid for a new one. "But in here," he tapped his head, "you can leave footprints wherever you like."

Before, differences in attitude of this kind created a middle ground where our minds could meet, or at least draw closer. Lately, though, neither of us seemed quite to get what the other one meant. I tried to tell myself it was because we weren't eating properly. Our constant hunger made us tetchy, that was all.

We played the last game of noughts and crosses more or less in silence.

Thoughts of family holidays brought Mum and Dad back to mind. That message I'd left on Dad's answering machine seemed an age ago. Several times, I'd come close to phoning home again: in Church Stretton, Bristol, Penzance. Each time, I hadn't made that call. What was I putting them through? Ivan, too. I knew how I would feel if my brother had "gone missing", yet I'd done that to him. Was still doing it.

"I've been so selfish," I said.

Uman looked at me. "How come?"

I told him what I meant.

"If you were selfish," he said, "you'd be too selfish to realize you were being selfish."

It was the kind of thing Uman sometimes came out with: clever and funny and wise at first glance, but not quite so profound once you took a closer look. I let it go, though.

The wind had really strengthened, so I suggested walking out onto the headland. On blowy days, it was impressive up there, I told him – watching the big waves rolling in from the Atlantic and crashing against the cliffs.

"Come on, then," he said. "Where you go, I go."

We scrambled up the rocks at the far end of the cove and through the broken-down fence above them. Uman held the strands of barbed wire apart for me and, once I'd ducked under, I returned the favour. But he still couldn't bend too well and his sleeve caught.

"Keep still, you're making it worse," I said, easing the metal barb from the cagoule and the sleeve of his hoodie underneath.

"Thanks," he said, when I'd freed him. "I could've been stuck here for days."

We were right in each other's space, pressed against that fence. I'm not sure we'd have kissed if it wasn't for that. But we did. Carefully, on account of his lip. Nervously, too. Like it was our first time. Or like we'd forgotten how.

Afterwards, as we followed the rough uphill track that would take us to the top of the island, Uman surprised me with a question.

"Do you wish we hadn't come here? To Bryher?"

"No, why?"

"All these memories."

"Yeah, but they're good memories."

"That's what I mean," Uman said. "This is your happy place. Maybe it would've been better to leave it that way."

"Is that what you think – that it was a mistake coming here?"

We'd climbed out of the cove, reaching the brow of the steep slope that led to the rockier terrain of Shipman Head Down, stretching ahead like a long knobbly finger. Up there, on the higher ground, the wind was stronger still, threshing our hair and buffeting our faces. One of the plastic toggles on the cords that fastened my cagoule kept whipping against my cheek.

"We should be doing new things, not old," Uman said.

"This is new. Being here together."

"We had an opportunity to do the things we'd always wanted to do."

"You were the one who suggested drawing one of our happy places out of a hat."

"It was a cup, actually."

A sudden gust caught me side-on, making me stumble on the stony ground. "You don't like Bryher, do you?" I said, as I regained my footing. "It's too quiet for you, too boring."

The conversation went on like this, never quite becoming a full-blown argument. It might just have been that wherever we'd gone after he got beaten up, his dip in mood would have turned him against the place. But, if you ask me, his problem with the island was that it was mine, not his – that he felt excluded by all my memories and associations, my tales of childhood holidays. We were there together, but it could never truly be ours. Despite my telling him no, he was right: I was beginning to wish we hadn't come to Bryher.

Whatever, we were stuck there. Broke, ravenous and stranded. Quarrelsome.

Shipman Head silenced us. Literally, with the roar of the wind in our ears, ripping away our words – our breath – if we opened our mouths to speak. It was all we could do to walk without being blown off our feet. It was *stupendous*. And scary as hell.

Up there on the headland at the very end of the island – perched on its fingertip, as close to the cliff edge as we dared to go – we were almost completely surrounded by the sea, exposed to the full force of the gale that raged from the west. One after another, great waves reared up a few hundred metres offshore and surged towards us before smashing themselves to a trillion pieces on the rocks below – sending explosions of spray so high into the air that the water arced above us, then fell to earth like a sudden burst of rain. Uman and I were drenched in an instant. Barely time to recover from one soaking before the next, then the next.

We clung to each other, legs braced, feet planted on the rocky ground, flinching at the fallout from each wave. We were so frail against the onslaught of the wind, it was as if it might lift us into the sky at any moment like a pair of kites and whisk us out to sea.

We shrieked, we whooped, we yowled … and we laughed and laughed and laughed.

It was as if standing on that headland – wind-blasted, scoured by sea spray – had stripped away all of the crap of the previous few days to leave us bright and fresh and zingy. I've never been more alive than I was up there, with Uman, and the feeling coursed through me for the rest of that day and most of the next. Our final hours on the island.

Same for him. I saw it in his eyes.

Same for us. Like we'd been blown to pieces and put back together again.

"It's just so *empty*!" Uman hollered, on the cliff top, mouth pressed hard to my ear but still having to shout to make himself heard.

The ocean, he meant. Anywhere else on Bryher, you can see the neighbouring islands, the offshore rocks, a lighthouse or two, even the faint grey line of the mainland on the horizon. But from the tip of that headland, there's nothing but sea in all directions, unfurling for hundreds of kilometres, *thousands* of kilometres: to Ireland, to France, to Greenland, or all the way to Canada and the United States. All the way down to South America and Antarctica.

"This is the very *end* of *England*!" I yelled back.

Just then, though, it felt like the beginning of everything. As if all possibilities opened out before us across the surface of that ocean – that, far from being stranded, far from having reached our final destination, we could do anything we pleased, go anywhere we wished, be anyone we wanted to be.

For the best part of a day and a half I let myself believe it.

Q20: You coming with me?

The next day was glorious. The wind had died down, the sky had cleared and the island sparkled in the morning light. We ate breakfast outside – the last of the stale bread we'd scavenged from the hotel the night before. In my fresh, zingy mood, even that tasted OK. From the direction of Great Par, the shrill cries of oystercatchers drifted across the abandoned daffodil fields as if the birds were calling to us, inviting us to pay another visit.

"The good thing about this 'artisan' bread," Uman said, inspecting his piece, "is that the mould might just be bits of walnut or olive."

"Don't be down on mould," I said. "It's our only source of protein."

He shot me one of his grins – even more lopsided now that one side of his mouth had healed more quickly than the other. At least the stitches had dissolved, so he no longer looked like he had a zip in his top lip. His nose was less swollen, if still red and a little crooked, and the bruising

269

beneath his eyes had faded to pale greenish yellow. I'd taken to stroking his injuries, brushing my fingertips over his face as if to magic away the last traces of damage at night as we lay together, drifting off. In the day, too, sometimes. I did it then, at breakfast – reaching out to caress him.

"It's like my face is covered in Braille and you're trying to read it," he said, softly. "Or trying to commit my features to memory in case you forget what I look like."

"Ssshhh," I said, pressing a finger against his lips.

It was our last morning, although we didn't realize it. At least, I didn't. If Uman already knew, he hid it well. Or maybe I just wouldn't let myself notice the difference in him.

We spent the next few hours swimming and sunbathing at Green Bay. We had the beach pretty much to ourselves. The bay was speckled with boats of various sizes. Some criss-crossed between the islands or headed out to sea while others lay a short distance offshore, bobbing at anchor. During what would have been our lunch break if we'd had any food, Uman pointed out some of the boats, identifying them by type and telling me their "spec".

"What's funny about 'spec'?" he said, when I failed to keep a straight face.

"Nothing."

"It means 'specification'."

"I worked out what it means," I said. "I just wish you'd told me you were a geek before I agreed to go on the run with you."

"A *geek*? Gloria in Excelsis, they'd run out of geek genes by the time I got to the front of the queue so they had to give me extra cool genes instead."

"How come you know so much about boats, anyway? Oh wait, don't tell me, your dad owned a yacht."

"Two, actually. One for family holidays, the other for tax purposes."

Uman said he learned to sail when he was eight years old. I thought he meant boats with sails, but he was referring to ones with engines, like some of those anchored in the bay. Looking back, it's obvious where he was heading with this; but, at the time, it was just one of the things we talked about on the beach that day. Besides, just then I spotted a Frisbee half-buried in the sand. It had bleached from red to pink and a bit was missing from the rim, but it worked OK. Well enough to take my mind off boats altogether.

"Look," I said, "my hands are shaking."

Uman took my hands in his. "Low blood sugar."

I was wiped out by the Frisbeeing. My stomach had started to cramp and I had come over so faint we'd broken off from the game to sit down. My whole body was in a cold sweat. Uman said he felt the same, although he looked in better shape than me. We drank the last of the water we'd brought with us; it was tepid, even though we'd kept the bottle in a shady rock pool, and there wasn't enough left to trick us into feeling full.

"Are you up to walking to the hotel?" Uman asked.

"In daylight?" We'd only ever raided the bins behind the kitchen after dark.

"It's either that or we 'borrow' some more food from the shop."

I shook my head.

"You sure, O famished one?"

"Please. No more thieving."

"OK, how about we amputate one of your legs with my Swiss army knife and barbecue it right here on the beach?"

"Why not one of your legs? There'd be more meat."

"We could just slice off a calf, if you don't want to lose the whole thing," he said.

I leaned into him, clutching my stomach because it hurt so much to laugh.

We set off for the hotel together, but I only made it half-way, I was so weak. So dizzy. I had to stop in the lane and puke into the verge, even though there wasn't much to throw up. Uman helped me back to the tent and, once I was settled inside my sleeping bag, he headed off on the "bread run" by himself.

I woke to find Uman stroking my hair, saying my name. It was still afternoon, judging by the light spilling through the open tent-flap, although I felt as if I'd been asleep for hours.

"Did you get any bread?" I asked, slowly coming to.

"I did a bit better than that."

I pushed myself into a sitting position. He was rustling

around in a carrier bag, pulling out two cans of regular Coke, two Mars bars, two apples and a packet of crackers.

"You stole from the shop?" I was torn between being cross with him and wanting to grab my share of the food and eat it right away.

"Not exactly, no. I mean, they don't give carrier bags to shoplifters, do they?"

"What, then? You can't have paid for it."

"I took the money from the honesty box at the community centre," Uman said. "There was only a few quid or I'd have bought more."

"The box wasn't locked?"

"Not once I'd taken it to a discreet spot and smashed it open with a rock."

After we'd eaten, we walked out to Great Par and sat on the rocks where we'd gone before to watch the oystercatchers. They weren't there this time, just the usual gulls. It was almost dusk, the sea turning honey-coloured in the dying light of the afternoon.

"Would it help if I apologized again?" Uman said.

From the first time I'd set eyes on him breezing into the tutor room without knocking, he hadn't behaved how other people thought he should. It was one of the reasons I liked him as much as I did. Even so.

"We talk about things," I said. "That's the deal. That's always been the deal."

273

"We do talk about things. But sometimes…"

"We don't."

"Yes, sometimes we don't. Nicely put."

"I'm so pleased we've sorted that out."

"Anyway, the important thing is … this." Uman patted my belly.

I wondered if his felt as bloated as mine. There hadn't been much to eat, really, and I'd finished my half slowly, pacing myself to make it last, savouring each mouthful. Yet I still felt as full as if I'd been at a banquet. I lay on my back on the flat slab of rock, gazing up at the sky as the first stars appeared. It reminded me of that time on the bench at school after we'd shared his pizza order. Uman lay back too and rested his left hand against my right, the little fingers touching.

"Why can't I stay pissed off with you?" I asked.

"Because I've bamboozled you with calories."

It was true. I was so grateful for the food I could've wept. "Bamboozled. I like that word."

"When I started at my last school, my father gave me a five-year diary to, and I quote, 'record my journey from childhood to adulthood'," Uman said. "But I only ever used it to collect new words. Each morning, I'd scroll through the dictionary and note down my Word of the Day – the more obscure, the better. Then, the rest of the day, I'd use it at every opportunity."

"I bet the teachers loved that."

"Frankly, the masters found my autodidactic displays somewhat ostentatious."

I smiled. "Do you still do it – write down a new word every day?"

After a pause, he said, "The diary was in the house."

The house his father burned down.

Neither of us spoke for a while. The slab was hard but not uncomfortable; the rock still held a faint residue of heat from the hours of sunshine it had absorbed that day. Or maybe it was my own warmth I could feel. I was about to ask Uman which was more likely, when he said, "We have to leave, Gloria."

The remark came out of nowhere. Yet, the moment he said it – so casually – it was as if the entire conversation had been leading to this.

"I know," I said.

"We can't stay here like this." Starving, he meant. Falling out with each other.

"I said I know."

I heard him exhale. "I really *am* sorry. I've spoiled your happy place."

"Uman, you don't have anything to be sorry for. It was a good idea at the time, coming here – then it turned out not to be. That's all." I hooked my little finger in his. "Anyway, *places* aren't happy. You have to carry happiness around with you – or make a fresh batch wherever you happen to be." I laughed. "God, how pretentious am I?"

He rolled onto his side towards me, his face looming over mine with a kind of wonder in his eyes, as if he couldn't believe he'd found me lying right there beside him.

"What you are is *extraordinary*." He said it with such feeling I couldn't help blushing.

"I am, aren't I? Extraordinarily extraordinary."

"No, but you are. All day I've been not quite saying it — the 'we have to leave' thing — and then, when I do, you're like, 'Oh, yeah, *that*.' It's like our thoughts are synchronized."

I poked him in the chest. "So, I'm extraordinary when I agree with you?"

He leaned in for a kiss. He tasted of chocolate and Coke. I don't tell Mum or D.I. Ryan about the kissing, or how long we kissed for, or any of that stuff. Or about my suggestion to Uman that we could simply lie there on that rock, kissing, until the police eventually found us. In fact, the kissing stopped when Uman had one of his coughing fits.

"You have to carry happiness around with you, or make a fresh batch," he said, once he'd recovered. "I wish I'd thought of that."

"I'm not sure I'd have thought of it before I met you."

"Oh, I reckon you would."

We let that idea settle over us. We were sitting up by now, my palm still tingling from where I'd massaged his back while he coughed. After a moment, Uman pulled the deck of playing cards from his jacket and set them down between us.

"What's this?" I asked.

"*These* are the Cards of Destiny. Frankly, I thought you'd recognize them by now."

I looked at the cards, then back at Uman. "We have *options*, plural?"

"Yup. Plan A and Plan B. There's always a Plan B."

"So, I'm guessing Plan A is we give up. Turn ourselves in."

"Exactly. Plan A in a nutshell." He didn't say any more, just sat cross-legged, rubbing his hands so vigorously on his knees I was sure he'd get friction burns.

"I, um, might need some help figuring out Plan B."

"Oh, right, of course." Nodding at the playing cards, he said, "Plan B is, we steal a boat and skedaddle to France like a pair of desperadoes."

I laughed. Then I saw he was deadly serious and I laughed again. "*Uman!*"

He had it all worked out, though.

Once it was late enough for everyone on the island to be asleep, we would break into the shop, force open the till and help ourselves to a wad of cash (and some food while we were at it). Then we'd head down to Green Bay and wade out to one of the boats lying at anchor. We'd climb aboard, raise the anchor and paddle the boat into the channel between Bryher and Tresco. As soon as we were well away from the shore, we'd start the engine. Then we'd sail to France. From there, all of Europe lay before us: a vast adventure play-ground of dodging and weaving.

"*Vives les dweaveurs!*" he said, eyes shining. "*Je dweave, tu dweave, nous dweaverons.*"

"OK, setting aside the fact that we are not breaking into the shop and smashing open the till ... what if the shop's alarmed?"

"This is Bryher we're talking about. It's still the 1950s here."

"Anyway, how are you even going to start the engine?"

"Grocery shops don't have engines, Gloria."

I just fixed him a look.

"OK, one of the boats out there" – Uman waved a hand towards the other side of the island, in the vague direction of Green Bay – "is a souped-up dinghy, really – but, substantial. Sea-going. And it looks like the same model my father had before he upgraded to something bigger. The ignition is dead easy to override if you know what you're doing."

"And you reckon you can drive it to—"

"Sail."

"Sail it all the way to France. In the middle of the night."

"We have our trusty compass," he said. Then, indicating the sky and the sea in turn, "We have the stars, a three-quarter moon ... the water's calm." He coughed. "The hardest part will be finding a safe place to put ashore without anyone spotting us when we get to France. Not to mention the amount of garlic they put in their food over there."

"Uman, this is so crazy it's beyond crazy. Even for you."

"Good crazy or bad crazy?"

"Bad crazy. Like, we're-going-to-end-up-dead-at-the-bottom-of-the-sea bad crazy."

"I could sail that mother with my eyes shut. Not literally, obviously. Do you know how hard it is to capsize one of those things?" With a shake of the head, he went on, "Worst case scenario, the coastguards intercept us. We spend a few hours in a French police cell and come home in a blaze of glory."

After a moment, I said, "Sail that *mother?*"

"Sorry, I go all urban when I'm excited."

I laughed. "OK, delete 'crazy' and replace with 'unbelievably stupid'."

"So, you'd rather just stick with Plan A?" Uman said. "We tell someone who we are and ask them to call the police to come fetch us. We go home. How unbelievably, crazily unexciting."

I kept my voice steady. "We're not going to France."

"All we're doing is consulting the Cards of Destiny. They might choose Plan A."

"I don't care. I'm not doing Plan B."

"Gloria—"

"Look, the last couple of weeks have been brilliant – the best time of my entire life by a million miles. Even the rubbish parts. And I love you so much. I really do." I studied his face in the moonlight to see if I was making any impression. His glazed eyes reminded me of Tierney's, when I talk to her before I realize she's plugged into her iPod.

I placed a hand on his knee, willing him to focus. "I mean, it's not like giving up stops us from being together, is it?"

"But this is what we are now," he said. "This is what we do."

"It doesn't have to be the only thing. We can be anything we want."

Uman didn't respond. He simply picked up the cards, tapped them out of their box. Shuffled them. "D'you remember the Arabic proverb about living like a river?" he said. "Never standing still or turning back, but always flowing onwards?"

I said I did. Said I'd always remember that story, and the morning he told it to me – just before that guy appeared and brought an end to our time in the Stretton Hills. In that moment, though, there had been only the beauty of a new day together and the tale of a river that reached the edge of a desert.

"Gloria, this is our desert." He meant the sea between Bryher and France. "We can stop. Give up. Go back to what we were before. Or we can become clouds and float across the desert" – he fluttered his fingers in the air – "and fall as rain to form a new river on the other side."

In that instant, I imagined myself saying yes, a grin spreading across my face as I flung my arms round him and told him what he hoped to hear.

Yesyesyes.

But gently, almost whispering, I said, "This is real life, Uman. Not a proverb."

He carried on even so, his hands a pair of pale birds in

the moonlight as he shuffled again, split the pack and set the two stacks down on the rock. One for him, one for me. Although for all the attention he paid me, I might as well have not been there. The evening chill made me shudder and I drew my jacket tighter. I just wanted to hold him, to make him stop.

"I'm not doing this, Uman."

"Your top card is Plan A: we quit," he said. "Mine is Plan B: France. Highest wins."

"Are you even listening?"

"If it's a tie, we go to the next two cards. Agreed?"

"Not agreed, no."

He indicated the half of the pack closest to me. "Go on, you first."

The easiest thing would have been to stand up and walk away; refuse to play his game. What did it matter, though? I wasn't going to obey the cards in any case.

My fingers were cold and clumsy as I turned the top card over.

Five of Clubs.

Uman nodded. "Only a five to beat," he said.

I thought he would draw it out, crank up the tension by taking an age to turn his card. But he did it right away – quick and neat, like he was ripping a sticking-plaster off his skin.

Two of Diamonds.

We were going home.

Uman stared at that card for the longest time, then

281

gathered them all up – the whole pack – and scattered them high in the air like they were scraps of bread for the gulls.

"You won?" D.I. Ryan asks.

"Didn't feel like it," I tell her. "It felt like we'd both lost."

Since that night, I haven't stopped asking myself the question: *What if?*

What if I'd called best-of-three, best-of-five, best-of-seven? What if I'd told Uman to ditch Plan A, that we should just go for Plan B and to hell with the Cards of Destiny?

What if we'd set off together in that boat?

After two weeks on the run with him – saying yes to everything – I'd become the sort of person who might have said yes to that, too.

Might have. But didn't.

When it came to it – when it really mattered – I wasn't as daring, as transgressive, as I'd imagined myself to be. I'd taken a few steps on the high wire. I'd felt it sway beneath my feet. I'd looked down at the ground way below. I'd retreated.

I think Uman always suspected things would turn out that way. That at some point he'd have to go it alone. That I wasn't quite the pink-and-purple stripy girl he had hoped I'd be.

How I hated him for what he did that last night on Bryher.

Ending it like that. Leaving so much unsaid. After all we'd been through together, I didn't understand how he could do that to me. Part of me still does hate him, even though you could say that he saved my life. Because the answer to the question *What if?*, I know now, is that I would be "missing, presumed dead" as well. Or one of two washed-up bodies on a French beach.

I didn't know it then, though. That night, if he'd asked me again – if he'd told me what he was going to do – I'd have said *yesyesyes* for sure if the alternative was to lose him right there and then. But Uman never said a word. And by the time I discovered Plan C, it was too late.

In my sleeping bag, I dreamt we were walking along a glass path that hovered above the ground, winding through dark forests and snow-capped mountains, across grassy plains and fields of wheat, past vineyards, olive groves and orchards of trees weighed down with fat citrus fruit, beside fast-flowing streams and vast, placid lakes, through toy-town villages where tiny plastic people lined up to wave us by and to offer us baskets of fresh-baked bread. At some point, the path turned to gold and I realized I was dreaming of myself as Dorothy in *The Wizard of Oz*.

The dream changed again, into a nightmare. Or maybe the nightmare came later.

It woke me, anyway. We're sailing across the desert when a sudden sandstorm whirls up and dashes the dinghy to pieces … and I'm thrashing about, half-blind in the dust – coughing, yelling Uman's name – desperately searching for him in the wreckage. But each ghostly shape I crawl towards, each arm or hand I grab hold of, turns out to be another piece of boat.

Uman! Was that in the nightmare or had I shouted his name for real?

My whole body was slick with sweat. I opened my eyes, but it was almost as black as when they were closed – just the faintest hint of moonlight was visible beyond the tent's dark-grey skin. When I tried to sit up, the sleeping bag was twisted around me like rope, and in my still-sleepy state the more I struggled the more entangled I became.

By the time I'd wrestled free, I was breathless and panicky.

"Uman?"

No reply. Nothing. Not even the wheeze of his smoke-damaged lungs or the shape of him in the dark or the musty, yeasty, sleepy warmth of him lying beside me.

I reached out to touch him but he wasn't there.

Even as I fumbled for a torch and hurried out of the tent, calling his name, I knew I was lying to myself. He'd gone outside to pee, that was all. He'd gone outside for some fresh air. No. He'd gone outside to think, to contemplate our last night on the run before we turned ourselves in. I would find him sitting on a wall, or a rock, or in the middle of the old daffodil field, cross-legged like the Buddha, bathed in moonlight.

None of these things was true. And I knew it.

I'd been so frantic, pulling on my boots and yanking at

the laces, tying them any old how, that one boot nearly came off as I sprinted towards Green Bay. I had to stop, refasten it. Each wasted second beat like a pulse in my brain. *Come on!* Running again, dabbing at the ground with the torch, the breath burning in my throat.

He's left the tent behind. I remember thinking that. Registering it as a sign of ... something. Hope. The sudden flare of hope that, if Uman hadn't taken the tent, he couldn't really be leaving the island without me. Or leaving at all.

Another of the lies I told myself.

He'd abandoned the tent because he couldn't take it without waking me, without telling me what he was doing. He'd abandoned the tent *exactly because* he wanted to leave without me.

How quietly, how carefully, he must have snuck out to avoid disturbing me. To avoid having to ask, "You coming with me?"

To avoid having to say goodbye.

Tears were leaking down my face by the time I stumbled through the scrub and the hummocky dunes at the back of the beach. I came to a halt, hands on hips, panting, scanning the shoreline. There was no sign of him. No shadowy figure crossing the sand, or wading into the shallows; no suggestion of movement on board any of the boats anchored offshore; no sounds of a paddle splashing the water. If it wasn't for the lapping of the waves, everything would have been utterly still and silent.

I wiped my face on my sleeve. Went on looking for him, listening for him.

"Uman!" My cry sounded obscenely loud in the dead-of-night hush.

No response.

How long had he been gone when I woke up? I had no idea. For all I knew, Uman might already have been halfway to France. Or still breaking into the shop.

That was where he'd be, for sure.

All I had to do was turn back and follow the track to the shop and I'd find Uman there, or intercept him on his way to the bay. Even as I was thinking it I heard what sounded like a chainsaw starting up somewhere behind me, on the island. In the quiet, the noise made me jump. It might have been coming from ten metres away or a hundred. As I tried to locate it the sound became higher pitched and more intense, then dipped again, settling to a steady drone. Which was when I realized that what I'd heard behind me was its echo in Bryher's hills and, in fact, the noise was coming from the opposite direction. From the channel of deeper water beyond Green Bay. I realized, too, that it belonged to an outboard motor.

His name made it as far as my throat but, this time, it stuck there.

What was the use? No way would he have heard me calling to him above the thrum of the engine when he was so far out.

286

I never saw the boat, the dinghy, or whatever it was he'd taken. Never saw Uman at the controls. Backdropped against the inky sea and the long, black streak of the neighbouring island, all I could make out – the last I saw of him – was a greyish line of wake that scarred the surface of the water for a few seconds before dissolving into the darkness.

Uman wouldn't have seen me, either.

He wouldn't even have known I was there, unless he happened to look back at the shore at that exact moment and spotted the torch laying a pale disc of light on the sand between my feet.

One last question

These are the Days of Next. They'd seemed impossibly far off when Uman and I shared the Days of Now and an unending life of fugitivery was imaginable.

It's a month since they found the boat.

They still haven't found whatever remains of Uman Padeem.

Tomorrow we fly to New York: Mum, Dad, my brother and me. Later than planned, but even so: *ten days in New York City.* I should be excited. I am excited. Just nowhere near as much as other people expect me to be. Uman is dead, but I should look forward to something?

Tierney's hyper enough for both of us. She keeps saying how lucky I am, putting on an atrocious American accent, asking if I like my eggs over easy, telling me which shops I should visit (even though she's never been there).

"You *have* to take a selfie outside Central Perk," she tells me.

"Central Perk doesn't actually exist, Tier."

She pulls a Rachel-style *what-are-you-talking-about?* face. I can't help laughing.

We're sitting on the rocks above the disused quarry at the Hangingstones, watching the climbers. At least, that was the plan. Only there are no climbers today. We sit here even so, talking, drinking Pepsi Max, pretending things are the same as they always were between us. It's a school day, but we've skived off – me, because I'm *special circs* and can get away with pretty much anything at the moment (not that I push it too far); Tier, because she doesn't like to think of me "mooching around" on my own. I've pointed out to her that being alone isn't the same as being lonely, but you'd think I'd said a lizard is a type of vegetable.

I expected her to hate me. But the day after the police had run out of questions, Tier returned my call and asked if she could come round.

"We still have photographers outside," I warned her.

"I know. Why d'you think I want to come round?"

"Tierney with an i-e!" I heard her call out to them from the doorstep. "Best friend since primary school." Inside, I'd barely shut the door when she wrapped me up in a hug and burst into tears. We were both in a state, to be honest. For the next two hours, we lay on my bed – head to toe, like we always did – and just talked and talked.

The awkwardness took a little longer to find us. It's still here, at the Hangingstones.

"I came here with Uman one time." I nod towards the

289

mouth of the quarry. "A guy walked across on a tightrope. No safety clip or anything."

Tierney seems only half-attentive. For all that we've talked since I came home, she has shown surprisingly little curiosity about Uman or my time on the run with him. It's as if she and I were a couple and I've cheated on her – and, now we're back together, she's trying to forget it ever happened.

She edges towards it now, though. "Is that the real reason you wanted to come up here today?"

"No." I can tell she doesn't believe me.

The school counsellor thinks it's "unhelpful", my visiting the places where Uman and I hung out. The riverside park, the Twelve Disciples, the bench where we ate pizza. I even called at his grandmother's house, but she didn't understand me or have any idea who I was. I never got to see Fatima, either, because the old woman had shut her in the lounge before opening the front door. I heard her yapping, scrabbling to be let out, but that was all. The other day, while Mum and Dad were at work, I took the train to Shipley and walked along the canal to Drop Bear Woods. In the clearing where we'd camped, I found a bent tent peg among the leaf litter at the base of a tree. It's on a shelf in my bedroom.

"It's like you're torturing yourself," Tierney says. Kindly, not harshly; all the same, there's the faintest trace of criticism in her tone.

I just shake my head.

It's breezy. The cold grey of the rocks has seeped into the

sky. We shouldn't have come. At least, I should have come by myself.

"He isn't here, Glo-Jay."

"I know that."

"So why, then?"

It's not about "finding" Uman, or "being close" to him, or anything like that. It's not about being in denial or refusing to let go. I've tried to explain it to the counsellor. I try explaining it to Tierney, now.

"He never said goodbye." I pick at the cap of the Pepsi bottle. "This is my way of saying goodbye to him. Place by place."

Tier doesn't understand. She nods like she does, but she doesn't.

"New York's exactly what you need," she says.

Somewhere that holds no memories of Uman, I presume she means. But I remember what he said on the beach at Bryher – about how we can make footprints ahead of ourselves on the sand, as well as leaving them behind. Besides, Uman (or my *Uman episode*) is the very reason we're going to New York. How can I not carry him there with me?

I wonder how far it is from New York City to Niagara Falls. One of his special places – from the Canadian side, anyway – although I don't see how one side of a waterfall can be any different from another. That didn't occur to me before. Now I'll never be able to ask him about it. And he'll never get there again.

I won't go to Niagara Falls while we're in New York.

"He had all these places he wanted to visit, all these things he wanted to do," I say.

Tierney doesn't respond.

"After the fire, it was like Uman had so much ... life bursting out of him. Too much, maybe. Is that possible?"

"I don't know," Tier says, quietly.

I try to explain it better, but the words catch in my throat. I half turn away so she won't see the tears in my eyes. We fall silent.

After a bit, Tierney reaches out to run her fingers through my hair. "The blonde will almost have grown out by the time you come back," she says. "You going to dye it again?"

"Probably not."

She's still stroking my hair. We used to do this a lot – groom each other like chimps. I consider kissing her on the mouth, but shut the idea down right away. I don't really want to kiss Tierney, I'm just curious to see how she'd react if I did. And to see how I would.

"I'm going to miss you," she says, letting her hand drop back into her lap.

"Same here." But, really, my capacity for missing people is pretty much used up just now.

I missed you so much. That's what she said, between sobs, when she hugged me in the hallway. I'd been missing. I'd been missed.

In all the hundreds of questions I've been asked since it

ended, no one – not one single person – has thought to ask: *Do you miss him?*

What's strange, though, is that whenever I return to the places we visited together, Uman's absence is more of a comfort than a torment. They were happy times, these were our happy places. Nothing can erase that. He is gone, but he was here, with me, and nothing can erase that, either.

The media leaves me alone now. I did the press conference, the interviews – "throw them a few bones and they'll stop barking", as D.I. Ryan put it – and after a couple of weeks they moved on to the next story. It all flared up again for a day or two when some tabloid journo tracked down that girl – Dominique – from Uman's posh school, and she admitted she'd made up the whole thing. Uman hadn't abducted her, or held her hostage, or done any of the stuff she'd accused him of. *How did I feel about that?*, the press wanted to know. I didn't feel anything about it, apart from wishing she'd said it while he was still alive. I'd known all along that Uman wasn't what they thought he was.

None of it will be news again until his body washes up somewhere.

D.I. Ryan phoned the other day.

"It's not about Uman," she said, right off, no doubt picking up the anxiety in my *hello?*.

She just wanted to know how I was doing. Which was good of her. I think she'd stopped disliking me by the end of the second day of questioning. We spoke for a couple of minutes, that's all, the phone becoming warm and clammy in my hand. Her voice took me straight back to the interview suite. As though reading my mind, she finished up by saying, "Gloria, I'm sorry I gave you such a hard time."

I replied, "I was just about to say the exact same thing to you."

At the Hangingstones, I tell Tierney, "I'm searching for myself."

She gives me a puzzled look.

"When I come to these places … if I'm searching for anyone, it's not Uman. It's me."

"I don't know what you mean," she says.

Me neither, I think. The words have spilled from my mouth while the thought is still forming in my head. "I'm not the same person I was before all of this." I set the half-empty Pepsi bottle down on the rock beside me. "I'm just trying to figure out how I've changed. Who I am now. You know?"

Tier looks like she regrets coming up here with me.

I laugh. "We don't do 'heavy', do we?"

She laughs too. "Not if I can help it, no."

"It's true, though, isn't it? I *am* different."

"Are we still doing heavy?"

"Seriously, Tier."

She exhales. "You're not different. Not really. Not deep down inside."

"You think?"

"Look, when you fall for a guy you become a bit like

him." She shrugs. "Then, eventually, you go back to being yourself again."

I'm turning this over in my mind a little later. We're eating ice creams at the tables outside the snack cabin in the car park just below the old quarry. We've been discussing the school holidays, our plans for the summer. I don't have any after New York, so Tier has been taking me through hers. Getting an all-over tan seems to be high on the agenda. Her phone pings and she breaks off from what she's saying to open the message. I watch her as she taps out a reply. She sneezes twice and I wonder if her hay fever is kicking in despite the cool, dull day.

My Danish friend. Are we even friends any more or is this just habit?

The breeze stiffens, cracking the flags on the poles by the entrance to the car park. The red-and-white of England, the white rose of Yorkshire. An Italian flag, too, because that's where the cabin's owner comes from. Tier has the hots for his son, who helps out here sometimes. He isn't working today.

When you fall for a guy you become a bit like him.

That was true: I had fallen for Uman; I had become a bit like him. But I'd become a bit like myself, as well – the carefree spirit I used to be as a young girl, anyway. With Uman, I had rediscovered that earlier version of myself. I'd forgotten how much I liked that "me".

You can't stay seven, eight, nine, ten years old for the whole of your life, though, can you? You can't run away, either. Not for ever, or even for very long. Not when you're fifteen. Maybe not at all. The world Uman had shown me was a false one, I saw that now. False hope. False promise. I couldn't burst with life like he did – I couldn't be that full-on, that transgressive, that reckless about whether I lived or died.

OK, so we'd been happy together for a while, but that happiness had nowhere to go.

"You're seeing everything in black-and-white just now," the school counsellor told me at our latest session. "Rebellion or conformity, freedom or constraint. Total adventure or total lack of adventure."

In time, she reckons, I will see that there are shades of grey. *Shades of pink and purple*, was what she said.

In time, I will be old enough to colour my life any shade I choose.

In time, I will plot a route between the black and the white. And it will be my route – not Uman's, not mine-and-Uman's.

"You don't need Uman to liberate you, Gloria." (She calls me Gloria, the counsellor. I asked her to.) "You don't need anyone. Only you."

She has an uncanny knack of telling me things I've already worked out for myself.

Tierney shuts off her phone and places it on the table. She's nearly finished her ice cream, but I've barely touched

296

mine. I pick off a strip of the chocolate coating with my teeth and let it dissolve on my tongue. It's quiet up here today; only one other table is in use – a young mum, breaking off pieces of sausage roll and feeding them to a curly-haired toddler in a buggy. On the path that rises past the old quarry, two elderly hikers pause to consult a map in a clear plastic holder. For a moment, I'm back in the Stretton Hills with Uman, planning our next pitch.

"Shall we go back to mine?" Tierney asks. "Watch a film or something?"

"I should pack," I say. "We have to be at the airport at stupid o'clock in the morning."

"I have cinnamon bagels. I have triple-chocolate brownies."

The boy in the buggy is staring at me. He has a flake of pastry stuck to his top lip, like a moth has settled there. I smile at him, but he doesn't smile back.

I won't go to Tierney's.

She'll be pissed off with me. There was a time when that would have mattered.

By tomorrow, I'll be thousands of miles away. New York suddenly seems very real and very imminent, and yet impossibly remote and unbelievable. But, then, everything is like that. The places I go (or don't), the people I'm with (or not), the things I do (or don't do). Each moment of each hour of each day for the rest of my life hovers on the turn of a (make-believe) card – held in perfect suspension between that which happens and that which doesn't. Between the questions I say "yes" to and the ones I say "no" to.

I am the sum of my choices. Did I read that somewhere, or hear someone say it, or have I just thought of it for myself?

We are the sum of our choices.

When you think of it like that, it's possible to be anyone you want to be, to live any kind of life you please. More or less.

I had a choice that final evening on Bryher, when Uman spoke of stealing a boat. All I had to do was say the word he hoped to hear.

Yes.

I had a choice – later, in the night – as I stood on the beach, listening to the engine noise and peering into the blackness for a last glimpse of him. All I had to do was raise the torch. Aim it across the water. Signal to him before it was too late.

Come back for me. Take me with you.

Those choices are gone. But there will be others. Thousands and thousands of them.

At the end of the footpath where Uman tricked us that time, Tierney and I hug and say our goodbyes and go our separate ways.

"Eggs over easy!" she calls after me.

"Sunny side up!" I call back.

Now it's just me, heading up the street, up the drive, up the steps, tugging the key from my pocket and letting myself into the house.

It's dead quiet and still. Mum and Dad are both at work and my brother won't surface from his bed till at least mid-afternoon. I'm thinking, home-made waffles. I'm thinking, a long soak in a hot bath so deep the water slops over the side when I slide in. I'm thinking, Van Morrison on the iPod.

I shut the front door behind me and stoop to gather the post from the mat. The usual glossy junk mail and flyers and boring bank credit-cardy stuff, along with a free newspaper and a charity collection bag. I stack it all on the side in the hallway.

Which is when I notice a postcard, half-hidden between two pieces of junk.

I ease it out.

The photo on the front shows a sheer-sided gorge with a narrow path winding its way along the rock face, and a rib-bon of white-water river far, far below. In the strip of clear blue sky at the top of the picture, the text says:

El Caminito del Rey, Andalusia.

My hand trembles so badly I almost drop the card as I turn it over.

I only saw his handwriting once – on the "happy places" slips he showed me after we'd drawn "Bryher" – but I'd rec-ognize it anywhere.

Four words. One underscore. And a question mark.

Wish <u>you</u> were here?

Acknowledgements

Way back at the beginning, this novel was going to be called *The Fourth Wish* and would feature a genie. While I was still roughing out a plan for the book I visited Scissett Middle School, near Huddersfield, in West Yorkshire, to run some creative writing workshops. While I was there I invited the students to enter a competition by answering the question: "If you were granted three wishes, what would you wish for?" The prize? I would choose the answer I liked the most and name one of the characters in my novel after the winning student.

In the end, I picked two winners: Jade Ellis ("The ability to see myself in the future so that I could work on the things that I did not like") and Tierney Rhodes ("To be able to see my future so I could see if there is anything that I would change"). And so the fictional Gloria Jade Ellis and her best friend, Tierney, were born. The novel altered beyond recognition on its journey to becoming *Twenty Questions for Gloria* – no genie, for one thing, and no time travel – but the

243 wishes produced by the 81 students who entered the competition were an invaluable part of the process. So I am very grateful to those young people at Scissett and to their brilliant English teacher, Maura Ryan (who also has a character named after her), for such enthusiastic support.

My heartfelt thanks also go to my agent in the UK, Stephanie Thwaites, for steering this novel back on course when I'd taken it walkabout, and to my London editor, Mara Bergman, and my New York editors, Wendy Lamb and Dana Carey, for their incisive notes during redrafting.

Finally, and most importantly, I am grateful to the two people who read this novel before anyone else and told me what they thought of it: my wife, Damaris, and my daughter Polly.

NEVER ENDING
How can she live with what she did?
MARTYN BEDFORD

It happened during a family holiday in Greece,
and now Shiv is tormented by guilt.
Nothing her parents have tried has helped her move on.

With its unconventional therapy, the Korsakoff Clinic
is her last hope. It is there she must confront the events
that have torn their lives apart.

By the author of Flip, shortlisted for the Costa Award
and winner of the Sheffield Children's Book Award,
the Calderdale Book of the Year Award, the Bay Book Award
and the Immanuel College Book Award.

"Beautiful and illuminating but as hard as therapy" – *Kirkus Reviews*

"A fine and serious novel" – *Books for Keeps*

"A moving portrayal of love and loss, beautifully written" –
Children's Books Ireland Recommended Read